EP

D

Little shop of horror . . .

Emma closed her eyes, clenched her fists and forced herself to stop screaming. Deep breaths. Like yoga class. In . . . out . . . in . . . out. Her heartbeat slowed and steadied in time to the measured rhythm. When she opened her eyes, everything looked perfectly normal—morning sun streaming through the dusty front windows; Arabella dressed for work in a long black-and-white batik-print dress, her hair pinned into a knot on top of her head; the interior of the shop silent and smelling faintly of fresh sawdust. Everything was perfectly normal. She looked down.

Except for the body at their feet . . .

Murder UNMENTIONABLE

MEG LONDON

BERKLEY PRIME CRIME, NEW YORK

THE BERKLEY PUBLISHING GROUP
Published by the Penguin Group
Penguin Group (USA) Inc.
375 Hudson Street, New York, New York 10014, USA

Penguin Group (Canada), 90 Eglinton Avenue East, Suite 700, Toronto, Ontario M4P 2Y3, Canada
(a division of Pearson Penguin Canada Inc.) • Penguin Books Ltd., 80 Strand, London WC2R 0RL,
England • Penguin Group Ireland, 25 St. Stephen's Green, Dublin 2, Ireland (a division of Penguin
Books Ltd.) • Penguin Group (Australia), 250 Camberwell Road, Camberwell, Victoria 3124, Australia
(a division of Pearson Australia Group Pty. Ltd.) • Penguin Books India Pvt. Ltd., 11 Community
Centre, Panchsheel Park, New Delhi—110 017, India • Penguin Group (NZ), 67 Apollo Drive,
Rosedale, Auckland 0632, New Zealand (a division of Pearson New Zealand Ltd.) • Penguin Books
(South Africa) (Pty.) Ltd., 24 Sturdee Avenue, Rosebank, Johannesburg 2196, South Africa

Penguin Books Ltd., Registered Offices: 80 Strand, London WC2R 0RL, England

This is a work of fiction. Names, characters, places, and incidents either are the product of the author's
imagination or are used fictitiously, and any resemblance to actual persons, living or dead, business
establishments, events, or locales is entirely coincidental. The publisher does not have any control over
and does not assume any responsibility for author or third-party websites or their content.

MURDER UNMENTIONABLE

A Berkley Prime Crime Book / published by arrangement with the author

PUBLISHING HISTORY
Berkley Prime Crime mass-market edition / September 2012

Copyright © 2012 by Penguin Group (USA) Inc.
Cover illustration by Nathalie Dion.
Cover design by Rita Frangie.
Interior text design by Laura K. Corless.

ISBN: 978-0-425-25157-7

BERKLEY® PRIME CRIME
Berkley Prime Crime Books are published by The Berkley Publishing Group,
a division of Penguin Group (USA) Inc.,
375 Hudson Street, New York, New York 10014.
BERKLEY® PRIME CRIME and the PRIME CRIME logo are trademarks of
Penguin Group (USA) Inc.

PRINTED IN THE UNITED STATES OF AMERICA

10 9 8 7 6 5 4 3 2 1

ALWAYS LEARNING   **PEARSON**

Acknowledgments

First I would like to thank Lieutenant Tom Lankford of the Paris, Tennessee Police Department for kindly answering my many questions. Any mistakes in police procedure are strictly my own.

I would like to thank Katelynn Lacopo, who worked tirelessly with me to perfect my proposal and first three chapters.

I would also like to thank my agent, Jessica Faust, for her guidance, and my editor, Faith Black, for showing me how to make my manuscript considerably better. And a thank-you to the Berkley Prime Crime copyeditor Megan Gerrity who worked so hard and saved me from some really embarrassing errors!

I apologize to the people of Paris, Tennessee, for adding in a number of stores and restaurants that don't actually exist in your charming town, among them, the Sweet Nothings vintage lingerie shop.

And finally, a big thank-you to my family and friends who have been so supportive of me on my writing journey!

Chapter 1

EMMA Taylor stifled a gasp as she pulled the garment out of the drawer at Sweet Nothings, her aunt's lingerie shop. "Aunt Arabella," she said, dangling the questionable piece of lingerie in the air. "What on earth is this?" She already knew her aunt's stock was hopelessly out-of-date—did anyone even wear half-slips these days?—but she didn't realize it was going to be this bad.

"Coming, dear, just a second." Arabella pushed aside the curtain from the back room. She was carrying a tray with a sweating pitcher of iced sweet tea and several glasses. Her French bulldog, Pierre, trotted obediently at her heels. He had one black ear and one white one, and he was getting quite round in the middle. Arabella claimed she didn't have the heart to put him on a diet. She set the tea and glasses on the counter and went over to where Emma was standing.

"This." Emma dangled the undergarment in front of her aunt. "I've never seen anything like it."

Her aunt laughed and ducked her head. "Oh, that. Just a

little hobby of mine. I got interested in it when Sally Dixon of La Tour Eiffel Antiques dragged me to some estate sales."

Emma's brows rose even higher. "But this looks like some kind of . . . of . . ." She couldn't bring herself to use the word *fetish* in front of her aunt.

"It's vintage, dear. Vintage. Early 1950s Maidenform. It's called a bullet bra. It's their Chansonette model. See"—her aunt pointed to the circular stitching—"this is what gave the famous sweater girls their shape. You know, like Marilyn Monroe, Lana Turner. That crowd."

Emma examined the reinforced stitching. "Did you wear—?"

"Of course. We all wore them. We actually used to iron them to get the shape just right. Some girls were known to stuff the tips of theirs." Arabella sniffed. "Then in the 1960s we all burned our bras and started going au naturel." She laughed as she poured a tall glass of tea. "I bet they don't serve sweet tea like this in New York." She handed Emma the glass.

Emma closed her eyes as the cool, sweet liquid slid down her throat. She held the glass to the back of her neck. She was glad she'd cut her hair short. She'd forgotten how muggy Tennessee could be in the summer.

Her aunt wore her long silver hair in a single braid down her back. She was dressed for the heat in a gauzy looking tunic and flowing pants. The all-white of the ensemble was relieved by a splash of color from an enormous coral necklace—the kind of piece that Emma had often heard called "important."

"I have several drawers full of vintage lingerie that I've cleaned and repaired, and lots more at home ready to be worked on." Arabella pulled open another drawer. "What intrigues me about vintage things is that they're a glimpse of another era—an era when women strove for feminine glamour instead of wanting to look like . . . like . . ." She waved a hand in the air. She turned and opened a cupboard and sorted through the padded white hangers. "This"— Arabella pulled out a garment—"would have been the crowning jewel of any woman's trousseau." She laid the nightgown and peignoir set out on the counter carefully. "Early 1940s. Silk charmeuse," she said, fingering the peach fabric lovingly. "And Point de Venise lace."

The bodice of the nightgown was indeed lace, and touches of the same lace graced the cuffs and collar of the matching peignoir.

"It's beautiful," Emma said as she took in the meticulous detailing on the matching set. The gown had a circular skirt and was made with only one seam running up the back.

"Would you like me to save it for you?" Arabella's eyes twinkled as she looked at her niece.

"Save it for me?" Emma repeated blankly.

"For your trousseau, dear. You're twenty-nine. I'm sure that any minute now you'll—"

Emma shook her head vehemently.

"Don't tell me there isn't someone . . . ?"

Emma shook her head again. "Nope. I'm as free as a bird." Emma thought about Guy and crossed her fingers behind her back. "Besides, women don't really have trousseaus anymore, do they?"

"True. What a shame. I remember reading an old Emily Post etiquette book that detailed everything the modern woman of the 1930s needed in her trousseau—from day dresses and evening dresses to sports clothes to the right number of sets of monogrammed towels for her bathroom."

Arabella opened another cabinet and took out a gown. "Look at this." She carefully smoothed out the fabric. "It's a 1930s peach Satin Dasche slip gown." Arabella pointed to the lace at the throat. "With beige Alençon lace. It needed a slight repair here," she pointed to a spot under the arm, "but I think I've managed it very nicely. You can't even tell."

"This is just what we need!" Emma exclaimed so suddenly her aunt jumped and even Pierre paused in his attempts to hoist his considerable bulk onto the padded bench by the window.

"For what, dear?"

"To put your shop back on the map! We'll specialize in vintage lingerie! People will come out from Memphis and Nashville just to shop at Sweet Nothings!"

"Do you really think so, dear?" Her aunt pulled her braid over her shoulder and fiddled with the ends. "The way things are going, I'll have nothing but my social security when I retire. And we know what they're saying about that." She made a face.

"I know this will be a success!"

She had to make this happen for her aunt, Emma thought. She owed Arabella. Arabella was her mother's older sister. She'd never had children or even married, and when Emma was born, she had taken a real interest in her, sending gifts from whatever port of call she was calling home at the time. The summer between Emma's sophomore and junior years in college, Arabella had used some of her connections to secure Emma an internship at Vera Wang. It had changed Emma's life. Before that, she'd assumed she would have a career, eventually get married and settle down in Tennessee. New York had opened her eyes to a much bigger world.

She still thought she would like to be married someday, but she wasn't so sure about staying in Tennessee. She did have to stay long enough to help Aunt Arabella get back on her feet, and then she planned to return to New York and her old life.

Everything hinged on making Sweet Nothings the success Arabella deserved.

Emma looked around at the shop and her heart sank slightly. The decor had been new in the 1970s, the last time her aunt had renovated the shop. The floors were swathed in pea-green shag carpeting that must have been all the rage back then. The bright orange, yellow and hot pink accents had faded over time to slightly less horrific pastel hues, but they added nothing. The stock wasn't in much better shape. It wasn't new enough to be saleable, but it wasn't old enough to be vintage, either. But if her aunt already had a significant amount of vintage lingerie, they could add some new lines to round things out. She thumbed through the BlackBerry in her mind. Chantelle DeLang was a buyer for a very exclusive shop in SoHo and always found the most unique things. Emma knew she'd be happy to share her sources. She felt a sharp tingle of excitement. What a fun challenge to turn around Sweet Nothings for her aunt! They'd combine vintage lingerie with one-of-a-kind pieces from Italy and France.

But first they'd have to redecorate.

"About the shop . . ." Emma began, and took another sip of her tea.

"I've already thought of that," Arabella said, pouring herself a glass of sweet tea. "As a matter of fact, Brian should be here any minute. He's agreed to do the renovations for us."

"Brian?"

"Brian O'Connell. Your friend Liz's brother. You remember him, don't you? Tall fellow, brown hair?"

"The last I heard he was in Nashville working for that architecture firm."

Arabella shook her head. "Their father isn't doing well—had a triple bypass last year—so Brian came home to help him with the hardware store."

Emma's glance strayed toward the front window of Sweet Nothings. She could see O'Connell's Hardware diagonally across the street. Was that Brian in the window rearranging the display?

When she turned around, Arabella had a strange, smug look on her face. "What?"

Arabella shook her head. "Nothing. Nothing at all."

"I figured you more for the Paris, France, type but now here you are, back in Paris, Tennessee." Brian O'Connell threw his arms around Emma and all but crushed her in a big bear hug.

Emma felt flutters starting in her stomach, like tiny bubbles of champagne. She'd always been a little in love with Liz's older brother. She'd been a freshman in high school when he was a senior and captain of the soccer team. He'd always been friendly—saying hi when they passed in the hallway and stopping by to say hello when she visited Liz. But he treated her like he treated Liz—a kid sister to tease. She remembered the time she and Liz were huddled under the covers watching a scary movie, and Brian and his friends decided to climb the tree outside Liz's window. They'd pressed their faces to the pane of glass and sent both Liz and Emma screaming downstairs. Another time when Emma and Liz decided to camp out, Brian had snuck a plastic snake into each of their sleeping bags. Once again, they'd been sent off screaming. Liz had insisted that these pranks meant he liked Emma, but Emma didn't think that was the case.

Then Brian went off to study architecture at the University of Tennessee, and Emma didn't see much of him again until she was there herself working toward a degree in art history. But by that time, he was a senior, and their paths hardly ever crossed.

He was even better looking than Emma remembered. Tall and broad-shouldered with strong-looking forearms visible beneath the rolled-up cuffs of his light blue shirt. His brown hair had gold streaks in it, and there were now crinkles around his blue eyes. Looking at him, Emma felt like a tongue-tied adolescent again.

"So what brings you home?" Brian stepped back and looked at Emma, holding her at arm's length.

"My mother called to say that Aunt Arabella needed help with her shop. It seemed like the perfect time to make a change." Emma glanced away so Brian wouldn't see the look in her eye.

"I remember your mom. Is she still making those . . . those . . . things?"

"Ceramics?" Emma nodded. "Dad built her a studio at their place in Florida. And she's teaching at the local community college. It keeps her busy while Dad perfects his golf game."

Arabella bustled over just then. Always the perfect Southern hostess, she had a pitcher of homemade lemonade ready. "Tell Brian about your job in New York." She turned toward Brian. "Emma was a stylist at *Femme* magazine. She's worked with some very famous photographers and models."

Emma thought of Guy and felt her face getting warm.

"Pardon my ignorance," Brian said, laughing self-deprecatingly, "but what does a stylist do?"

Emma explained how she was in charge of creating the look, feel and theme for magazine photo shoots by choosing the clothes and accessories, the background props and sometimes even the model's hair and makeup.

Brian looked impressed. "I thought you wanted to be an artist or something."

"I majored in art history—which is still a passion. But museum jobs are few and far between and pretty much require you to have an independent income if you hope to live anywhere near New York City. Besides, I fell in love with the art of fashion."

"So, what are you two planning?" Arabella poured out

glasses of lemonade and handed them around. Pierre hovered near her feet, sensing that food might be in the offing.

"I'm thinking something along the lines of shabby chic," Emma said. "Whitewashed armoires for displays, soft pastel accent colors, lacy window treatments." She turned toward Arabella.

Arabella clapped her hands. "I love it." She looked at Brian. "What do you think? Can you manage it?"

Brian shook his head. "No problem. There's nothing major involved structurally. But you will have to close for a few weeks."

"Don't worry about it. I've been planning on it." Arabella turned toward Emma. "What are you thinking for colors?"

Emma furrowed her brow. "I'm not sure. Maybe the palest pink for the walls?"

Arabella nodded. "I know just the shade you're thinking of." She opened a drawer and began rummaging through the contents. She pulled out a puddle of silk satin and spread it out on the counter. It was the barest whisper of pink.

"This is what they call a teddy. Sort of like a full slip but with a tap pant bottom."

"It's beautiful." Emma stroked the fabric gently. "It must be very old. It looks like something they would have worn in the twenties."

Arabella shook her head. "Actually, it isn't, but I couldn't resist it since it's in such beautiful shape. It was made for the J. Peterman Company sometime during the 1990s. The same company made a lot of the pieces that were worn in the remake of the movie *Titanic*."

"I brought some paint samples with me." Brian pulled out a fan of colored paint chips. "O'Connell's Hardware will be pleased to offer you a discount." He grinned and the dimple in his right cheek deepened.

"That's very kind of you."

"We have to go above and beyond to compete with the

big box stores these days. We're even opening half days on Sunday; otherwise the weekend DIY crowd will head to one of the big stores that do keep Sunday hours. So many mom-and-pop places are closing their doors."

Emma nodded. "That's why Sweet Nothings needs something special to compete with the chain places at the malls. But I'm confident we've found it." She stopped for a minute as a thought formed in her mind. "What if we had a grand opening complete with a fashion show?"

"That's a wonderful idea," Arabella said.

"We can have models showing off your best vintage pieces."

"Will you be modeling some of the styles yourself?" Brian grinned at Emma.

Emma felt the heat rush into her face, and when she looked at her aunt, Arabella was giving her that smug smile again.

Emma and Brian spent the rest of the afternoon with their heads together over the new design for Sweet Nothings, their talk punctuated by the faint sounds of Pierre's snoring. Arabella ghosted about, occasionally gifting them with that same smug smile she'd bestowed on Emma earlier. Emma was dying to ask her what was up, but she had the feeling she'd find out soon enough.

Finally they poured the last glass of lemonade and pushed their chairs back.

"So what really brings you back to Paris?" Brian asked suddenly.

Emma stammered. "I told you. My aunt needed help with the shop, and my mother thought that with my experience I could . . ." She trailed off at the look on Brian's face.

"Really?"

"No. Not really, but I'm not ready to talk about it yet. How about you?"

"I came back to help my father with the store." Brian

drained the last of his lemonade and wiped a hand across his mouth.

"Really?"

He laughed. "Yes, really." He was quiet for a moment. "I'm glad I came back. Liz's kids are getting bigger, and I want them to know who their uncle Brian is."

He gave Emma a look she couldn't quite read—wasn't even sure she *wanted* to read.

Arabella came out of the back room with her purse over her arm. "If you don't mind keeping an eye on Pierre, I'm heading down to Angel Cuts for a wash. Angel Roy gives all of us shop owners a discount so if you need a trim, that would be the place to go. Of course you'll have to listen to Angel go on and on about her latest conquest—she figures herself to be Paris's femme fatale, but at least the cut's cheap." She gestured at Emma. "I love what you've done with your hair, by the way. Very Audrey Hepburn in *Roman Holiday*."

Emma put a hand to her head. "Thanks." Cutting her hair short had been a whim, but she liked it. Guy said it played up her eyes, which he'd told her were almost as violet as Elizabeth Taylor's. Emma had laughed at his outrageousness, but she'd been pleased, too. She shook her head. She didn't want to think about Guy right now.

Arabella glanced toward the window and frowned. "Is that Deirdre Porter?" She moved closer until her nose was almost pressed to the glass then turned around with a sigh. "The mayor's new daughter-in-law—I don't know who she thinks she is. Speeding through town in that expensive red sports car of hers."

"I thought she was rather pretty," Brian said.

Arabella and Emma both swiveled in his direction.

He held his hands up in defense and laughed. "Okay, okay, I didn't mean anything by that."

Arabella sniffed. "I know you didn't," she said in a soothing voice. "But there's something about that girl that gets my dander up. It's as if we're not good enough for her. The other day I heard her getting all snippy with Jim at the Meat Mart because he didn't have *foie gras*. Folks here want their pork for a good barbecue, their turkey for Thanksgiving, their ham for Easter and a decent chicken or rib eye the rest of the time. None of this *foie gras*. Not that I didn't love it when I had it in France." She sighed. "Yves Aubertin introduced me to the pleasures of a fine foie gras. And a rich, ripe St. Andre . . . And . . ." She stopped abruptly.

"And?" Brian prompted.

Arabella shook her finger at him playfully. "Never you mind!"

ARABELLA had offered Emma a room in her house—a large, rambling Victorian done up in yummy sherbet hues, with a deep front porch that always seemed to catch a fresh breeze. Sitting on the swing watching the world go by had been one of Emma's favorite pastimes. Instead, Emma had opted for the one-bedroom apartment above Sweet Nothings. She'd become something of a night owl and didn't want to disturb her aunt.

The apartment had escaped Arabella's seventies renovation craze. Emma looked around at the charming living room with the built-in window seats, wall of bookshelves, polished wooden pieces and jewel-toned Oriental carpets. The apartment was small by most standards, but enormous by the standards Emma was used to—a hideously overpriced studio on Manhattan's Lower East Side where the bathtub stood in the middle of the room, and in order to entertain guests, she had to cover it with a board and a cloth and disguise it as a table.

Tonight, Emma was glad to be alone. She kicked off her shoes, pulled a pitcher of iced tea from the refrigerator and poured herself a glass. She curled up on the window seat and looked down at Washington Street below. She loved living right in the center of town. Shop owners were flipping their open signs to closed and shutting and locking their front doors. Emma thought she saw a shadow move behind the window at O'Connell's Hardware Store, and she squinted trying to make out the shape. It looked like Brian, but she couldn't be sure.

Not that it mattered. She was done with men—at least for the moment. Guy Richard had trampled her heart, leaving it broken and shopworn. She moved away from the window, and noticed that the message light on her cell phone was blinking. She dialed voice mail, but the message, from Guy's assistant, Kate Hathaway, was brief—just that she'd call back later. Emma was relieved. The last thing she wanted to do at the moment was talk about Guy.

EMMA felt a strange sense of proprietorship when she put her key in the lock of Sweet Nothings the next morning. Dappled morning sun lit the white brick façade that hadn't changed much since the early 1900s when the building was erected. A glossy black-and-white striped awning with SWEET NOTHINGS penned in elegant script shaded the front door. Emma paused and plucked some dead leaves off the white geraniums that sat in twin plaster urns on either side of the entrance.

Someone was standing at the front door of The Toggery, the oldest store in Paris. It had been in its original location since 1917 and had been spared by the fires that had destroyed a number of other buildings around the square. The door opened, and the person disappeared inside. Shortly afterward, Emma saw lights go on, and the shade over the front window was rolled up. Downtown Paris was waking up for business.

She felt better than she had in a long time. She'd come

up with a unique angle for her aunt's failing business, Brian was ready to start the renovations she'd suggested and she'd had a good night's sleep with the windows open, listening to the chirp of the crickets and feeling the soft breeze scented with honeysuckle and pine. It was a far cry from the city, where the night sounds consisted of a cacophony of taxi horns and people shouting, and where the air was fouled with car exhaust and bus fumes.

Emma was starting the coffee when she heard the front door open and the jingle of Pierre's leash.

"Hello! Good morning," Arabella called out. "Pierre," she turned her attention toward her dog, "Stop pulling on the leash like that."

"Good morning." Emma greeted her aunt and gave her a quick hug. She glanced down at Pierre, who was still straining at his collar, attempting to reach the front door. "What's up with Pierre?"

Arabella sighed. "It's that dachshund across the street. Bertha. A most unsuitable match for a French bulldog, but try telling Pierre that. It was love at first sight. I can't imagine what he sees in her."

Emma closed the front door, and Pierre finally sulked over toward his dog bed.

"I hardly slept a wink last night," Arabella admitted as she tucked her handbag under the counter. "I'm so excited about all your ideas for Sweet Nothings."

"I know," Emma replied. "I'm very excited, too. I was thinking that we really need to organize a grand opening with a bang."

"I finished some more repairs last night." Arabella pulled a tissue-wrapped bundle out of a black-and-white Sweet Nothings shopping bag. She placed it on the counter and opened it. "Look at this." Arabella held up a green silk tap-pant-and-bra set.

"They're beautiful," Emma breathed.

"The straps are actual silk ribbon and in perfect condition."

"Is this . . . what did you call it . . . Point de Venise lace?" Emma asked.

Arabella shook her head. "This is Alençon. Its name comes from the town of Alençon in Normandy, France. A local needlewoman, attempting to duplicate Venetian lace, ended up creating her own pattern, which they named after the town."

A knock sounded on the front door, and they both jumped. Pierre catapulted from his dog bed and approached the door, head down and a low growl emanating from his throat.

"That must be Brian—" Arabella began.

"That must be the armoire I ordered—" Emma said at the same time. "I'll get it."

Emma smoothed a hand over her hair, and Arabella gave her that little smile again. Emma dropped her hand to her side and strode toward the door.

She pulled it open half expecting to see a couple of burly men ready to hustle the white distressed armoire she'd ordered into the shop.

But it was Guy Richard.

Standing on the doorstep of Sweet Nothings, his Nikon slung over his shoulder, a bunch of slightly bedraggled flowers clutched in his hand and a very repentant look on his face.

Chapter 2

"GUY!" Emma's jaw dropped and her stomach flip-flopped at the sight of him standing on her doorstep. "What are you doing here?"

"I've got something for you." There was an earnest look in his eyes that Emma had never seen before.

"Flowers?" She gestured toward the wilting bouquet in his hands.

"*Non.*" He handed the flowers to her. "Something else. Can we go somewhere and talk?" He gestured toward the street with his shoulder.

Emma wasn't sure she could move. She felt rooted to the spot, as if she had been planted there.

"Well, well, well. Who do we have here?" Arabella cooed as she glided toward Guy with her hand outstretched.

Guy turned toward Arabella and took hold of her hand, his lips hovering above it. "*Enchanté, madame.*"

Pierre tried to muscle between Arabella and Guy, his upper lip pulled back in a snarl.

Arabella fluttered her eyelashes in response. "*Voulez-vous couchez avec moi?*"

"Aunt Arabella!" Emma hissed. "Do you know what that means? You just asked him if he'd like to sleep with you!"

Arabella put a hand over her mouth. "Oh, dear. Is *that* what that means?"

"We're going to go get coffee," Emma said firmly. "The Coffee Klatch should be open by now."

"Nonsense." Arabella said. "I can put on some coffee *tout de suite*."

"Please," Guy held out his hands. "I don't want to be a bother."

"It's no bother at all."

Guy shot Emma a helpless look, but she knew better than to try to sidetrack her aunt. Once Arabella got going, she was like a locomotive steaming toward its destination.

Emma helped Arabella retrieve cups and saucers from a cabinet in the back room and carried them to the front of the shop. Shock had made Emma's movements awkward and clumsy, and she clutched the porcelain tightly for fear she would drop something.

Guy was looking through Arabella's stock of vintage lingerie and had taken out the peach peignoir set and laid it on the counter. He spun around when he heard Emma coming.

"These are so beautiful, *cherie*." His camera was out of its case, and he was adjusting the lens. "Have you thought about making an online catalogue? Beautiful things like these would be bought up like that." He snapped his fingers.

Emma set the tray down on the counter, relieved to note there was the barest rattle of crockery. "I hadn't thought about that." With an online presence, the shop wouldn't be totally dependent on local customers for its revenue.

"That's a wonderful idea," Emma said cautiously. "I don't suppose it would cost that much to get started."

"*Non*, not at all," Guy reassured her. "Besides, now that I am here, I can take the photographs for you."

"Really?" Emma felt her excitement build. "Arabella," she called toward the back room. "Guy has had the most wonderful idea."

"What's that?" Arabella emerged, wiping her hands on a dish towel.

Emma explained Guy's proposition to her.

"What a brilliant idea," Arabella exclaimed.

"You can be my model," Guy said to Emma, turning toward the negligee spread on the counter. "This looks like it should fit perfectly. And this color, with your complexion . . ." He kissed the tips of his fingers.

"No!" The word burst out of Emma. "We can put it on a mannequin to be photographed."

Emma glanced at the negligee and peignoir set again. It was certainly a far cry from the old T-shirt she normally wore to bed. And there was no way she was going to allow pictures of herself in it to be displayed on the Internet. Arabella had offered to save it for her trousseau. Would she ever need a trousseau, she wondered. She'd told Guy they were finished, and she meant it. And the way she felt right now, it would be a long time before she was ready to risk the pain of a broken heart again. She'd rather sit alone in front of the television eating ice cream out of the carton.

Guy shrugged, a casual Gallic tossing of his shoulder.

Emma took the nightgown from him and started to replace it on the hanger. She didn't notice the jingle of the front door opening. Brian strode into the room and stopped short when he saw her.

Emma dropped the negligee as if it had scalded her hands. Brian looked almost as flustered as she felt.

"Sorry if I'm interrupting . . ." He waved a hand in the air. "Something."

"Not at all." Guy smiled at him reassuringly, but Brian continued to study Guy rather like a scientist might study a parasite under a microscope.

"I don't want to interrupt anything. I was going to start on those alcoves we talked about . . ."

"*Pas de problème*, no problem." Guy answered quickly. He turned around and began fiddling with his camera lens.

Brian continued to stare, his mouth in a grim line, for several seconds before turning on his heel and heading toward the other end of the shop. After an uncomfortable silence, the whine of the saw filled Sweet Nothings.

Despite Guy's sudden appearance, Emma and Arabella still had work to do. Whatever Guy wanted to discuss would have to wait until later. Fortunately, he had become immersed in taking photographs as Emma had suspected he would. They'd been working for a few hours and were about to break for lunch when they heard the door open and a feminine voice call out, "Yoo-hoo!"

Arabella rolled her eyes. "We should have locked the front door."

"Where's that gorgeous Frenchman I heard you've been hiding, Arabella?"

"In here, Angel."

"How—" Emma began.

"It's a small town, and, as they say, news travels fast."

Angelica "Angel" Roy was preceded into the room by a cloud of Opium. She was wearing polka-dot capri pants and a halter top, and she had her fire-engine-red hair teased and sprayed into a massive bouffant mixture on top of her head. Her nails were painted hot pink, and a tattoo of a cat was inked above her left ankle.

She stopped short when she caught sight of Guy.

"Close your mouth, you're drooling," Arabella said.

Angel ignored her and tottered purposefully toward Guy on her high-heeled sandals.

He took her outstretched hand and kissed it. "*Enchanté, mademoiselle.*"

Angel preened and patted her hair. "The same to you, I'm sure." She looked around the shop, where stock was piled on the counters. "What are you all doing?"

"Renovating. My niece is here from New York to help." Arabella gestured toward Emma.

Angel gave Emma the once-over. "I don't know how long you're staying, but if you need your hair cut or a mani and pedi, come on down to Angel Cuts. It's just past A Good Yarn and right next to The Taffy Pull. If you get a hankering for something more than just eye candy," she glanced at Guy from beneath her lashes, "they do some of the best fudge I've ever tasted. Made right on the spot." She licked her lips suggestively.

Angel turned toward Guy. "You helping Miss Arabella with her renovations?"

Guy shook his head. "Not exactly, *non*. I am going to help photograph her catalogue."

"Right here in the shop?"

"Maybe. But also outdoors, I think."

"I know just the spot! You can take some snaps right next to the Eiffel Tower. It'd be perfect seeing as how this is Paris, Tennessee. Get it? Paris, *Tennessee*?"

Guy looked confused. "*Mais La Tour Eiffel?*"

"Exactly! Didn't anyone tell you? We've got one of our very own right here in Paris. It's over at Memorial Park and stands sixty feet tall!"

"*Non!*"

"Yes." Angel cracked her gum loudly. "Well, come on, big boy. What are you waiting for? You don't mind, do you?" She glanced at Emma as she headed toward the door.

Emma opened her mouth, but before any words came out, Angel was gone, high-heeled sandals slapping, whisking Guy along in her wake.

"Are you going to let her steal your boyfriend like that?" Arabella looked up from the nightgowns she'd been folding.

"He's not my boyfriend, and she's welcome to him." Emma opened a drawer and began making note of the contents.

Arabella opened her mouth but then, after a glance at her niece, shut it again. Instead, she shook her head and went back to what she was doing.

EMMA was alone in the shop, closing up, when Angel returned Guy. He looked exhausted, and his shirt was damp with perspiration. He sagged against the counter where Emma was finishing an inventory of one of the drawers. Arabella had never bothered to keep track of the stock and had no idea what she had in all the cupboards and cabinets.

His cologne drifted toward Emma, and she closed her eyes against the memories it stirred up. She remembered their first shoot together, and how she'd been enchanted by his consideration toward everyone on the set—ordering in lunch at his expense for everyone from the magazine's assistant to the assistant to the models themselves. She'd quickly developed a crush on the handsome, dark-haired Frenchman.

"Have dinner with me, *cherie*, please?" Guy's eyes had a pleading look in them, which surprised Emma.

"Tonight?"

He nodded.

"I'm sorry," Emma looked down and made a notation on her clipboard. "My friend Liz has invited me to dinner tonight."

"Are you busy tomorrow then?"

Emma hesitated.

Guy reached out and took her hands in his. "I want to tell you something."

Emma's heart rate ratcheted up to warp speed.

"I've missed you." He turned her hand over and traced the lines on her palm with the tips of his fingers. A shiver ran down Emma's spine. "I want you to come home."

Emma opened her mouth, but he squeezed her hand to stop her. "I've arranged an interview for you next week with La Moda Italiana." He looked at her face as if judging her reaction.

Emma's mouth opened but no sound came out. La Moda Italiana! It was one of the biggest fashion houses in the world! For one heady moment her entire career flashed before her eyes—an entry position to start, quick promotion to something more substantial, years of fun and work traveling the globe for La Moda Italiana, finally an executive vice presidency, a fantastic New York apartment, several walk-in closets filled with the latest fashions, an adoring husband—Guy?—by her side. Maybe a baby or two . . .

She dropped back to earth suddenly.

"Don't say no. Say you'll think about it." Guy spread her palm open again and began kissing and nibbling it.

Emma snatched her hand away. "I can't. I can't leave Aunt Arabella. She needs me."

"I need you." Guy looked deep into her eyes, and Emma felt her knees tremble.

She raised her head and stiffened her spine. "What about Monique? And Gabriella? And Donna?" Hurt washed over her with a sharpness that took her breath away.

Guy shrugged. "They meant nothing." He hung his head. "*Cherie*, I wish I could find the words to tell you how sorry I am. I was very, very—" He waved a hand as if he could pluck the right words from the air. "Very foolish." He made a sad face. "Sometimes I have to remember that *on ne peut avoir le beurre et l'argent du beurre.*"

Emma looked blank.

"It means, how do you say it in English? You can't have your cake and eat it, too."

Emma laughed bleakly.

"You must give me another chance."

"I can't do it again." Emma's shoulders sagged.

"Don't say anything right now. Think about it. And have dinner with me tomorrow night. I'll put some Veuve Clicquot on ice *chez moi,* for afterward."

Emma knew she should say no. But she didn't.

EMMA couldn't wait to see Liz again. Liz had come up to New York once to visit, but that had been six years ago, before the children arrived, and before Emma had started spending all her holidays in Florida where her parents now lived. She had to bite back her impatience as she settled Arabella in the front passenger seat of her MINI, Pierre at her feet. Arabella had baked a pie to bring, and Emma secured that carefully in the backseat before sliding behind the wheel herself.

Liz and her husband had moved into a house just outside of Paris. It had belonged to Liz's father, and his father before that, but after his heart attack, he'd moved to an assisted living community in town. Emma knew that Liz and her husband had completely renovated the place, preserving the best of the old while adding new features and amenities.

The fifteen-minute drive seemed to take forever, but then finally they were turning onto Liz's street. Emma felt her pulse quicken as the house came into view. It was built in the old-fashioned farmhouse-style with a huge wraparound porch out front. All the paint had been renewed, and brightly colored Adirondack chairs provided a warm welcome.

Liz was standing on the steps when Emma pulled into the drive. She was tall, with a wide-open, freckled face and strawberry blond hair that was a total contrast to Emma's petite frame, heart-shaped face and dark hair. They embraced heartily and, with an arm under Arabella's elbow,

Liz led them up the steps toward a small table set with a pitcher of Tennessee Tea.

Liz ensconced Arabella in a bright red Adirondack chair and handed her a sweating glass of the cold Tennessee Tea. Matt Banning, Liz's husband, gave Emma a hug that nearly took her breath away before taking a seat on the floor, his back against one of the porch railings. He had the looks of a handsome cowboy, and Emma half expected to see a horse tied to the railings.

Their daughter, and Emma's goddaughter, Alice, was playing on the swing set with her younger brother, Ben, beside her, her blond ponytail whipping back and forth. All of a sudden they jumped off the swings and began running toward the drive, shouting "Uncle Bri, Uncle Bri!"

A red pickup truck was coming down the drive, kicking up dust and pebbles. It stopped and Brian got out—more like unfolded himself, Emma thought. He was immediately tackled around the knees by two small munchkins who continued to chant "Uncle Bri, Uncle Bri!" He pulled something from his pocket and handed it to them.

"It's for after dinner," he shouted as the children scampered toward their mother, demanding, "Can we eat it now, can we?"

Liz shook her head. "No more candy, Brian, please. It will be impossible to get them to bed tonight."

"An occasional treat isn't going to hurt them." Brian mounted the steps to the porch, swiping a hand across his forehead.

"You're going to spoil them rotten!" Liz admonished.

Brian faked surprise. "I thought that was my job!"

Liz took a playful swipe at him, and he ducked. "Just wait till you have kids," she said.

"If that ever happens," Brian said, his expression suddenly serious.

There was an awkward pause that Liz rushed to fill.

"Tea?" She grabbed the pitcher from the table and held it toward Emma and Brian.

Brian glanced at the pitcher. "Is it the real deal?"

Liz nodded. "One part Jack Daniel's, one part triple sec, one part sweet and sour mix and two parts cola," she recited.

"Then I'll take a big ol' glass." Brian smiled.

Matt heaved himself up off the floor. "I'll go get the grill started. Want to give me a hand?" He glanced at Brian.

The rest of the evening went by in a blur, everyone seeming to talk at once in their effort to catch up on all the news. The children had retreated to the family room to watch television, and when Emma went in to peek at them, they were on the sofa, fast asleep.

"They look like angels, don't they?" Brian said as he came up behind Emma. He tiptoed over and pulled up the light throw that was folded over the arm of the couch.

"You two want some pie?" Liz came out of the kitchen, wiping her hands on her apron.

"Coming!" Brian said as they followed Liz back out to the porch.

"I haven't had chess pie like this since I left home." Emma closed her eyes as she savored the first bite of her aunt's homemade dessert. She scraped up the bits of flaky pastry and licked them off the tines of her fork.

"Absolutely delicious." Brian declared and put his plate down with a sigh of satisfaction.

A lone car came down the street, its headlights picking out a row of honeysuckle bushes and a white picket fence.

"I wonder why they call it chess pie?" Emma took a sip from her coffee cup.

"I've heard a lot of different stories about the origin of the name." Arabella dabbed at her lips with her napkin. "But my favorite is that the housewife who created it, when asked by her husband what kind of pie it was, answered, 'I dunno. It's ches pie.'"

"Yours is definitely some of the best." Brian took a gulp of his coffee. "I like the hint of lemon in it."

Arabella nodded. "It cuts the sweetness. Some people use vinegar, but I prefer the citrus taste from the lemon."

Liz began to collect the plates and cups and saucers.

"Here, I'll help." Arabella got to her feet. "I need to move, or I'll get as stiff as a board."

They heard a thud as Pierre jumped off the swing where he'd been sleeping and padded out to the kitchen behind them.

They piled the dirty dishes on the granite-topped counter. Liz had knocked two rooms into one to expand the kitchen. There was now a large island encircled with stools, with a pot rack suspended over it, as well as a fireplace with two overstuffed armchairs pulled up in front of it.

"Finally we can talk." Liz leaned her arms on the island. "Have you told Liz about your delicious Frenchman?"

"Guy? I'm afraid that's over." Emma fiddled with a loose thread on one of Liz's dish towels.

"But he seems quite smitten with you," Arabella said. "Besides, he's come all this way . . ."

Emma grabbed one of the dishes and began rinsing it. "Oh, I'm sure Guy is convinced that he's in love with me. It's just that he can't give up Donna and Gabriella and Sophie and I don't know how many others."

"Those Frenchmen," Arabella sighed. "Cheating seems to be in their DNA or something." She fiddled with one of the pins anchoring her French twist. "Were you serious about him?"

Emma nodded.

"You poor baby." Arabella put her arms around her niece. "You must have really been hurting if you were willing to come back to Paris, Tennessee, to help your old aunt! When your mother told me you were coming, I couldn't believe my good luck." She rubbed Emma's back absentmindedly.

"But I'm sorry to hear it's because your heart has been bro-ken." She gave Emma a squeeze. "But he's come after you—that must mean something."

Liz nodded. "Yes! He's come all the way here from New York. He must be pretty serious."

Emma grabbed a cloth and wiped at a spot on the counter. "I don't know. He says he is, but . . ." She scrubbed a little harder, although the spot was virtually gone. "He claims it's because he was sickly as a kid. He grew up really skinny with ears that stuck out." Emma made a noise that was half-way between a laugh and a sob.

"He certainly turned out to be handsome enough. You should see him." Arabella turned toward Liz.

Emma nodded. "I know. But he says it haunts him still—all those years when none of the girls would even say hello to him. When gorgeous models virtually throw themselves at him now, he can't resist." Emma swiped at a tear that was making its way down her cheek. "Every day, everywhere I went, I saw Gabriella, Monique, Sophie and the rest of them staring down at me from billboards all over Times Square. Wearing nothing but a push-up bra and a lacy thong." She smiled. "It's hard to believe in yourself, when you're sur-rounded by so much perfection."

"Airbrushing!" Arabella declared firmly. "I read all about it in a magazine. None of them really look that good."

Liz nodded vehemently.

"And none of them could possibly hold a candle to Emma."

They hadn't heard Brian come out to the kitchen, and Emma, Arabella and Liz all jumped.

"You scared me!" Emma accused to hide her confusion. She could feel heat flooding her face.

"Just saying." Brian picked up a dishcloth and began dry-ing the glasses. "You deserve the best. And I'm not sure that Guy is it."

"Well!" Arabella and Liz exchanged glances, and Arabella whispered to Emma as Brian was taking out the trash. "If you decide not to go back to New York, it looks as if there might very well be something for you here in Paris."

Chapter 3

EMMA felt strangely shy around Brian the next day at Sweet Nothings. Not that she believed Arabella—Brian wasn't interested in her, she was just his kid sister's best friend.

It didn't help that Arabella kept referring to them as "you two" all day. Fortunately, Guy had gone out to scout locations for the Sweet Nothings online catalogue shoot. Emma didn't think he was the jealous type, but she was glad she wouldn't have to find out.

"There you are, you two!" Arabella interrupted Emma's thoughts. She was carrying a huge stack of glossy white boxes and could barely see around them.

"Let me," Emma began, but before she could complete the sentence, Arabella took a tumble and the boxes skittered across the floor.

"Are you all right?" Emma and Brian asked in unison.

"Of course, of course." Arabella began to struggle to her feet. Emma and Brian each put a hand under her arms to help her up.

"Are you sure you're okay?"

"Of course. Couldn't be better." Arabella put her foot down. "Ouch."

"What's wrong?"

"I must have twisted my ankle."

"You'd better sit down." Brian picked her up in his arms as if she were a child and carried her to a chair. "Let's see that ankle."

Arabella stuck her leg out, and Brian gingerly rotated her foot. "Ouch," she said, wincing again.

"I don't think it's anything serious. A sprain at the most. It's probably best if you stay off it as much as possible."

"I can run down to the drugstore and get you a cane."

"Bah," Arabella exclaimed. "Those ugly things! I've got a collection of walking sticks in an urn by the door. Bring me one of those."

Emma hurried to the urn and chose a hefty ebony stick with an ornate silver head. "Here. This should work."

Brian took the cane, weighed it in his hands and swung it in an arc as if batting a ball. "Well, if anyone tries to mess with you, you can clobber him with this. I don't doubt it would do a good bit of damage."

"I'll be fine. Stop fussing, you two." Arabella smiled benignly at them.

BY the time the day was over, all Emma wanted to do was go upstairs, shower, microwave a frozen dinner and veg out in front of the television. However, Guy had made reservations for the two of them at L'Etoile and would be waiting for her there.

Emma was about to step into the shower when her cell rang. "Drat." She pulled on her terry robe and went in search of the ringing phone.

"Hello?"

"Emma? It's Kate."

"Kate." Emma perched on the arm of an upholstered wing chair. Kate Hathaway was Guy's longtime, and long-suffering, assistant. She and Emma had hit it off right away—bonding over Guy's many and varied idiosyncrasies. Emma suspected Kate had put up with Guy so long because she was a little in love with him herself.

"I'm sorry. I tried to reach you to warn you that Guy was on his way, but I was too late."

"I appreciate the effort." Emma swung her foot back and forth. She really needed a pedicure, she thought, as she examined her toes. Maybe she would give Angel a call.

"Has he persuaded you to come back with him?" Kate laughed as if she understood the absurdity of that.

Emma sighed. "I don't know, Kate. On the one hand, I'm having a blast here with my aunt Arabella, helping her redo her shop . . . on the other hand, Guy did manage to get me an interview at La Moda Italiana next week. You know I'd kill to work there."

Emma thought she heard Kate give a strangled gasp. "Are you okay?"

"Fine. Some water just went down the wrong way." She paused. "So? Are you coming back with Guy or not?" Her voice got higher at the end of the sentence—as if Emma's answer had assumed an unnatural importance.

"I haven't decided." Emma pushed off from the chair and got to her feet. "But I'll let you know, okay?"

"Fine. Just let me know."

Emma clicked the phone off, shrugged out of her robe and plunged into the steamy shower.

THE parking lot of L'Etoile wasn't too crowded when Emma got there, and she managed to find a space fairly near the front door, where a green and white striped awning stretched out to the sidewalk.

The interior of L'Etoile was dimly lit and soothingly cool after the mugginess of the Tennessee evening. Emma pulled her pashmina shawl up around her shoulders. L'Etoile was Paris's most upscale restaurant—the go-to place for special birthdays, memorable anniversaries and popping the question. The tables were covered in white linen, the silver was heavy, the waiters wore dinner jackets and there wasn't a revolving rack of cakes and pies for sale by the hostess stand.

Emma walked through the bar, where the bartender paused briefly in his glass-polishing to give her the once-over. Judging by the smile on his lips, she passed.

The maitre d' stood behind a wooden console, a stack of menus in his arms.

"Mademoiselle." He bowed and tugged at the collar of his dress shirt. A couple sat on the banquette just outside the dining room, waiting for their table. They were holding hands and looked nervous.

"I'm meeting a friend." Emma scanned the dusky restaurant. Only half the tables were filled—it was late by Paris standards—but she didn't immediately see Guy. Drat, she was hoping he would have already arrived.

A couple was tucked into the darkened corner in the back, and something about the girl caught Emma's eye. Even seated, Emma could tell she was very tall, and thin, with long, honey-colored hair. Her arms were draped around her companion's shoulders like a sweater, and their heads were together in a whispered tête-à-tête. The girl moved slightly, and Emma caught a glimpse of the man's face.

It was Guy.

No wonder the woman looked familiar—it was Nikki St. Clair, the model Guy was rumored to have been playing around with before Emma had fled New York. Emma had styled a number of shoots with her and Guy. You couldn't open a magazine or newspaper these days without seeing her posing half clad for some advertisement or fashion layout, and her photos were plastered on billboards from New York to California. Emma noticed the other patrons glancing at her and whispering to each other.

Guy looked up and caught sight of Emma. She saw the shocked look on his face. Had he been planning on ditching Nikki before she got there? She didn't stay long enough to find out.

She turned on her heel, flew past the astonished maitre d', past the bartender whose head swiveled to follow her as she blew by, out the door and into the car.

Loose gravel churned up and hit the side of the car as she blasted out of the parking lot and down the street.

EMMA didn't cry until she got back to her apartment and slammed and locked the door behind her. Her mind was whirling, and her hands were shaking with fury. She leaned against the closed door as hot tears ran down her cheeks. Guy Richard was nothing but a sniveling, lying, cheating *bastard*!

And she was through with him. Finished. *Finito. Finis.* No matter what language you used, the result was the same—she was through!

She kicked off her high-heeled sandals, dropped her dress on the bed and pulled on a T-shirt and a pair of yoga pants. Her stomach rumbled loudly, but she couldn't face the prospect of eating. What she needed was some chocolate. And a glass of wine.

Arabella had left the refrigerator stocked with basics like ketchup, eggs, bread and a wedge of Brie. Fortunately, Arabella's idea of the basics included an ice-cold bottle of pinot grigio. Emma rummaged in the drawers until she found the corkscrew. She grabbed a glass from the shelf, poured the wine and put the bottle back in the refrigerator. She went through the cupboards again, but the only chocolate she could find was a half-finished bag of semi-sweet chocolate chips. She undid the twist tie and poured out a handful. She nibbled them one by one as she sipped the wine and scrolled through four hundred and fifty cable television channels without finding anything she wanted to watch.

Finally, she switched the television off and dialed Liz. She glanced at her watch—hopefully she wouldn't be waking the children up.

Liz answered on the third ring. "Hello?"

"Liz," Emma said with a groan.

"What's the matter? You sound as if you've been crying."

"I have."

"Is it that Frenchman you told me about?"

Emma sniffled. "Yes. This time I thought he meant it, but when I got to the restaurant, that girl was there." She rummaged in her pocket and pulled out a slightly torn and dusty tissue.

"What girl is this?"

"She's a Claudette model—tall, thin, long blond hair. Perfect. You know the type." Emma dabbed at her nose with the tissue. "Everyone in New York was saying that she and Guy were a couple, but he told me that wasn't true. It was me he wanted." Emma gave a loud hiccough. "But there she was, draped all over him. She must have flown down with him."

"What a bastard!"

"That's what I said." Emma hiccoughed again.

"Do you want me to come over?"

Emma hesitated. It would be so good to see her friend, but it was late, and she knew Liz had her family to take care of. "I'll be okay. I think I'm going to go to bed. I drank a bit of wine." She picked up the bottle and checked the level. "A lot actually. I think I'll be able to sleep now."

She hung up the call and sat staring at the phone. She punched in Guy's number. Her thumbs flew over the keys as she typed in her text. *We are through. Leave me alone.* She wanted to tell him what she thought of him, but it would have taken up more than the 160 characters her texting program allowed. She hesitated for a split second, and pressed send. Minutes later, her cell phone rang once, but she didn't answer, and turned it off instead. Then she stuffed it behind the sofa cushion for good measure. She finished the bag of chocolate chips and stretched out on the couch. Her eyes were getting so heavy, she really needed to rest them for a bit.

EMMA dreamt someone was screaming, and sat bolt upright, surprised to find herself on the sofa with the morning sun streaming in the windows. She saw the wineglass and empty Hershey's bag on the coffee table, and slowly the evening before came back to her.

There was another scream, and this time it was definitely not part of her dream. It was coming from downstairs—from Sweet Nothings as far as she could tell. Emma grabbed her keys from the kitchen counter and bolted down the stairs. Her head pounded dully and her mouth felt thick and dry.

A third scream curdled the air, and Emma flung herself down the last few steps, out the door and around to the front of Sweet Nothings. Her hand was shaking and she had trouble getting the key in the lock. She swore in frustration as she missed a second time. It wasn't until she got the door open that it occurred to her she ought to be afraid. Who knew what she was going to find?

It was certainly the last thing she expected. Arabella's hands were over her mouth, stifling another scream, and she was leaning over something on the floor. It looked like a body.

Emma stopped short when she saw who it was.

Guy Richard.

Blood pooled on the carpet beneath him, and his eyes were open. Emma was pretty sure he was dead.

She, too, began to scream.

Chapter 4

EMMA closed her eyes, clenched her fists and forced herself to stop screaming. Deep breaths. Like yoga class. In . . . out . . . in . . . out. Her heartbeat slowed and steadied in time to the measured rhythm. When she opened her eyes, everything looked perfectly normal—morning sun streaming through the dusty front windows; Arabella dressed for work in a long black-and-white batik print dress, her hair pinned into a knot on top of her head; the interior of the shop silent and smelling faintly of fresh sawdust. Everything was perfectly normal. She looked down.

Except for the body at their feet.

Guy's body.

Pierre circled Guy, sniffing furiously. His one black ear twitched back and forth like an antenna looking for a signal.

"Pierre, no." Emma made a shooing motion with her hand. Pierre gave a disdainful snort and proceeded to ignore her.

Arabella pointed at Pierre's dog bed with an imperious

finger. "Pierre Louis Auguste! Now!" Pierre lowered his head and slunk toward the bed, with the occasional backward glance at Guy.

"We need to call an ambulance."

Arabella shook her head. "I think it's too late for that." She got down on one knee beside the body and put her index and forefinger against Guy's neck. "Give me a hand," she said to Emma as she struggled back to her feet. She shook her head again. "There's no pulse." She looked at Emma, her mouth quivering.

Emma felt tears spring into her eyes. Her knees wobbled dangerously. "Are you okay?" Emma whispered with a worried glance at Arabella.

Arabella nodded her head. "I think so. Sixty-eight years of living do prepare you for a lot, but even so, this is still a shock." Her hand trembled as she wiped it across her forehead. "How about you? You're deathly pale."

Emma took a shuddering breath and stood a little straighter. If her aunt Arabella could cope with this, then so could she. Her relationship with Guy flashed in front of her eyes—Guy wooing her with compliments and flowers; Guy cooking her his famous coq au vin; Guy whispering in her ear in French.

Zoe at Vera Wang had introduced them. Emma had needed a portfolio to interview for the job at *Femme*, and Guy had been willing to let her style a couple of his shoots. He'd taken to asking for her as his stylist even after she got the job. One night he'd invited her to join him and one of the models and her agent for a drink. Emma and Guy had sat and talked for hours at the bar long after the other two had left.

A tear slid down Emma's cheek, and a knot formed in her throat.

"We'd better call 9-1-1." Emma reached into her pocket for her cell phone but then remembered stuffing it behind the sofa cushions. She looked around helplessly.

Arabella pulled an iPhone from her macramé tote bag. She saw the look on Emma's face. "What?"

"Nothing." Emma shrugged. "I'm just kind of surprised you have one of those."

"I'm not *that* old," Arabella shot back as she punched in the numbers.

They stood huddled together, waiting. Emma thought she saw the door to O'Connell's Hardware open and she found herself wishing that Brian would stop by. His presence always made her feel secure. She guessed that's what big brothers were for.

Finally, they heard the long, low wail of a siren in the distance.

"Sounds like the cavalry are on their way." Arabella said. "Let's just hope they've sent someone with a brain."

Emma went to the front door and peered out the window. A silver Crown Vic slewed into a parking space in front of Sweet Nothings, its siren trailing off as it came to a halt.

A large, beefy policeman shouldered his way into the shop. His forehead shone with perspiration, and he had his hat pushed back to the center of his head. His damp blond hair curled around the brim.

"You reported a body?" He skidded to a stop just inside the shop. Emma noticed his glance stray to a mannequin in a lacy bra and panties, and she watched as his face flushed a deep red.

Arabella opened her mouth, her lips working furiously but no sound emerging.

Emma quickly spoke up. "Yes."

The front door banged open again, and another policeman entered. He was broad shouldered, with red hair cut really short and a wide face peppered with freckles.

"What have we got here?" He pushed his hat farther back on his head and scratched behind his ear.

"Looks like a body," the other policeman answered. "We

got ourselves a real, live dead body." His face paled suddenly, and he swayed slightly.

"No kidding, Einstein." The other policeman shuffled from foot to foot, staring at Guy's body. "We haven't had one of these since 2004 when Mrs. McGillicuddy came home early and found her husband in bed with the neighbor. Missed the neighbor, but she nailed him good." He circled Guy slowly then looked at Emma.

Emma glanced at the shiny badge pinned to his uniform. Officer Joe Kenny.

"Who is this guy? Do you know him?"

"I don't think I've ever seen him around these parts before," the other policeman said. His badge indicated his name was Patrick Flanagan. He swallowed hard and kept his eyes averted from the floor of Sweet Nothings.

"Me neither." Kenny scratched the other side of his head as he stared at Guy. "Know who he is?" He looked at Emma.

She began to stutter. "His name is Guy Richard. He's a photographer."

"What's he doing here?" Flanagan asked.

"Dunno," Kenny answered.

Emma gave him a stern look

"He a friend of yours?" Kenny asked.

Emma nodded her head.

"Boyfriend?"

Emma began to nod her head again but then stopped. "Ex. Ex-boyfriend. We dated, but it was over." She crossed her arms over her chest definitively. She wished her head wasn't pounding quite so hard. It was putting her at a disadvantage.

"Okay, so let's start from the beginning." Kenny nodded toward Arabella. "Who found the body?"

Arabella finally got her voice back. "I did." She fiddled with the strands of jet beads at her neck. "Would you mind if I sat down?" She moved toward a chair. "I've had quite a shock."

"Aunt Arabella, are you okay?" Emma helped her to the chair. "Would you like a drink of water?"

Arabella shook her head. "I'd rather get this over with as soon as possible. She perched on the edge of the chair, her back rigid, her head high.

"So you found the body." Kenny turned toward Arabella. "When did this happen?"

"Obviously a few minutes before I called you. I certainly didn't sit around polishing my nails first," she added with a sharp edge to her voice.

Pierre lifted his head and gave a low growl.

Take that, Emma thought, and shot an admiring glance at her aunt.

"So the body was here on the floor when you arrived?"

Arabella gave a quick nod. "I came in through the front door," she waved a hand in that direction, "and there he was."

"Was the door locked?" Kenny pulled a small, worn-looking notebook from his pocket and scribbled in it.

"Yes. I used my key to get in. Then I locked the door in back of me."

"Why?"

"Obviously so no one would come in."

"Were you expecting someone to come in?"

Arabella gave a hiss of annoyance. "Of course not. But occasionally customers try the door, and if it's not locked, they assume we're open for business."

"And you aren't?"

"No. We're in the process of renovating the shop. We plan on being closed for a few weeks."

"So let me get this straight." Kenny took his hat off and tucked it under his arm. "You come open up the shop as usual and bam, you fall over this dead body lying in the middle of your floor."

"I didn't fall over him," Arabella protested.

"In a manner of speaking, only," Kenny reassured her.

"And this guy is your niece's ex-boyfriend. And it looks like someone clonked him over the head with something." Kenny squatted down next to the body and examined the wound. "Nasty." He shook his head and stood up.

Emma noticed a glint of something shiny underneath the edge of one of the cabinets. She bent down to get a better view. It was Arabella's silver-headed walking stick. She reached out a hand.

"Don't touch it!" Kenny snapped.

Emma jumped and pulled her hand back. "I was only—"

"That could be our murder weapon." Kenny yanked a slightly tatty-looking handkerchief from his back pocket, wrapped it around his hand and reached under the cabinet. He pulled out the walking stick.

"Do you really think it's murder?" Arabella's face turned even paler.

"Unless our victim tripped on something and hit his head hard enough to cause that kind of damage." Kenny pointed toward the body.

"I suppose that is possible." Arabella looked at Emma eagerly.

Kenny gave a harsh bark of laughter and Pierre half rose from his dog bed, his upper lip pulled back in a snarl.

"I think this is our murder weapon right here." Kenny brandished the walking stick under their noses. "See? There's blood."

Emma recoiled, her stomach doing Olympic-worthy flip-flops.

"The detectives will have a field day with this. Hopefully we'll be able to lift some prints if the perp wasn't smart enough to wear gloves."

"It's going to be covered in prints," Arabella pointed out dryly. "Mine, specifically. My niece's, too, since she handled it. And probably half a dozen other people."

"Is that so?"

They all heard the front door open and turned to look in that direction.

Brian strode in but stopped short when he saw what was going on. "What happened?" He moved swiftly toward Emma and Arabella.

"And who might you be?" Kenny asked, his pencil poised above his battered notebook.

"Brian. Brian O'Connell."

"As in O'Connell's Hardware Store?" Kenny gestured toward the front window.

"Yes." Brian turned to Emma and Arabella. "Are you ladies okay?"

They both nodded.

"What's going on?" Brian addressed Kenny and Flanagan.

"I might ask you the same question." Kenny replied. He moved toward Brian and stood toe-to-toe with him. "What are you doing here? According to these ladies"—he swept a hand in Emma and Arabella's direction—"the shop is closed."

"I've been doing the renovations," Brian said.

"Were you acquainted with the deceased?" Kenny indicated the body with a nod of his head.

"I met him once. The other day."

Kenny brandished the walking stick, which he still had in his hand. "I take it this is yours?" He looked at Arabella.

"Yes, that belongs to me." Arabella responded.

"It does, does it?"

Emma bristled at the tone in Kenny's voice. "What is that supposed to mean?" she snapped.

"Nothing, nothing," Kenny said soothingly. "Just trying to confirm ownership, that's all."

"When did you last see this walking stick?" He turned back to Arabella.

"Yesterday. I was using it to get around after I'd tripped

and twisted my ankle. But it was feeling much better, and I didn't think I needed it anymore."

"So what do we have here?" Kenny looked around at them, sounding like Hercule Poirot in one of Agatha Christie's Golden Age mysteries. "We have a body." He indicated Guy with a flourish of the walking stick. "We have the murder weapon." He brandished the stick again. "We have no sign of a forced entry." He glanced toward the front door. "Ergo, our murderer must be someone with a key." He looked around his assembled audience. "Who has a key to this place?"

"Obviously, I do." Arabella spoke first. "And my niece."

"Me, too," said Brian.

"Really?" Kenny said, and Emma did not like the tone of his voice.

"I'm going to be doing the renovations on the shop, so Arabella thought I ought to have a key."

"Anyone else?" Kenny asked. "A neighbor, friend, boyfriend . . ." His voice trailed off as they all began shaking their heads. "No?"

"Don't you think we ought to call this in to headquarters now?" Flanagan reached for his walkie-talkie. "Get one of the detectives out here?"

"All in good time." Kenny slapped his notebook shut and stuffed it back in his pocket. "This case seems pretty simple to me. Open and shut." He pointed a finger at Emma. "You got mad at your ex-boyfriend and clonked him over the head with your aunt's walking stick."

Chapter 5

STUNNED silence greeted Officer Kenny's pronounce-
ment. Then everyone began talking at once. Emma sputtered, she was so mad. Arabella hissed and Brian bellowed.
They sounded like a steam engine roaring to life.

Before any of them could complete a sentence, Kenny
was at the front door of Sweet Nothings. "Coroner's here,"
he called over his shoulder as he ushered in a stoop-
shouldered man with untidy gray hair.

"District attorney's on his way," the coroner said, pulling
a pen from his shirt pocket. "Luckily, I was just down the
block getting a cup of coffee." He approached Guy's body.
"What have we got here?"

"You might not want to watch this," Kenny said to
Emma, Arabella and Brian. "Why don't you go on down to
The Coffee Klatch and get something to drink?"

Emma looked down at her yoga pants. At least she wasn't
in her pajamas. She would be more than glad to get away

from Sweet Nothings and Guy's body. The longer she stayed, the more real things became.

"I'll just go put Pierre in his crate." Arabella looked at Pierre and he lowered his head and obediently followed her into the back room.

As soon as Arabella rejoined them, they trooped out the door and into the warm, humid morning air. Emma had started to shake and the warmth felt good.

They were closing the door behind them when they saw someone waving from across the street. Emma didn't recognize him, and she stared, puzzled, as the man darted across Washington Street, just missing a red minivan that had to swerve to avoid him.

He stopped in front of them, breathless and panting. "Is everything all right? I saw the police and I couldn't imagine what had happened." He glanced at Arabella. "I was so afraid you'd taken ill or something." He smoothed a hand across his head where several long strands of white hair had blown across to the wrong side.

Arabella gave a dry smile. "Well, as you can see, I'm perfectly fine." She turned toward Emma and Brian. "Les, this is my niece, Emma. She's down from New York to help with my shop. And this," she said, turning toward Brian, "is Brian O'Connell. He's helping with the renovations. His father owns O'Connell's Hardware."

Arabella turned toward the small, dapper gentleman at her side. "And this is Les Wallace. He runs The Toggery just down the street."

Emma looked from Les to Arabella and back again. Was Les a gentleman caller, as they used to say in the old days? There was a twinkle in Arabella's eye that hadn't been there before, and Emma swore her cheeks had a faint blush to them. Of course, it could have been the heat, but somehow she didn't think so.

"We're on our way to The Coffee Klatch. Would you care to join us?"

"But what's happened?" Les spluttered, adjusting his tie, which had become slightly askew in his dash across the street. "What are the police doing outside your shop?"

"Come with us." Arabella linked her arm through his. "And I'll tell you all about it." She glanced over her shoulder where a small crowd of people had gathered in front of Sweet Nothings. "It's probably best if we keep this among ourselves for as long as we can."

That won't be long, Emma thought, remembering how quickly word of Guy's arrival had spread.

FOR most of its life The Coffee Klatch had been known simply as The Paris Diner, and several of the letters were still faintly visible behind the sign announcing its new name. Although the name had been changed, the staff and customers remained much the same. The young couple that had taken over the diner after the previous owner died had invested in a fancy espresso/cappuccino maker that retained its original polish these many years later. Orders for anything fancier than coffee with cream and sugar were few and far between. And despite now being called "baristas," the waitresses still wore frilly white aprons and called all their customers, male and female alike, "honey."

A long line snaked from the takeout counter to the back of The Coffee Klatch, but most of the tables were empty. Emma, Brian, Arabella and Les slid into a booth near the back.

"Hopefully no one will find us here," Arabella said, as she swiped a paper napkin across the table. "The less we say to people, the better."

A waitress arrived at their table, pad in hand, piece of gum tucked firmly behind her back molars. Her glance kept straying to the front windows of The Coffee Klatch.

"Something's going on down the street," she said even before she asked for their order. "A whole lot of police cars went screaming past." She cocked her head toward the chef flipping eggs on the griddle. "Hank said they stopped in front of Sweet Nothings. That's your shop, isn't it, Miss Arabella?"

Arabella fiddled with her menu. "Yes," she agreed reluctantly. "And how is Marshall?" she asked firmly. "Marshall is Mabel's son, and he's just about to start first grade," she explained to the rest of the table.

"Oh he's fine," Mabel glowed, adroitly deflected. "He's so excited about taking the bus to school for the first time." She tucked her pad into the pocket of her apron. "Just coffee then?" she asked, reaching out a hand for the menus.

"Could I get some green tea?" Emma asked.

"Green tea? I'll see if we have any. I think they bought some a couple of years ago, but no one ever asks for it."

Mabel tossed her yellow curls and strode off.

"That was close." Brian smiled at Arabella.

"We won't be able to hold the questions off forever—"

"Speaking of that," Les cleared his throat timidly. "What is going on? Do you know?"

Arabella hesitated. "There's been an unfortunate accident at the shop, and a young man has been killed."

Les gasped. "But . . ." he sputtered.

Before he could say another word, Angel Roy rushed up to their table. Her French twist was coming down around her ears, and her face was flushed with excitement. "What is going on?" she demanded before even saying hello. "There are all these police cars outside your shop, Arabella. Are you okay?"

Arabella sighed. "Just an accident. Nothing for everyone to get so worked up over."

Angel looked at her watch and groaned. "Of all the days for me to have an early appointment. Gertrude Bloch is coming in for a perm. She's going to visit her daughter in Nashville and wants to get it done before she leaves." Angel heaved another sigh. "See you all later," she called over her shoulder. "I'll be by as soon as I'm done with Gertrude."

"Is that a threat or a promise?" Arabella muttered under her breath. She fell silent as Mabel approached with their coffee.

Mabel put the cups down with a bang, sending coffee sluicing over the sides. She pushed a mug of pale liquid toward Emma. "You're in luck. Hank found that old box of green tea." She tossed a stack of napkins on the table. "I got a quick look-see out the door while I was getting your coffee, and I swear the cops were wheeling a body out of Sweet Nothings!"

Arabella sighed again.

Mabel lingered by their table, adjusting and readjusting the packets of sugar in their ceramic holder. They all stared glumly into their cups until Hank shouted for Mabel, and she went running toward the counter.

"We're not going to be able to keep this to ourselves." Emma took a sip of her tea, trying to look normal, but her hand was shaking and her stomach revolted as soon as the hot brew hit bottom.

"You're right, of course." Arabella ripped open a packet of sugar and dumped it into her mug. "I just can't stand gossip." She took a sip and squared her shoulders. "It's so destructive. Better to wait until the police know something and let them announce it to the public. Their people will know how to put the appropriate spin on things."

As if on cue, the front door of The Coffee Klatch banged open, and Officer Kenny barged in, blinking against the lights like a mole. He caught sight of Emma and Arabella in the back booth and headed their way with obvious determination.

He was puffed up like a blowfish with self-importance,

his eyes popping. He didn't waste any time. "Detective Reilly wants to speak to you. Stat!"

"Me?" Emma's voice quavered in spite of herself.

"Yes." He glanced at his watch. "Now."

Emma followed Kenny out of the restaurant. All heads swiveled in her direction, and she had the urge to grab one of the brown paper bags from the stack by the takeout window and pull it over her head. She gave one last backward glance at her friends and let the door shut in back of her.

EMMA trotted down the street after Officer Kenny, trying to keep pace with his lumbering gait. Flanagan was standing outside Sweet Nothings, attempting to keep the crowd at bay. All heads swiveled toward Emma as she arrived, breathless and perspiring, in Kenny's wake.

"Excuse me. Step aside, please."

Kenny elbowed his way past the curious stares of Emma's neighbors and fellow shopkeepers and shepherded her safely through the door and into the relative quiet of Sweet Nothings. Emma noticed a camera flash as Kenny led her past the scene of the crime, his broad shoulders partially blocking the view. She averted her eyes quickly. As it was, she doubted she'd ever get the image of Guy sprawled on the floor out of her mind.

The stockroom was in shadow, the only illumination coming from the small lamp on Arabella's desk. A man was standing with his back to Emma. He was of medium height, wearing a boxy suit and had dark hair curling over his shirt collar in back. Something about his stance seemed familiar.

He turned around and Emma gasped.

"Chuck Reilly!"

"Emma Taylor," he answered smoothly.

"What are you doing here?" they both asked simultaneously.

Chuck indicated for Emma to go first.

"I'm here helping my aunt with her store." Emma realized she sounded defensive, which was ridiculous. She had every right to come back to Paris if she wanted to.

Chuck pulled out his wallet, flicked it open and held out his badge. "I'm a sergeant now. Made the CID, Criminal Investigation Division, that is, last year."

"Oh" was all Emma could say. Last she'd heard, Chuck was still a patrolman chasing down jaywalkers and helping get cats out of trees. They'd dated briefly in high school, but she'd quickly broken it off. Chuck hadn't taken it well. He had been Henry County High School's star running back and wasn't used to being rejected.

He'd made life miserable for Emma after the breakup. She hoped he was over it, because he was in a much more powerful position now. Just the thought made her palms sweat.

"I want to ask you a few questions," Chuck said quietly. Too quietly.

Emma's mouth went dry. "Okay."

He had her walk through the whole thing again—hearing Arabella scream, running down to Sweet Nothings, finding Guy's body. All familiar territory now.

Emma felt herself sag with fatigue. Chuck pointed toward the desk chair, and Emma sank into it gratefully. He pulled an armless folding chair toward him, spun it around and straddled it. "This was your ex-boyfriend, you say? What was he doing here?"

Emma cleared her throat. She wouldn't lie—she couldn't. Her face would get as scarlet as Rudolph's nose, and she'd be busted immediately. "He was here to . . . to try to make up with me."

Chuck gave a slow smile. Emma's palms got slicker.

"Another one of your victims?"

Emma jerked as if she'd been jolted by an electrical current. "What do you mean—one of my victims?"

Chuck gave a nasty laugh. "I mean another victim who felt the sting of your rejection."

"Look . . ." Emma began.

Chuck held up a hand. "How about you let me do the talking, okay?"

Emma sank back down into her seat. Chuck held all the cards in this round. It wasn't fair. Why wasn't he still giving out speeding tickets and directing traffic?

He was a good-looking man—even better looking than he'd been in high school. Maturity had added to his attractiveness, along with the ice blue eyes and cleft chin that had drawn Emma to him in the first place. But Emma had soon discovered that Chuck's attractiveness wasn't more than skin deep. He oozed fake charm, but as Abraham Lincoln had so famously said, you can't fool all the people all the time. Emma had come to her senses quickly.

Chuck rested his hands on the back of the chair. "So, the boyfriend tracked you down in order to try to get you back?"

Emma flashed back to the scene at L'Etoile and Nikki St. Clair draped around Guy's shoulders. Guy had certainly chosen a strange method of trying to win her back.

"And you met the boyfriend in the shop and had it out?" Chuck began a thorough examination of his fingernails.

"No!" Emma protested.

Chuck raised an eyebrow in disbelief. "Really?"

"Look," Emma held her hands out, palms up. "If I'd killed Guy, wouldn't it have been the other way around?"

"What do you mean?"

"I mean," Emma took a deep breath, trying to calm the sledgehammering of her heart. "If I'd hit Guy over the head, wouldn't it make more sense if I'd been the one trying to get him back?"

Chuck raised an eyebrow.

Emma sighed in exasperation. "It's like this. Imagine that I wanted Guy to take me back. He refuses. So I"—she clenched her fists—"grab Aunt Arabella's walking stick and clobber him over the head." She swung her arms in an arc as if wielding a deathly blow.

"So, that's what happened," Chuck declared over his steepled fingers.

He leaned back with a smug expression on his face.

Chapter 6

LATER that afternoon, Arabella sat in a pool of light from the gooseneck lamp that was trained on the bundle of silk in her hands. She was repairing a slight tear in a section of lace with silk thread ordered especially from a shop in New York City. Emma noticed her hands shook slightly, although Arabella insisted she was fine after the shock of that morning.

"The police can't possibly think you had anything to do with it!" Arabella eased her needle into the garment in her lap.

"That's ridiculous," said Liz. As soon as news of the murder had reached her, she had come running to Sweet Nothings, double-parking her station wagon in her haste. She was now perched on a stool in front of the counter, one eye trained on the street outside.

Emma shrugged and tilted the lid of her laptop slightly. Chantelle DeLang had sent photos of several wonderful lingerie lines. "I get the impression I'm Chuck's only suspect. He kept pointing out how I didn't have any alibi."

"Lots of other people don't either." Brian put down the block of wood he was sanding. "Why pick on you?"

"Think about it." Emma bookmarked the site she was exploring and powered down her laptop. "Who else had any reason to kill Guy? No one knew him before he arrived here. Except me," she added glumly.

"That may be true, but what's more important," Arabella said, knotting the end of her thread, "is what are we going to do about it?"

"What do you mean?" Emma ran a hand through her hair. She rolled her shoulders forward and back. She was so tired. She couldn't wait to crawl into bed and put this day behind her.

"Do you mean we should do some of our own investigating?" Brian wiped his hands on a rag, balled it up and stuffed it into his toolbox.

Arabella arched an eyebrow as she deftly slid her needle through the periwinkle blue silk in her hands. "Why not? Surely among us we can muster a few more brain cells than that pathetic Chuck Reilly."

Brian laughed, and Emma managed a small smile in spite of her worries.

"Sure, why not?" Emma shrugged and glanced at Brian.

"I'm in." Brian gave Emma a big smile.

"Me, too, although I'll have to work around Ben and Alice's schedule." Liz slid off her stool in her excitement.

Emma felt her spirits lift. "There's Nikki St. Clair, although Chuck didn't seem to think much of that angle."

"Nikki?" Brian's head swiveled in Emma's direction. "Who's Nikki?"

"She's the blonde who was with Guy that night at the restaurant. When I arrived at L'Etoile." Emma shuddered. "She was draped all over him." Her lips curled in disgust.

"Oh, no!" Arabella exclaimed, dropping the peignoir she was working on.

"What's the matter?" Emma, Brian and Liz all rushed to her side.

"It's nothing. I just pricked my finger."

"Do you want me to get—"

"No." Arabella shook her head. "I was just afraid I might get blood on the fabric." She examined the stretch of lace carefully. "Fortunately, I don't seem to have done any damage."

Emma thought of the blood pooling under Guy's head and felt her stomach turn over.

"I think we need to track down this Nikki." Brian began putting his tools away. "Was she someone local?"

"Uh, not exactly. She must have come down with Guy from New York. You'd know her if you saw her. She's a rather well-known lingerie model." Emma thought Brian's eyes lit up, and she had a pang of what felt an awful lot like jealousy.

"Do you think she's still here in Paris?" Arabella snipped the end of her thread.

"It's possible. I know Guy's return flight was for tomorrow. If she came down with him, she probably planned to leave with him as well."

"I wonder where she's staying?" Brian said.

"Probably the Beau. That's the Beauchamp Hotel and Spa," Liz explained, obviously noticing the confused look on Emma's face. "It's brand-new. And very swanky. Just the type of place a model would want to stay."

"I think it's time someone had a chat with this Nikki St. Clair," Emma said.

"I'll go with you," Brian said quickly.

"I'll—" Liz began at almost the same time, but she bit off what she was about to say, and Emma noticed her exchange a knowing glance with Arabella.

"Why don't you call the hotel and see if Miss St. Clair is registered, and I'll go get cleaned up." Brian brushed at his jeans.

"Sure." Emma pulled her cell phone from her pocket.

"And tomorrow I'll start chatting with some of the other shopkeepers." Arabella piped up. "Maybe someone saw something last night." She folded the garment she'd been working on and turned off the lamp. "I know Angel lives over her shop, although how she can stand it with the smell of all those hair chemicals, I don't know, but perhaps she just happened to be looking out the window."

"Or someone might have been working late taking inventory," Brian added.

Emma felt a flicker of hope. Maybe they could find some other suspects for Chuck to chase, and maybe then he'd leave her alone.

THEY got a later start than anticipated. Brian's father needed help creating a new window display. While Emma waited, she made herself her favorite dinner, one that she hadn't had since departing for New York—grilled cheese and tomato soup. She'd called the Beauchamp Hotel earlier and discovered that a Nikki St. Clair was, indeed, registered there.

Since Brian was going to be late, she ran through her evening yoga series. A few downward facing dogs, cobras and forward folds took the kinks out of her muscles and back, and five minutes in child's pose helped restore her equilibrium. She felt almost cheerful when Brian knocked on her door. He led the way down the stairs and out to the parking lot, where he gestured apologetically toward the red pickup truck waiting in one of the spots. "I hope you don't mind riding in the truck. It's perfectly clean," he reassured her, glancing at her dress.

"You forget. I'm used to riding the subway. Having your own wheels is a real luxury." Emma smiled. She stood for a moment, taking in the warm Tennessee night. Stars sparkled in the midnight blue sky, and the air was perfumed with the scent of honeysuckle and pine. She paused by the truck and took a deep breath. Brian reached for the door handle, and his fingers accidentally brushed hers. Emma blushed and moved her hand away.

Brian held the door open, and Emma hesitated. The seat was a lot higher than she was used to.

"Put your foot here." Brian indicated the running board.

Emma did as he suggested, and Brian put a hand under her elbow, giving her a boost. She slid onto the seat and her dress rose up. She tugged it down to her knees, conscious of Brian's gaze on her legs.

As they headed away from town, the inky darkness of the night intensified. Emma thought she saw the occasional luminescent glow of an animal's eyes as they sped through the countryside. She shivered and gave a sigh of relief when they spotted the entrance to the Beauchamp Hotel and Spa. It was a low-lying building, modern, with lots of wood and glass. An island in the center of the circular drive was thick with striped ornamental grasses.

The interior matched the outside, with soothing sage green walls, polished light-wood floors and scattered Oriental rugs. The reception desk was a slab of polished concrete mounted in a rock wall. Water trickled over the wall and pooled in a small trough lit with dozens of pinpoint lights. The air was gently perfumed with the aromas of lavender, vanilla and mint.

Emma inhaled the delicious scent and looked around. A room in this place must cost a fortune, but she supposed supermodels made plenty of money. She recalled one of them saying once that she didn't even get out of bed for less than ten thousand dollars.

"May I help you?" The woman behind the counter wore a pair of black yoga pants and a white tunic, and had her hair pulled into a low bun at the nape of her neck.

"We're here to see Ms. St. Clair." Brian glanced at the piece of paper. "Room 251."

"Let me see if she's in." She picked up the telephone, but before she put it to her ear, she glanced inquiringly at Brian and Emma. "Who may I say is calling?"

Brian hesitated, and Emma spoke up quickly. "Guy. Guy Richards."

"And you are?" The woman tilted her head in Emma's direction.

Emma shook her head. "Just an assistant. It isn't important."

The woman raised an eyebrow but proceeded to dial the telephone. She spoke briefly and listened even more briefly. She put the telephone receiver back in its cradle. "You may go up now." She pointed across the lobby. "Take the elevator to the second floor and turn left."

"I think Ms. St. Clair is going to be quite surprised when she opens her door and sees us," Brian said as the elevator whisked them silently toward the second floor.

"I'll be curious to see just how surprised she is."

"Do you think she had something to do with it?"

"She was the only other person around who already knew him. Except for me."

The elevator doors opened with a gentle ping, and Emma and Brian stepped into the silent, softly lit corridor.

They turned left and found room 251 halfway down the hall.

"Here goes nothing." Brian smiled at Emma and knocked once.

He was about to knock again when the door was flung open.

"Oh." Nikki stood in the doorway wrapped in a short silk robe that bared the better part of her long, colt-like legs. She tried to look around Emma and Brian but then realized that no one else was there. Her hair was messy, as if she'd been lying down, and she wasn't wearing any makeup, but she was still striking.

The look she gave Emma made her suddenly feel tatty in the dress and sandals that had seemed so perfect when she put them on earlier.

Nikki bestowed a glittering smile on Brian. She hooked her arm through his, her robe parting to show a little more skin than Emma was comfortable with. "Why don't you . . . and your assistant," she hissed the word through narrowed lips, "come in and tell me what you're doing here and why you pretended to be Guy Richard."

Emma couldn't tell if Nikki was mocking her for the lie she'd told the receptionist or if she really didn't recognize Emma despite their having worked together on several occasions. Emma sighed. It was probably the latter. People like her were invisible to people like Nikki.

Nikki's suite was cavernous, and Emma wondered if all the rooms were this big. The walls were the same soothing sage green as the lobby, and the sofa and chairs in the main area were sleek and cream colored. An irregularly shaped coffee table with a thick glass top stood between them. Cream-colored drapes were pulled against what looked to be a wall of windows. In front of them was a freestanding spa tub big enough for several people. Emma could see into the bedroom beyond, where a huge platform bed dominated the room. The sheets were rumpled, and Emma wondered if they had woken Nikki.

"Well?" Nikki rounded on Emma. "Are you going to tell me what this is about?"

"It's bad news, actually." Emma decided to opt for boldness. "Guy is dead. He's been murdered."

Nikki's professionally plucked eyebrows rose as one. "What?"

"It's true." Brian followed her into the room. "I'm very sorry to say that Guy Richard is dead."

"Why should I believe you?" Nikki stalked over to the corner and grabbed a pack of Marlboro Lights off the teak end table. She shook out a cigarette, oblivious to the no smoking sign plastered on the door to the room. She pulled a pack of matches from the pocket of her white silk robe, struck one and held it to the cigarette at her lips.

"Well?" She inhaled deeply and blew out a stream of smoke. "What makes you think Guy is dead?" She got so close to Brian their noses were almost touching. Brian stuttered and took a step backward. Nikki took another step forward, as if they were locked in a bizarre tango. "Well?"

Emma grabbed the telephone receiver and waved it at Nikki. "Call the police. They'll tell you. Ask for Chuck Reilly." She shuddered thinking about how obnoxious Chuck would be if he had the opportunity to talk to Nikki. She could imagine his eyes undressing her from head to toe. Of course her modeling assignments didn't leave much to anyone's imagination, even Chuck's overactive one.

Nikki stuck out her lower lip in a pout and heaved her thin shoulders. "All right. So I believe you. Guy is dead." She stabbed her cigarette at the ornamental glass bowl she was using as an ashtray.

Nikki glared at Emma and turned toward Brian. She tossed her hair back and let her robe slip open a little farther. "So. What happened?" She shook another cigarette from the pack, handed the matches to Brian and leaned in close as he held the flame to her cigarette.

Emma began a slow burn. Was Guy nothing more to Nikki than her latest conquest? Had she ever cared for him at all, or was it just a game to her to see whose boyfriend she could steal next? Emma started to open her mouth, but bit her lip and stopped herself. It wouldn't do any good to antagonize Nikki.

"No one really knows what happened." Emma watched Nikki carefully. "Do you know where he went after leaving L'Etoile last night?"

Nikki perched on the arm of the sofa and pulled her hair over her shoulder. She began raking her fingers through the long, honey-colored strands. "I have no idea. We had a fight." Her lower lip trembled slightly. "I tried to get him to stay, but he refused. He wanted to go after you." She threw the words at Emma as if they were poisoned darts.

"You don't know where he went?" Brian said.

Nikki shook her head.

"How about you? What did you do after leaving L'Etoile?"

"Me?" Nikki looked startled. "Nothing. I came back here." She glanced around the room. "I was . . . waiting for someone." She looked down and away from Emma and Brian.

"What time was it?"

"I don't know." Nikki's tone was petulant. She fiddled with a loose string on her bathrobe tie.

Emma thought back to the previous evening. It seemed a million years away all of a sudden. She'd arrived at the restaurant shortly after eight o'clock. Had Guy stayed behind to try to calm Nikki down?

"Was it nine o'clock? Ten o'clock?" Emma said

"I told you. I don't know." Nikki stared at her feet. She shrugged. "Nine o'clock, maybe?"

"And you came back here?"

"Yeah." She jumped up, tossing her hair back. "What is this all about? Why are you asking me all these questions?"

"Sorry," Brian said. "We don't mean to upset you. It's just that we're trying to figure out what happened."

"It sounds to me like you're trying to say I had something to do with it." Nikki stalked toward the small kitchenette that formed an *L* off the main room. She opened the refrigerator and pulled out a bottle of water.

Emma recognized the blue and white label and the unique shape. It might only be water, but it sold for almost five dollars a bottle.

Nikki twisted off the top and took a long swallow.

"How did you get back here?" Brian stood with his arms crossed over his chest.

"Well I didn't walk," Nikki sneered. "I have a rental car." She perched on the edge of the sofa again, swinging one bare foot. Her toes were painted a deep midnight blue.

"Did anyone see you?" Emma tried to keep her tone light.

"Look. I don't know who you think you are, but you have no right barging in here like this asking me all these questions." She glared at Emma then turned to Brian with a smile. "Why don't you get rid of your 'assistant'? Then you can ask me all the questions you want." Her voice dropped to a low purr.

Brian took a step back. "I don't think that's necessary." He paused. "Did anyone see you after you got back here?"

Nikki scowled. "I don't know. Maybe. The lobby was pretty empty, and I can't remember if there was anyone behind the desk." She picked up a throw pillow and held it to her chest. "Now will you please leave me alone?"

Emma and Brian obligingly headed toward the door. They heard the soft thud of the pillow hitting the door as it closed behind them.

THE night was even blacker as they drove back toward downtown Paris. Emma's head was swirling with all the information they'd gleaned. Nikki was definitely not telling them everything she knew. That didn't necessarily make her the murderer, but there was certainly a lot more than met the eye where Nikki was concerned.

"Do you think Nikki's telling the truth?" Emma turned to Brian.

He glanced back briefly. "Some of it, at least. But certainly not all. I got the impression she's trying to hide something."

"Me, too."

BRIAN insisted on waiting until Emma was safe and sound behind her closed and locked apartment door. It wasn't as if a serial killer was on the loose in Paris, Tennessee—she was pretty sure Guy had been singled out to be killed—but she was still grateful for Brian's chivalry. In spite of herself, she made a cursory inspection of the apartment—no one under the beds or hiding in the closet—before she kicked off her shoes and poured herself a glass of sweet tea.

Her cell phone rang as she was about to sink into the large comfy chair and ottoman drawn up in front of the television. Emma rummaged through her purse trying to find it, finally dumping the contents out onto the rug. She grabbed her cell and pressed the button.

"Hello?"

"Emma. It's Kate."

Emma gave a silent groan. Kate! She'd forgotten all about her! How was she going to tell her Guy was dead? Although Kate denied it, Emma was quite certain Kate was in love with Guy. She pictured Kate's open and honest face. She wasn't good at hiding her emotions or her thoughts. This was going to break her heart.

"Hi, Kate." Emma debated putting off telling Kate until tomorrow, but by then reporters might have picked up on the story. She didn't want her friend opening the paper over breakfast to learn of Guy's death.

"You sound . . . upset."

Emma took a deep breath. "I am. Kate, I don't know how to tell you this, but Guy's dead. He's been murdered."

Kate was silent for so long, Emma wondered if the

connection had been lost. Finally she heard a sound like a kitten mewling.

"I'm so sorry, Kate. I know this must be very difficult for you."

"What happened?"

Emma gave Kate an abbreviated version of the story. No need to upset her with all the gory details. She wished she hadn't had to witness them herself. The memory still made her feel slightly queasy.

"Did you say Nikki was there?" Kate gave a loud sniff, and Emma heard her blowing her nose.

"Yes. She came down with Guy." Emma felt disappointment wash over her again.

"Be careful, Emma."

"What do you mean?" Emma stretched her legs out on the ottoman and leaned against the chair cushions. She rubbed the back of her neck where the muscles were tangled up in knots.

"Nikki St. Clair is trouble. One time she—well, I don't like telling stories about other people. Let's just say you need to watch your back."

"Don't worry, I will." Emma could picture Kate's earnest face, her eyebrows drawn together in concern, her glasses half-slipping down her nose. "I just have to convince the police that I didn't have anything to do with the murder." Emma felt a dark cloud settle around her at the thought.

"Why don't I come down there and help?" Kate's voice brightened slightly.

Emma didn't want to disappoint her, but she couldn't imagine what Kate would be able to do. "That's really not necessary. I know how busy you are . . ."

"It's no problem. Really. I'll check on flights and let you know when I'm arriving. It'll be better for me than sitting here twiddling my thumbs and wondering what's going on. Is there somewhere I can stay?"

Emma glanced around her small apartment. "You could stay here with me. I don't mind bunking on the couch."

"You're sweet, but I don't want to put you out of your own bed."

"I think there are a few bed-and-breakfasts within walking distance of downtown. I'll check with Aunt Arabella and make the arrangements."

"It'll be good to see you again, Emma."

"You, too," Emma answered and hung up. Her spirits perked up at the thought of seeing Kate's familiar face again.

Chapter 7

WHEN Emma arrived at Sweet Nothings the next morning, the lights were already on and the front door was unlocked. She was about to push it open when she noticed the newspaper lying on the mat. She bent down, picked it up and tucked it under her arm.

Brian was already at work and he looked up and smiled when Emma entered. He'd transformed the wall of particle-board cupboards into white, floor-to-ceiling, glass-fronted cabinets. Emma would be able to hang stock in them without having to fold it. Arabella had hired someone to iron all the vintage negligees and peignoirs so they would be perfect when Sweet Nothings opened again.

Perhaps the armoires would come today, Emma thought. She planned on having one in each corner of the store, with their doors propped open and enticing bits of silk and lace spilling out.

"Morning," Brian called above the noise of the electric

screwdriver as he fastened the last knob on the last cabinet door.

Emma gave a brief wave. She couldn't help but notice how attractive Brian looked with his sleeves rolled up for work and his hair slightly tousled. He turned around and she looked away quickly.

"The cabinets look fantastic."

"They did turn out well." Brian stood back to admire his handiwork.

There was the sound of scratching at the door followed by excited yelps. Arabella pushed open the door, and Pierre shot into the room, tail wagging furiously. He greeted Emma, then Brian, then, after turning around three times, settled on his toile dog bed, panting happily.

"Oh, they're magnificent!" Arabella exclaimed when she saw the new cabinets.

Brian beamed. "You like them?"

Arabella nodded her head. "Very much so." She turned toward Emma. "Excellent idea, my dear." She opened one of the cabinets and peered inside.

Emma tossed the newspaper on the counter and joined Arabella. She tried the doors, opening and closing them. "They're gorgeous." She smiled over her shoulder at Brian.

He ducked his head. "Glad you like them."

Emma stuck her purse under the counter, and was about to tuck the newspaper next to it, when she noticed the front page. Her heart jumped into her throat as she spread open the paper and read the headline.

"Oh, no."

"What's wrong, dear?" Arabella turned toward Emma with concern.

Emma held up the newspaper where the headline *Murder At Sweet Nothings—Owners Questioned* made a bold, black slash across the front page.

Arabella put a hand to her chest. "That almost makes it sound as if the police think we're guilty."

Emma put the paper on the counter and began skimming the article.

"The headline sums it up," Emma said when she'd finished reading, her stomach flipping over and plummeting to the level of her knees. She looked from Arabella to Brian.

"You know what they say," Arabella put an arm around Emma. "There's no such thing as bad publicity."

Emma glanced at the headline again. "I wish I could believe that."

Two sharp knocks sounded on the front door. *The armoires?* Emma wondered. She remembered how she'd thought that the last time and instead had found Guy standing on the doorstep. She hesitated momentarily, then hurried to the door and pulled it open.

"Oh."

A very diminutive woman stood on the mat. She had a paisley scarf tied gypsy-style around her head, and large hoops dangled from her drooping earlobes. A portable oxygen tank stood slightly behind her, and a recently extinguished cigarette was by her right foot. Surely it was dangerous to smoke around oxygen. It was lucky they all hadn't been blown to kingdom come.

"Can I help you?"

The woman stared back at Emma. "Who are you?" Her heavy New York accent came as a surprise.

"Sylvia." Arabella rushed over to the door. "Come on in."

The woman eased her way into Sweet Nothings, the oxygen tank bumping along in back of her.

"This is my niece, Emma Taylor. She's down from New York to help me with the shop." Arabella turned toward Emma. "This is Sylvia Brodsky. She's from New York, too. She moved down here last year with her son and daughter-in-law when her son was transferred."

"I'm not living with them, though. Got my own place above The Taffy Pull." Sylvia gave a long, hacking cough. "Didn't want to be an inconvenience. Besides, I got my little side business going and don't want to disturb my son and his wife the princess with people coming and going."

"Side business?" *Is she the woman Arabella had hired to do the ironing?* Emma wondered.

Sylvia shook her head, and her earrings bobbed back and forth. "I do tarot readings and hold séances. Last week we contacted Loralee's late husband. She's the one who runs A Good Yarn, the craft and knitting store on the corner."

"Oh." Emma honestly couldn't think of a single other thing to say.

"That's what I wanted to talk to you about." She maneuvered her way farther into the shop and perched on the end of a chair. "The night that young man was killed in your shop." She pointed a finger at Emma. "He was your fellow, wasn't he?"

Emma opened her mouth, but Sylvia didn't wait for an answer.

"I was looking out my window. Billy Bob Winthrop— he's the football coach over at the high school—had booked a reading, and he was late. So I'm looking out the window and a light goes on over here at Sweet Nothings. I'm thinking to myself, What on earth is Arabella doing at the shop so late?"

It must have been Guy, Emma thought. *And his murderer.* The thought gave her a chill.

"Then I drew the Tower card." Sylvia nodded so vigorously her earrings slapped against the side of her face.

"The Tower card? What on earth is that?" Arabella asked.

"It's a tarot card. And let me tell you, it ain't good. It signifies death or destruction. And here that very same night that young man was killed!"

"Did you see anything besides the light?" Emma said.

Sylvia's shoulders rose and fell. "Nah. I thought I might've seen a shadow in the window, but I couldn't tell who it was." She looked disappointed. "Besides, just then Angel Roy next door started up a real racket with that boyfriend of hers. They live right next door to my place." She drew a deep breath and began another hacking cough.

Emma waited as patiently as she could. "What were they fighting about?" She asked as soon as Sylvia stopped wheezing.

"I couldn't hear every word. You know in movies when they show some gal holding a glass to the wall and listening? Well, don't believe it. It don't work. But I did manage to hear the boyfriend say something about Angel hanging around with some guy."

That didn't help them much, Emma thought. Unless . . .

Unless the boyfriend hadn't meant "some guy" but had actually been referring to Guy. Guy Richard.

Could Angel's boyfriend have become jealous enough to kill?

Chapter 8

"MAYBE it's time you took Angel up on that mani-pedi she offered when you first arrived," Arabella said as she closed the door behind Sylvia Brodsky.

Emma was about to protest but then realized what Arabella was getting at. This would give her the chance to probe for more information. She thought for a minute. "Do you know Angel's boyfriend? What's he like? The jealous type?"

"Can't say that I know him all that well. Angel's boyfriends tend to come and go. At the moment it's Tom Mulligan. He owns the auto repair shop just outside of town on Route 69. I took my car there once, and he was polite enough. Did reasonable work, too."

"I don't know Tom, but I've heard some things." Brian straightened from where he'd been busy nailing molding around the cabinets.

"Do tell." Arabella settled back in her chair, her hands folded expectantly in her lap.

"I don't approve of gossip," Brian said, "but I've heard

the same thing from a number of people. He likes his drink, they say. And he can get a little hot under the collar after a few shots." He ran his hands through his hair, leaving it even more rumpled than before. Emma had to resist the urge to smooth it down for him.

"I heard he got into a fight with some guy outside the Rooster, the bar out on Route 69. Put the guy in the hospital. He would have gone to jail, but the fellow refused to press charges. Said it was his fault. He started it."

"This is beginning to sound interesting," Emma said. She glanced at her watch. Perhaps she could get in to see Angel sometime during the afternoon.

"Look." Brian came around the corner and stood toe-to-toe with her. "You'd better be careful. Someone—whoever it is—has killed already. What's going to stop him from doing it again? If they catch wind of you snooping around . . ."

Emma inhaled sharply. Brian was right. This wasn't some game or show on television. This was real. Someone was dead. *Guy* was dead.

But Chuck Reilly was threatening to pin the murder on *her*. If she didn't investigate she could go to jail. She shivered. Suddenly a mani-pedi at Angel Cuts didn't seem all that dangerous.

EMMA secured an appointment for two o'clock that afternoon. She was looking forward to a little pampering. It brought to mind her first days in New York, when she'd been so intimidated by all the high-maintenance women and their perfect clothes, hair, makeup and nails. The editor of *Femme* magazine had a standing appointment at seven a.m. every morning for a blowout, and the fashion editor's trademark was Chanel's Rouge Fatal polish, with the half-moons on her nails left unpainted. Emma had immediately started taking tuna sandwiches on day-old bread for lunch in order to save enough

money for manicures, pedicures, haircuts that cost more than
rent did back in Paris and expensive—and painful—wax jobs.
She looked down at her hands and cringed. She'd been back
in Paris for such a short time and already her nails were a
mess. It was high time she indulged in a manicure.

But first she dialed Kate Hathaway's number at work.
Arabella had recommended several small bed-and-breakfasts
that would be very suitable, and Emma wanted to run them
past Kate before making a decision.

Kate's extension at Guy Richard Photography rang and
rang. Emma was about to hang up and dial Kate's cell when
someone grabbed the phone.

"Hello?" The girl said breathlessly. She didn't sound
remotely like Kate.

"Is Kate Hathaway there?"

"I'm so sorry," the voice said. "She's been on vacation
all this week. We don't expect her back until Monday."

"Oh. Thanks. I guess I'll call her on her cell." Emma hung
up the phone, perplexed. Kate hadn't said anything about
being on vacation. With the news of Guy's murder, it had
probably slipped her mind.

Emma dialed Kate's cell phone. Kate answered on the
third ring. She laughed when Emma mentioned not knowing
Kate was on vacation.

"I took time off to get some things done around the apartment. I'm such a slob! My closets are a total disaster. I
decided to dedicate a week to getting them in order."

"I know what you mean!" Emma said. She'd taken her
share of days off to get her life in order. When you worked
so hard and put in such long hours, things got away from you
easily.

"My aunt has found you a couple of places you might
like to stay. Have you booked your flights?"

"Yes. Hang on while I grab the printout."

Emma took down Kate's flight details and offered to meet

her at the airport. Kate insisted that she'd be fine taking a taxi, and she promised she would stop by Sweet Nothings immediately upon arrival.

ANGEL Cuts was humming when Emma got there. There was a roller-bedecked head under each of the five dryers, and all four manicure stations were busy. Six chairs were lined up in front of a row of mirrors, and a customer was in each, getting a haircut, color or blow-dry. Angel's chair was slightly to the side and had its own niche, as befitted the owner of the salon. She was creating a foot-high updo for a blond, twentysomething bride.

"Hey." Angel greeted Emma with a wave of her curling iron. "We're kind of backed up. Sorry about that, but Heather went into labor during the night. It's a week early, but you know babies, they don't follow any kind of schedule."

One of the waiting ladies lowered her magazine and peered over the edge. "Did she have a boy or girl?"

"Neither." Angel wrapped a strand of the blonde's hair around the curling iron and clamped it shut. "Least not yet. She's still in labor last we heard. Going on eighteen hours by my count."

"Oh, the poor thing," the woman said, and went back to her reading.

Emma pawed through the basket of magazines by the front counter. She pushed aside the gardening tomes and fashion titles until she found a slightly worn copy of *Star* magazine. The cover promised lots of juicy gossip, and she settled happily into one of the empty seats.

Two tanned, expensively highlighted blondes sat next to Emma. They were both impeccably dressed in white linen slacks, silk blouses, strands of sizeable pearls and armfuls of gold bangles. One peered over the top of her reading glasses at someone passing the front window of Angel Cuts.

Her nose rose a fraction of an inch in the air, and she elbowed her companion gently.

Emma glanced out the window to see a woman striding past in a red Polo shirt, well-fitting jodhpurs and dark brown riding boots. She carried a helmet in one hand and a riding crop in the other. Her posture indicated she was someone to be reckoned with.

"Looks like Deirdre's been riding again," the one woman said to the other with a snicker.

"Yes, but the question is, what's she been riding." The other woman shot back, and they both laughed.

The first woman noticed Emma looking at them and leaned closer to her, gesturing toward the window with a shrug of her shoulder. "Deirdre Porter. She's the mayor's new daughter-in-law. Rumor has it that her new riding instructor is a bit," she cleared her throat purposefully, "more than just a riding instructor."

"Oh." Emma squirmed uncomfortably. It was one thing to read the stories in magazines like *People* and *Star*, which were about celebrities you didn't actually know. It was quite another thing to be confronted with such a juicy tidbit at the hairdresser's. She had to remind herself that if she was going to solve Guy's murder, she would have to give in and listen to the wagging tongues.

"I think Luanne's ready for you," Angel called above the roar of the blow-dryers and the din of chattering female voices. She gestured toward a woman with jet-black hair in a pink smock decorated with Barbie dolls.

As Emma walked past Angel's station, Angel tapped her on the shoulder. "Check these out." She pointed to a vase overflowing with two dozen red roses.

"They're gorgeous." Emma touched one of the silky petals and inhaled the rich perfume.

"Tom." Angel said succinctly. She winked at Emma. "Kind of makes the whole fight worth it, don't you think?"

"A fight?" Emma lingered by Angel's chair despite the encouraging gestures of Luanne.

"He is just so jealous! Honestly." Angel sounded more proud than irritated. "Can you believe he got his boxers all in a knot over me taking Guy sightseeing that day?"

"Really?"

Angel nodded vigorously, and the knot of flame-red hair on top of her head bobbed precariously. She moved her face closer to Emma's until Emma could smell the fruity scent of her gum. "Just between you and me, I was kind of nervous. You know that night Guy was killed? Tom didn't come home till late, and he refused to tell me where he'd been. Mama always said not to jump to conclusions, but I was worried. Turns out he'd been playing poker with the guys again. After promising me he wouldn't." She grabbed a chunk of the blonde's hair and pulled so vigorously the girl winced. "Sorry about that." Angel tapped her on the shoulder then turned back to Emma. "I think they're taking advantage of him. Last time he dropped a C-note, and he can't hardly afford to lose that kind of money."

By now Luanne's welcoming gestures had taken on a desperate edge. Emma reluctantly moved away from Angel's station toward the manicure carts in the back.

By the time Luanne was done, Emma had perfectly painted pink toes and fingernails.

But she was leaving Angel Cuts with oh so much more.

Chapter 9

CLOUDS rolled in on Saturday morning, and the skies were dark when Emma looked out her apartment window onto Washington Street. She hoped the weather wouldn't delay Kate's flight. She was really looking forward to seeing a familiar face.

Excited yelps greeted Emma as she pushed open the front door to Sweet Nothings. Pierre danced around her legs, tail wagging furiously. Emma dodged his leaps as she made her way into the shop. Brian was nailing up the last stretch of molding around the new cabinets. He'd happily agreed to work on Saturdays so that Sweet Nothings wouldn't have to be closed any longer than necessary.

"Coffee?" He proffered his thermos. "Homemade with freshly ground beans."

"Thanks." Emma shook her head. "I'm having my usual." She held up a travel mug. "Green tea."

Brian made a comical face. "Okay, suit yourself."

Pierre continued to circle Emma, giving little yips of excitement.

"Pierre!" Arabella pointed to his dog bed. He obediently trotted over, but instead of lying down, he sat upright, ears straight and alert, head scanning the room for anything interesting.

"Guess what—" Arabella and Emma said at the same time.

Emma laughed. "You go first."

Arabella's cheeks flushed with excitement. "Wait till you see what I've got!" She pulled a tissue-wrapped bundle from under the counter. "Sally Dixon went to a sale at the old Kilpatrick Estate out near Green Acres Lake. Mrs. Kilpatrick finally departed this life at the age of 105. She outlived some of her own children and grandchildren." Arabella shook her head, and her white bun quivered. "I don't think I would like that."

"What is it?" Emma moved over to the counter and leaned her elbows on it.

Arabella fumbled with the bit of tape that held the edges of the tissue together. "You won't believe this. As soon as Sally spotted it, she called me, bless her heart." She wrestled the package open with shaking hands and pulled out a pink chiffon gown. "Heavenly by Fischer lingerie," Arabella exclaimed. "Mint condition. Never, ever worn. Look," she pointed to a small department store tag affixed to the bodice. "Here's the label," she pointed to a blue and white tag stitched to the seam. "See? There's the mermaid. That's their trademark." She put her hands on her hips. "This is museum quality Fischer."

Emma peered at the tag.

"Heavenly by Fischer is one of the most coveted vintage lingerie labels. A gown like this sells for over four hundred dollars!"

"Now we really need to get that web site up and running."

Emma turned toward Brian. "Do you think Liz would be willing to help?" Liz had given up a very lucrative web design business to stay home with the children.

"I'm sure she'd be delighted." Brian grinned. "I've gotten the impression lately that she would love to have something a little more challenging to sink her teeth into."

"Now that that's settled," Arabella said, beaming at the two of them, "why don't you tell us your news." She turned toward Emma.

Emma's mind had raced ahead to web site designs and colors and fonts and it took her a moment to remember what she'd been about to tell everyone.

"I had a very interesting visit at Angel Cuts yesterday." Emma wiggled her fingers in the air.

"I can see that. Love that color on you." Arabella glanced approvingly at Emma's manicure.

"But I picked up a lot more than just a new nail polish shade."

Arabella settled onto the stool behind the counter, and even Brian paused in his hammering.

"Do tell." Arabella prompted.

"Well . . ." Emma paused for dramatic effect. "Angel admitted that she and Tom had a big fight the night Guy was murdered." The word "murdered" stuck in her throat slightly. "And she also admitted that the fight was about Guy. Tom was jealous that Angel had been showing him around Paris."

"Lovers quarrel all the time, how do we—" Arabella began.

Emma held up a hand. "This was a fight. A big one. Two-dozen-long-stemmed-roses big."

Brian whistled. "Bet those set Tom back a few bucks."

"That's what I mean." Emma said. "I don't think he'd have gone to that expense if they'd just had a slight tiff. Besides, Sylvia said she heard them arguing straight through the wall."

"Which reminds me," Arabella said. "Sylvia offered your friend Kate a room at her place if she's interested. Said she wouldn't dream of charging her. She'd be glad of the company."

"Thanks. I'll let Kate know and see what she wants to do." Emma had a sudden idea. "Maybe she could listen in for any more fights between Angel and Tom."

"What makes you think Tom had anything to do with Guy's murder? Other than that he was jealous." Brian wiped his hands on a rag and took a sip of his coffee.

"According to Angel, he went out that night and refused to tell her where. Later he claimed he'd been at a poker game with some friends even though he'd promised her he was going to quit. If we could just find out whether or not he actually went . . ."

Brian furrowed his brow. "I know a couple of guys who usually play in that game." He ran a hand across the back of his neck. "Bobby Fuller for one. He works in our stockroom. I can run over later and ask him."

"That's wonderful, but you'd better be somewhat discreet about it." Arabella began smoothing out the pink chiffon negligee. She folded it carefully and placed it back in the tissue paper. "If Tom does turn out to be the murderer, we can't have you putting yourself in danger."

Emma felt her heart give a peculiar jolt at the thought of Brian in danger.

"Hey, give me some credit." Brian grinned. "Don't worry. I'll figure out a way to work it into the conversation naturally."

"It looks like you got your money's worth at Angel Cuts." Arabella finished wrapping the negligee and placed it in a drawer.

Emma looked at Brian's nearly completed cabinets. "I wish the armoires would come. I'm going to line them with black-and-white toile wallpaper. Then we can prop the doors

open and add a hook for displaying our best merchandise."
She pointed toward the drawer next to Arabella. "Like the
Fischer negligee."

Arabella clapped her hands. "It'll match Pierre's dog bed!
How perfect. But what about the carpet?" Arabella pointed
at the pea-green shag carpeting that had been part of her
1970s renovation.

"I really do think it needs replacing."

"I was very fond of this carpet." Arabella ran her foot
through the plush shag. "It was all the rage when I had it
installed. But you're right. Its time is past." Her face darkened. "Besides, I doubt we'd ever get that stain out." Arabella's glance strayed toward the spot where Guy had lain.
"What do you suggest?"

Emma frowned. "Something very simple and elegant . . .
but practical. I'm going to go down to the rug store and look
at some samples."

"As soon as I've finished the painting, we can rip out the
old stuff," Brian said.

"Sounds like unskilled labor." Emma smiled. "That's
just the kind I can help with."

"It's a date, then." There was an awkward silence. "I
mean . . ." Brian blushed.

"I just remembered something," Emma blurted out to fill
the void. She carefully avoided looking at Brian. "When I
was at Angel Cuts, two women were talking about this girl
in riding clothes who walked past the window." She turned
toward Arabella. "You mentioned her the other day. Deirdre
Porter?"

"Looks like she really is becoming the talk of the town."
Arabella sniffed. "Shame. The Porters are a nice family
even if Peyton isn't the sharpest blade in the drawer. It's a
lot of sour grapes, I suspect. Deirdre set people's teeth on
edge the minute she arrived in town. It's not completely her
fault. Everyone assumed Peyton and Marcie would be

married as soon as they finished college. And then he turns up with someone new, and she's not even a local gal. People around here hoped the Porter money would stay with someone in Paris."

"I thought she was attractive, though." Emma frowned. "Perhaps she'd be willing to model in our opening fashion show? She sounds like she's not afraid of a little scandal so parading around in a negligee should be right up her alley."

"Brilliant!" Arabella declared. "Hopefully she'll bring some of her moneyed friends."

Brian cleared his throat and glanced at his watch. "I could do with a break. Perfect time for me to do some detecting." He put down his drill and grinned. "I should be able to catch Bobby Fuller on his coffee break. Hopefully he'll know whether or not Tom Mulligan was at that card game the night Guy was killed."

Emma wanted to add her warning to Arabella's earlier one, but she settled for giving Brian a worried look. Hopefully he would be able to read her message loud and clear.

"LOOK at this," Emma called to Arabella and pointed at her computer screen.

Arabella put down the gown she was mending and went over to where Emma perched on a stool, her laptop open on the counter.

"Aren't they gorgeous? They'll go perfectly with the vintage pieces we already have."

Arabella peered over Emma's shoulder at the screen. "They're absolutely delicious."

"It's Monique Berthole's new line." Emma scrolled down the page. "The collection isn't nearly as expensive as it looks, but I've heard the quality is excellent." She clicked the NEXT button, and a whole new page of exquisite lace and satin creations filled the screen. "I'm going to order—"

The rat-a-tat-tat of someone knocking on the front door of Sweet Nothings made them both pause and turn in that direction. Pierre began yelping furiously, only abating when Arabella looked at him sternly.

"Finally!" Emma exclaimed. "It has to be the armoires." She jumped off the stool and headed toward the door.

"Third time's the charm," Arabella quipped. "I really am excited to see them. Too bad Brian's not here to help with the moving."

"I'm sure they'll put them where we want them." Emma reached for the knob, turned it and swung open the door. "Oh."

A very tall man stood on the step, his broad shoulders nearly spanning the doorway. He looked to be about Arabella's age and had thick, wavy, salt-and-pepper hair.

Emma was so startled she couldn't find her tongue. She'd been so sure she was going to open the door to find two burly men ready to manhandle her armoires into the shop.

Arabella glided forward quickly. "Can I help you? I'm afraid we're closed at the moment."

The man fumbled in the pocket of his rumpled sport coat, pulled out a billfold and flipped it open. "Special Agent Francis Salerno. Tennessee Bureau of Investigation."

"Oh," Emma and Arabella chorused together.

"The police have already been here—" Arabella began.

Francis stuffed his wallet back in his pocket. "I'm just following up on a few details, ma'am. We've been called in to help the local police with their investigation."

Thank goodness, thought Emma. Maybe they would no longer have to deal with the odious Chuck Reilly.

Arabella immediately went into hostess mode. "Can I get you anything? A glass of sweet tea, perhaps, or some lemonade?"

If Emma didn't know better, she could have sworn Arabella was actually *flirting* with Special Agent Salerno. Her cheeks had turned bright pink, and there was a glow in her eyes.

Francis gave a slow smile. "It sure is hot out there." He ran a hand around the back of his neck. "A glass of sweet tea would be pure heaven."

"You just wait right there. I'll be right back."

Arabella disappeared into the stockroom, and Emma was left alone with Francis.

He gave a reassuring smile. "Would you mind showing me where the crime took place?" He said as politely as if they were at a tea party and he was asking her to please pass the cream.

Emma pointed to the spot where the carpet was stained a dark brownish red. Brian had tried scrubbing the spot for them, but it had been impossible to remove it. Emma bit her lip and looked away.

"I'm sorry, this must be very difficult for you."

Emma felt tears explode against her lids. His manner was so different from Chuck Reilly's. He wasn't treating her like a suspect.

"We try to keep out of the local boys' hair as much as possible. Unless they request our help, of course. But I do like to visit the location of the crime and meet the people involved. That way, when I'm going through the thousands of documents, reports and interviews every case accumulates, I can picture the scene and the people involved myself."

Arabella bustled in with a pitcher and several glasses on a tray.

"I hope I'm not disturbing you." Francis took a sip of tea. He swallowed and licked his lips. "I think this must be the best glass of sweet tea I've ever tasted."

Arabella turned even pinker, and her hands fluttered like butterflies around her face. "Thank you."

Francis drained his glass and put it down on the counter. "I take it you're the one who found the body?"

Arabella nodded.

"I'm downright sorry that you had to go through that."

Arabella gave a small smile.

"This was your young man, I understand?" He turned toward Emma.

"We had been dating, but it was over." Emma explained.

Francis nodded. "Do you know of anyone who might have had a grudge against him? Someone who maybe followed him down here?"

Emma was already shaking her head. "No, not really."

Francis was thoughtful for a moment. "Well, I just came by to get the lay of the land so to speak, and to assure you ladies that we will do our best to track down all the facts and put the person who did this behind bars."

"We appreciate that." Arabella held the pitcher over Francis's glass questioningly.

He shook his head. "I've got an appointment at the Paris police station in . . ." He glanced at his watch. "Ten minutes. Much as I'd love to stay and enjoy your hospitality some more, I'd better be going."

"Well," Arabella said, as she closed the door behind Francis, "what an attractive man!"

"Aunt Arabella!"

"What?" Arabella looked at her niece with eyebrows raised.

"What about Les?"

"What about Les?" Arabella shot back.

EMMA frowned at her computer. She was seated on a stool at the counter with a spreadsheet open on her laptop. Bookkeeping was not her favorite chore, but it was a necessity when running a business. Numbers didn't come as naturally to her as did colors and fabrics and all things visual. She was glad she'd taken some courses in the fundamentals of bookkeeping and accounting. Arabella's accounting methods were just this side of an abacus. Emma was transferring everything to the computer and had set the store up for online banking and online accounts with their suppliers.

The door to Sweet Nothings eased open, and Brian stepped in.

All of Emma's senses went into overdrive as they always did when she was around Brian. She put her head down so he couldn't see the color she knew had flooded her face.

"I'm not interrupting anything, am I?" His dark brows lowered over his eyes.

Emma shook her head and closed the lid of her computer. "Just some bookkeeping," she wrinkled her nose. "Not my favorite task."

"I know what you mean."

Arabella came out of the stockroom at the sound of their voices. "Any news? Weren't you going to check with that fellow who works for you about that card game?"

"I did." Brian frowned in disappointment. "Unfortunately, Bobby was sick that night and skipped the game. He's going to ask around though, and see if anyone else knows whether Mulligan showed up or not."

Emma suppressed a quiver of frustration. It seemed as if every step they took forward led to a dead end. Why did Bobby have to get sick this one time? They had to get this wrapped up before Sweet Nothings's grand opening. They just had to!

Pierre, who had been napping in his canopied toile bed, suddenly sat bolt upright. He twitched his white ear, then his black one, then twirled them both as if they were antennae attempting to pick up sound. He gave a low growl deep in his throat that slowly escalated to a full-fledged bark.

"What is it, boy?" Emma went to pat the top of Pierre's head, but he jerked away as if to say "This is serious." Emma glanced at Arabella. "Maybe Bertha is going past outside?"

Arabella shook her head. "If that were the case, his bark would be very different. Someone must be outside."

Suddenly Pierre bolted from his bed and made straight for the door of Sweet Nothings, barking so excitedly that he levitated slightly off his paws with each bark.

"Maybe the delivery men are here with the armoires!" Emma exclaimed. She waited, but there was no knock on the door.

Pierre had stopped barking, but he continued to pace back and forth, his tail going like a metronome.

Emma strode toward the door and pulled it open to find a young woman standing there. She was at least six feet tall and very pretty, with long, blond hair. She was holding what looked like a bakery box fastened with old-fashioned string.

"Ohmygoodness," she said so quickly that the words all ran together. "You must be Emma."

Emma stood at the door, openmouthed.

The woman switched the box to her left hand and stuck out her right. "I'm Bitsy. Bitsy Palmer. Actually, it's Catherine Palmer, but everyone has always called me Bitsy."

Emma couldn't help it—she looked Bitsy up and down. Although she was very thin and trim, at six feet tall, she was definitely not bitsy!

Bitsy laughed. "I know what you're thinking. How did a long, tall drink of water like myself get a nickname like Bitsy? Well, it's like this. I was born real premature and barely any more than three pounds. My uncle Mike said, 'What a bitsy little thing,' and it stuck. I've been Bitsy ever since."

"Who—"

"I'm sorry. I should have said. I'm a friend of Liz's, and she told me I'd better come right down here and welcome you home to Paris. Here." She thrust the box at Emma. "I've brought you some cupcakes from my shop, Sprinkles. It's down the street and just around the corner." She motioned toward the window with one hand.

"Thank you." Emma took the box, still feeling slightly dumbstruck by the whirlwind that was Bitsy Palmer.

"Liz is just the best, isn't she?"

Emma nodded.

"You know that big old garden of hers, out back?"

Emma nodded again.

"She grows edible flowers for me. To decorate my cupcakes with." Bitsy took the box back from Emma, slid off the string and opened the top. "See?" She pointed to the beautifully colored flowers that topped the cupcakes.

Emma admired Bitsy's handiwork. If they tasted even half as good as they looked, they would be spectacular. Emma had an idea. "You know we're having a grand opening as soon as our renovations are done." She gestured toward the interior of the shop. "We'd love to order some of your cupcakes. They'd be perfect."

Bitsy's face broke into a huge grin. "It would be a pleasure and an honor."

Emma grinned back. She had the feeling she was really going to like Bitsy.

"And if you ever need anything, anything at all, as I said, I'm just around the corner."

"Maybe we could get together sometime—"

"That would be marvelous! And perhaps we can drag Liz away from those children and husband of hers!"

Emma laughed. "It's a deal."

"I almost forgot." Bitsy retrieved a piece of paper from under her arm where she'd stowed it. "I found this stuck to your window."

"Thanks."

"See you then. I've got to run."

"Not another circular," Arabella said with a sigh once

Emma had shut the door. "They usually shove them under the door, and I've nearly broken my neck slipping on them when I come in in the morning."

"I don't think it's a circular." Emma held up the note so that Arabella could see the printing on the front.

"Open it," Arabella encouraged, peering closely over Emma's shoulder.

Emma unfolded the damp paper. The writing inside was the same as the shaky capital letters on the front.

"What does it say?" Arabella fished for the glasses that hung from a beaded chain around her neck.

Emma shivered. "It says, 'Stop sticking your nose where it doesn't belong, or someone is going to get hurt.'"

"What is that supposed to mean?" Brian looked from Emma to Arabella and back again.

"I think it means someone doesn't like our snooping around. But who?" Arabella removed her glasses and let them fall against her chest.

Emma turned the paper over. "It looks like someone used gum to stick it to the window."

"Not a very sophisticated operator." Arabella quipped.

Emma held the paper closer to her nose. "It smells familiar."

"The gum? Something minty?" Arabella asked.

Emma shook her head. "Fruity. And I know I smelled this same gum somewhere." She took another sniff. "I know. Angel. She was chewing gum when I went to her shop for my manicure the other day. And it smelled just like this." Emma brandished the note under Arabella's nose.

"Angel!" Arabella's eyes widened in shock.

"Maybe she's trying to protect her boyfriend, Tom. She might have gotten wind of the fact that I've been asking around about him," Brian said.

Arabella frowned. "I can't picture Angel doing something like this, but then you never really know."

"Or," Emma paused as an idea formed. "Maybe Angel is protecting herself? She claims Tom wasn't home the night Guy was murdered. But what about Angel? If Tom wasn't home, then she doesn't have an alibi, either."

Arabella glanced at the note again and shook her head. "It looks like we've stirred up a real hornet's nest here."

Chapter 10

"WHEN did you say your friend Kate was arriving?" Arabella looked up from the boxes she was going through.

"She thought she'd be here around five o'clock." Emma glanced at her watch. "Oh. It's almost six already. Her flight must have been delayed because of the weather."

Just then a knock sounded on the front door. "The armoires!" Arabella and Brian chorused with a laugh.

"Very funny," Emma said over her shoulder as she headed toward the door. She saw Brian and Arabella exchange amused glances.

"Kate!" Emma exclaimed as she opened the door. "You made it. You must be exhausted. Was your flight delayed because of the weather?"

Kate looked puzzled. "No. We were right on schedule."

"Oh." Now Emma was confused. "I thought you said you'd be here around five."

"Did I?" Kate laughed. "I must have forgotten about the

time difference. As a matter of fact, I'd better change my watch right now."

Kate's suitcase had barely hit the floor when Arabella bustled out of the back room with glasses and a pitcher of sweet tea.

"I'm sure you could use a nice, cold drink."

"It's so good to see you." Emma threw her arms around her friend and hugged her. She hadn't realized how homesick she was until just now.

Splotches of water darkened the shoulders of Kate's dress, and the ends of her light brown hair were damp.

"Would you like a towel?" Emma offered. "It looks like you got soaked."

Kate shook her head. "I'm fine. I'm just so glad to see you." She smiled in a way that made her plain face light up. She accepted a glass of tea and looked around the shop. "This is so charming."

"It's all thanks to Brian," Emma said as she introduced them. "He's done all the renovations for us."

"It was something of a 1970s relic before Emma and Brian took over," Arabella acknowledged.

Kate looked around again. "Is this where it happened . . ."

Emma nodded. "Yes. I'm so sorry, Kate. As hard as it's been for me, I'm sure it's been even harder for you."

Kate swiped a hand across her eyes, then smiled and took a sip of her tea. "We all have to move on, I guess. I just wish they would find who did it."

"Me, too." Emma agreed. "We've been doing some sleuthing of our own but haven't come to any conclusions yet."

"Maybe I can help." Kate's face brightened.

"That'll be great." Emma thought about the note stuck to the front window of Sweet Nothings but decided not to tell Kate at the moment. She didn't want to frighten her.

"So." Kate put down her glass. "Where am I staying?"

Emma explained about Sylvia Brodsky. "She has a room available, but if you're not comfortable, we can always—"

"It will be fine. She sounds like quite a character. I can't wait to meet her."

EMMA eased her way up the stairs with a grocery bag balanced on each hip. Kate was settling in at Sylvia's, and Emma was going to make them both dinner so they could relax and catch up. Liz was coming, too, and Emma was excited to show her the apartment. It would be an opportunity to bring her two lives together—her past in New York and her current life in Paris.

Emma put a bottle of pinot grigio in the refrigerator to chill and began emptying the bags. She had boneless chicken breasts, cream, shallots, frozen peas and a box of risotto. She would sauté the chicken breasts in butter, followed by the shallots, then deglaze the pan with a splash of wine followed by a half cup of cream. The peas she would sauté with some diced onion and finish with a bit of beef broth. It was a recipe her Italian friend, Alessandra, had given her, and it elevated frozen peas to a whole new level. The risotto could be done in the microwave and finished with plenty of grated Parmesan.

Emma hummed as she set the table. She was excited to be entertaining in her new apartment. It was quite a departure from her space in New York—here she even had a proper dining table.

She fussed a bit with the place settings and spent a few minutes arranging a bunch of Peruvian lilies in a vase, which she placed in the middle of the table.

The chicken breasts and peas were being kept warm in the oven and the risotto was almost done when the bell rang.

"Oh, this is so charming," Kate gushed as Emma ushered

her into the apartment. Kate looked all around then walked toward the windows where she knelt on the window seat and peered out. "You can see the whole street from here!" She turned around with an expression Emma couldn't quite read.

Before Emma could answer, the bell rang again. Liz bustled in with a huge, ungainly parcel in her hands. Somehow, despite the size of the package, she managed to throw her arms around Emma and hug her fiercely.

Liz put her bundle down and turned toward Kate. "You must be Kate." She stuck out her hand. "Emma has told me so much about you." Liz indicated the small package in Kate's hands. "Looks like we've both brought hostess gifts. Go ahead, Emma, open them."

"Okay." Emma started with Kate's smaller box and peeled off the paper.

"Oh, Kate, thank you so much," she said as she examined the monogrammed crystal wine stopper. "It's perfect."

"I wish you'd come back to New York." Kate's expression was wistful. "I've missed you so much."

"No," Liz exploded. She threaded her arm through Emma's. "She has to stay right here."

Emma laughed. "Maybe I can clone myself."

"Go ahead and open mine." Liz indicated her rather haphazardly wrapped gift.

Emma tore off the tissue paper to reveal a large plant. "What is it?"

"It's a schefflera plant. I grew it from a cutting I made of one of mine. It needs plenty of indirect light."

"Thanks. I'll do my best to keep it alive, but I don't have the best track record when it comes to growing things."

Emma retrieved the bottle of white wine from the refrigerator and poured them each a glass. She curled up on the ottoman opposite Liz and Kate.

"So tell me what you've discovered so far." Kate took a sip of her wine.

"Unfortunately, the police still have me down as their chief suspect." The glass Emma cradled in her hand shook slightly.

"They can't be serious!" Kate's brown eyes widened.

"Brian said he's helping you and Arabella do your own investigating." Liz took a sip of her wine.

"Really?" Kate's eyes got even bigger.

"We are." Emma admitted.

Kate leaned forward eagerly, her glasses sliding down her nose.

"We have three possible suspects so far." Emma ticked them off on her fingers. "One, Nikki St. Clair. We only have her word that she went back to the hotel the night Guy was killed. Maybe she and Guy had argued about something? Two, Angel Roy's boyfriend, Tom Mulligan. Angel gave Guy a sightseeing tour of Paris, and it seems Tom began seeing the greenies shortly afterward." Emma paused and took a sip of her wine. "Three, Angel Roy herself. Maybe she read more into Guy's attentions than he meant for her to."

Kate snorted. "That wouldn't surprise me. She wouldn't be the first woman to make that mistake."

Emma realized ruefully that she'd made her own mistakes as far as Guy was concerned.

The microwave pinged and Emma went into the kitchen to check on the risotto. "Are you comfortable enough with Sylvia?" She called over her shoulder to Kate. "Otherwise we can find you somewhere else to stay."

"You can always bunk in with us," Liz offered.

"Oh, I'm fine. She's a real hoot. I'm definitely going to enjoy staying there."

"Oh, good." Emma carried the platter of chicken and

bowl of peas to the dining table. "She claims she heard Angel and her boyfriend arguing about Guy. Well, not about Guy exactly, but about some guy." Emma stuck a spoon in the bowl of peas. "Which I took to mean Guy himself since that was shortly after Angel's guided tour of Paris."

"Makes sense." Kate pulled out a chair and sat down.

"Their apartments are right next to each other, which is why . . ." Emma hesitated for a second. "We're hoping that you can listen in for any more arguments between Angel and her boyfriend."

Kate pushed her glasses up her nose with her index finger. "I'd love to." She gave an excited shiver. "This is going to be fun."

Later, after Kate left and Emma and Liz were cleaning up the dishes, Emma realized she still hadn't told Kate about the threatening note they'd found on Sweet Nothings's window.

Emma explained it to Liz.

"I suppose Kate does have a right to know about it, especially since you're asking her to help you snoop."

"I know," Emma said, vowing to call Kate in the morning. "If anything happened to Kate, I would feel terrible."

EMMA had a leisurely Sunday—church with Aunt Arabella in the morning, where she was introduced to so many people it made her head spin, a trip to the playground with Liz and her children in the afternoon. Kate was a huge sport and tagged along. Then a quiet dinner with Kate and an early evening in bed with a book. By Monday morning, she couldn't wait to get down to Sweet Nothings. Brian was finished painting, and the last step was at hand—ripping out the old green shag carpeting. Emma shuddered every time she saw it. She'd ordered a jute carpet bleached to a pale cream. It was environmentally friendly and very durable.

Now if only the armoires would arrive! She was going to check on them as soon as she got to work.

Brian was ready for action when Emma opened the door of Sweet Nothings. He had on old jeans and a ripped T-shirt and had set out several utility knives along with a serious-looking pair of scissors. Emma had dressed for the job as well in some old capris and a T-shirt she'd bought at a rock concert when she was barely out of her teens.

"I cannot wait to see how things look without this filthy old carpet in here!" Arabella declared.

"You might want to leave the shop until we're done," Brian said. "There's going to be a lot of dust."

"Oh, pooh, a little dust never hurt anyone. But I am glad I left Pierre at home this once. He was terribly unhappy, poor thing. Kept glaring at me with those big, dark eyes of his." Arabella sighed. "Fortunately, he'll get over it as soon as he sees the steak I bought for his dinner."

"Don't say I didn't warn you," Brian said, but there was a twinkle in his eye.

"Where should we start?" Emma was anxious to get going.

"Are you sure you don't mind helping? It's going to be a very dirty and dusty job."

"I'm dressed for it, don't worry."

Brian pointed toward the far corner. "Okay, then, I'd suggest we start over there. I've arranged for a Dumpster, which they've put in the back alley. We can tear the carpet into strips and dump it in there."

Emma went over to where Brian had indicated and began to tug at the carpeting. This was going to be harder than she thought. By the time she'd lifted up two feet of green shag, she was sweating, dirty and sneezing from the dust. But she was also determined. She gritted her teeth and yanked harder and another foot came away. How she was going to enjoy tipping this old rag into the Dumpster!

Emma was wrestling with her third section of carpeting when a timid knock sounded on the front door of Sweet Nothings.

Definitely not the armoires, she decided as she smoothed down her hair and blew some dust off the end of her nose. Surely a couple of muscle-bound movers could muster up something more manly sounding than that.

"Hey," Emma said, opening the door wider and ushering Kate into the shop. She was right. Definitely not the armoires.

"This place is going to look so different without that old carpeting," Kate exclaimed, looking around. "You've done a wonderful job, Emma."

"It was Brian's doing, actually." Emma smiled at Brian, and he tipped an imaginary hat in their direction.

"I'm afraid I'm not being the best hostess," Emma apologized. "But I'd promised Brian I would help him with the carpet."

Kate waved a hand. "Don't worry about it. I have a date with Sylvia. She's taking me sightseeing. Apparently there's an actual replica of the Eiffel Tower in a park somewhere."

Emma nodded. "There is. I don't think you're allowed to leave Paris without seeing it."

"I can't wait—" Kate was interrupted by the jaunty toot-toot-toot of a car horn.

They all looked toward the window just in time to see a black Cadillac go sailing past.

"Good heavens!" Arabella exclaimed. "Sylvia's not driving, is she?"

Kate nodded. "She said the car hasn't been out of the garage since it was shipped down here from New York."

They all cringed at the sound of screeching brakes and indignant horn honking.

"With good reason," Arabella quipped.

"Did you know that Sylvia is descended from Grand Duchess Anastasia of Russia?"

Arabella gave an unladylike snort. "Not that old chestnut again."

Kate tilted her head. "What do you mean?"

Arabella raised an eyebrow. "DNA tests recently proved beyond a doubt that Anastasia died along with her parents and siblings. She has no descendents. No matter how fervently Sylvia Brodsky would wish us to believe otherwise."

"Oh," Kate declared suddenly. "I almost forgot to tell you." She shook her head, and her mousy brown hair swung around her in an arc. "I overheard Sylvia's neighbor last night. Her name's Angel, right?"

Emma and Arabella nodded and crowded closer around Kate.

"It sounded like the BF was upset with her for being AWOL a couple nights a week. She was counting on him going to some poker game and not noticing, and apparently he was feeling under the weather one night and didn't bother to go."

Arabella glanced at Emma with her eyebrows raised.

"BF." Emma replied to the unspoken question. "Boy-friend."

Arabella nodded. "I see."

There was a sharp rap on the door, and they all turned in that direction.

Emma swung it open and found Sylvia on the doorstep exhaling the last puff of her cigarette, her oxygen tank standing perilously close by.

Sylvia poked her head into Sweet Nothings. "Kate here? We're going sightseeing."

Kate grabbed her purse. "Right here. I'm ready."

Arabella leaned toward Kate and spoke in a low voice. "It might be best if you drive."

"That's for sure." Emma joined the low-pitched conversation.

"I already offered," Kate whispered back. "But Sylvia insists."

Arabella rolled her eyes and made a quick sign of the cross.

"Be careful," they chorused together as Kate disappeared out the door with Sylvia. Minutes later they saw the Cadillac sail straight past the window, straddling the white line like an undecided politician, its left blinker flashing furiously.

"Back to work," Emma declared.

She really put her all into the next section of carpet. Each piece that came up added to the transformation of the Sweet Nothings space. Emma could just imagine how it was going to look with the armoires in place. If they ever arrived.

While she pulled carpet, she mused on Kate's news about Angel. It sounded as if she were stepping out on a regular basis. Maybe Tom had counted on that? If he already knew she'd be gone, he would have been free to go off and do anything he wanted—including murder Guy. Emma would like to know where Angel was going on those evenings. Perhaps one night she could follow her.

A piece of carpeting gave way, sending Emma plummeting to the floor on her backside.

"Whoa, careful there."

Brian walked over to where Emma was sprawled and stuck out a hand.

She grabbed it and he pulled her to her feet. Suddenly she became conscious of what a wreck she must look—her clothes all dusty and dirty, her hair rumpled from running her hands through it and goodness only knew how many smudges and smears on her face.

She found herself standing toe-to-toe with Brian, and her breath caught in her throat. She could feel telltale heat rising to her cheeks, and she looked down hoping he wouldn't notice. Why did she always feel like an awkward teenager around him?

She took a quick step backward and turned partially to the side. "Thanks."

"Anytime."

Emma glanced out of the corner of her eye to see Brian smiling at her. The heat in her cheeks intensified.

"Want to go out to dinner tonight?" Brian asked. "We deserve it after all this hard work."

"Sure." It was the last thing Emma expected. Of course Brian was probably just thinking they'd grab a bite when they finished with the carpet. It wasn't a date or anything like that. Just two friends getting something to eat together after a job well done.

"Great. I'll make a reservation at L'Etoile. Would seven o'clock be okay?"

Emma gulped. L'Etoile! Was Brian actually considering this a . . . a . . . date? There was nothing casual about dinner at L'Etoile. Her mind immediately raced ahead. What would she wear? She looked up to find Brian staring at her expectantly.

"Oh, yes, that would be great. Great." She turned away before the burning in her cheeks reached the boiling point.

FOR the rest of the afternoon, Emma kept her head down, hardly daring to glance at Brian for fear of starting the flames of fire in her face all over again. By four o'clock, all the carpet had been pulled up and cut in sections.

Brian straightened from where he was yanking up the last bit of pea-green shag and put a hand to his back. "Finished," he declared triumphantly. He looked down at his jeans, which were covered with bits and pieces of jute backing and carpet fibers. He brushed at them rather ineffectively. "Boy, I'm a mess."

The grin he gave Emma made her face flame up again. She wanted to tell him that he looked eminently desirable in spite of the dust and dirt, but she held her tongue and settled for grinning back.

"Me, too, I guess."

Arabella looked around at the shop now stripped of its 1970s green shag. "What a difference. It's hard to believe." She smiled at Emma. "I'm glad you talked me into getting something new. And now that you're done," she said, retrieving her purse from behind the counter, "I guess I'll go home and rescue poor Pierre. He must be feeling quite abandoned by now."

"Shall we get this nasty old rug out to the Dumpster?" Brian picked up a piece and held it aloft.

They carried it out, section by section, to the enormous metal container that had been left for that purpose in the alley. At one point, Emma staggered under the weight of the discarded rug, and Brian immediately rushed to her side.

"Here, let me do this. You can hold the door open."

Emma wanted to protest, but she realized that she was tired, and the carpet was indeed very heavy. She gratefully took her post by the door and leaned against it, propping it open.

Brian dragged the last piece of 1970s shag out of Sweet Nothings and was heaving it into the Dumpster with a showman's flourish when Emma heard a faint ping. She looked around but didn't immediately see anything. Suddenly Brian moved, and the sun lit on a small piece of gold metal lying to the side of the garbage bin.

"What's this?" Emma bent down and picked it up. It was an earring. The design was very unusual—it didn't look like something you would find in a store at the mall. It looked more handmade—in a good way. Perhaps it was Aunt Arabella's? She had a large collection of unusual pieces.

Brian peered over Emma's shoulder. "It looks expensive."

Emma held the earring up to the light. The stone was very unusual—a deep bluish green like the sea, with gold and tan veins running through it. The stone was round, and Emma thought the colors made it look like a tiny representation of the earth. A band of gold ran around it, looking much like the ring around Saturn. "I'll check with Aunt Arabella and see if it belongs to her."

She was putting the earring in her pocket when Arabella appeared at the back door.

She had a strange look on her face that Emma couldn't quite read. She cleared her throat. "Someone is here to see you, Emma."

Chapter 11

EMMA followed Arabella back into the shop. She made some ineffectual moves toward straightening her hair and brushing off her clothes, but whoever had come to see her was going to have to take her as she was. She couldn't imagine who had shown up at the end of the workday to say hello. An old friend from school, perhaps, who had gotten wind of her return?

A woman had her back to them and was browsing through the few garments Emma had already placed in the glass-fronted cupboards Brian had built. She was strikingly tall and thin with hair that nearly brushed her waist. Pierre was watching her carefully, his ears twitching as if tuning into psychic waves, his upper lip pulled back and ready to growl if need be. Emma felt herself stiffen. She had come to trust Pierre's instincts.

The woman turned around. She had Arabella's Fischer nightgown in her hand.

"I want this. How much is it?"

It was Nikki St. Clair. Emma stifled her surprise and pasted a smile on her face. "Welcome to Sweet Nothings."

Nikki smiled—a smile that didn't come close to reaching her eyes. "It's Emma, isn't it?"

Emma nodded warily.

"This place is charming." Nikki waved a hand around the shop, pointedly ignoring Pierre who was sticking to her like hair on a biscuit. "May I try this on?" She brandished the pink chiffon gown.

"I don't know. We're not really open at the moment . . ." Emma looked around for Arabella.

"What is it, dear?" Arabella emerged from the back room with her usual tray and pitcher of sweet tea. She placed them on the counter and poured out four glasses. "Where has Brian gotten to? I'm sure he could use a nice cold drink to wet his whistle."

At the sound of Brian's name, Nikki perked up. She took a glass of tea with one hand and shook the nightgown with the other. "Can I try this on?"

"I told her we're not officially open yet—"

Arabella tut-tutted. "It's okay, dear. We might as well make a sale while we can."

Arabella took the gown from Nikki and led her toward the dressing rooms. She hung the Fischer nightgown on the hook and pulled the curtain closed in back of Nikki. She went over to where Emma was standing behind the counter. "Do I dare charge four hundred dollars for the gown? My sources tell me that's what it's worth," she said in a low voice.

"Why not? If anyone can afford it, Nikki can."

"Is she that model who tried to steal your boyfriend?"

Emma nodded. Thinking of Nikki and Guy was like picking at a scab.

"If you'd rather I didn't sell it to her . . ."

"Don't be silly." Emma smiled. "But let's stick it to her. Tell her it's five hundred dollars."

Arabella giggled. "Done."

Nikki was certainly taking her time, Emma thought, as they waited for her to emerge from the dressing room. Suddenly she remembered the earring she and Brian had found outside. She took it from her pocket. "Is this yours?" She showed it to Arabella.

Arabella held it up to the light. "No, it's not, but it's lovely. Where did you find it?"

"It fell out of the carpet as we were tossing it into the Dumpster."

"We'll keep it just in case someone comes back for it, but it might have been in the carpet for decades."

They heard a sound and turned to find Nikki had emerged from the dressing room and was admiring herself in the large gold mirror in the corner.

Emma wondered how long she had been standing there. Had she overheard her and Arabella talking?

"It's divine. I must have it." Nikki turned around.

"It certainly leaves nothing to the imagination," Arabella whispered to Emma.

"I heard there was some of your delicious sweet tea to be had." Brian came in from outside, stopping abruptly at the sight of Nikki posing in front of the mirror in the sheer gown.

Emma expected Nikki to make the most of it, but after a brief nod, she retreated hastily to the dressing room.

"Our first customer?" Brian took off his work gloves and tossed them on the counter. "This looks delicious." He picked up the glass Arabella had filled for him. He wiped his mouth with the back of his hand. "Did you show your aunt that earring we found?"

"Yes," Emma whispered with a nod toward the dressing room Nikki had just disappeared into. "It's not hers."

Nikki reemerged from the dressing room in street clothes—a short, strapless sundress that barely hid more than the chiffon nightgown had. She didn't balk when Arabella quoted the five-hundred-dollar price.

"We should get together sometime," she said to Emma as she put her wallet back in her Louis Vuitton purse. "Why don't you give me your cell number? We could have a drink or grab a bite to eat. The police have insisted I stay in town, and I'm getting bored all by myself." She pouted prettily.

The phrase "when hell freezes over" ran through Emma's mind, but she just smiled and picked up one of the Sweet Nothings business cards that were out on the counter. She scribbled her number on the back. She would be very surprised if Nikki ever did call her.

"So the police are still investigating?" Emma said. Chuck Reilly hadn't been around to bother her in several days, although he still haunted her dreams, where she imagined him carting her off to jail in handcuffs.

Nikki stiffened. "I was questioned by the most obnoxious detective. It was terrible." She shivered.

That would be Chuck, Emma thought. She wondered if he'd now put Nikki at the top of his suspect list. The thought gave her a brief moment of satisfaction as she closed the door behind Nikki.

Emma glanced at her watch. She'd better get upstairs and start getting cleaned up for her dinner with Brian. She had a feeling it was going to take a good, long scrub to get rid of all the day's dirt and grime.

LATER, with a tall glass of well-iced tea in hand, Emma stood in front of her closet and moaned. She had nothing to wear. All the years she'd spent in the fashion industry scoring outfits at bargain basement prices or with drop-dead discounts had been for naught. She still had absolutely nothing to wear!

She shifted through the dresses in her closet. She'd

already worn the black sheath, her favorite go-to dress. The
silk was too fancy, even for L'Etoile, and especially on a
weeknight. She didn't think the prints struck the right note,
the sundresses were too bare and her old office dresses weren't
bare enough. If only she'd had time to go shopping!

Emma went through the hangers again, one by one. Her
fingers closed over an unfamiliar fabric, and she pulled the
hanger from the back of the closet. She'd forgotten all about
this dress! She'd only worn it once for fear of dirtying it—
New Yorkers tended to wear black for a reason. It was a
cream-colored silk sheath shot through with gold threads
and cinched at the waist with a gold rope belt. It was perfect.
Dressy and elegant but not overboard. Bare enough without
being too bare. She'd wear it with her high-heeled, strappy
gold sandals.

Emma laid the dress on the bed and went to turn on the
shower. She thought she heard the phone over the running
water and stuck her head out of the bathroom. Her cell trilled
from the depths of her purse where she'd left it. She managed
to grab it on the fifth ring.

"Hello?" She frowned. "Hello?"

A voice came over the line, muffled and raspy. "Stop
investigating now," the person said in a near whisper, "and
maybe then no one will get hurt."

"Who are you?" Emma demanded.

The line went dead.

Emma shivered. Someone was trying to scare her.

Was it the same person who had stuck the note to the
front window of Sweet Nothings?

"I don't like it," Brian frowned when Emma told him about
the telephone call. "It sounds like someone is getting desperate. I don't want you to get hurt."

They were walking toward the parking lot when he

stopped abruptly and put his hands on Emma's shoulders. "I'd never forgive myself if anything happened to you."

Emma attempted a brave smile. "I'll be careful. Don't worry."

Brian was wearing gray slacks, a navy blazer, a blue shirt and a striped tie. Emma couldn't remember ever having seen him so dressed up before. She was suddenly very conscious of the way he towered over her, the width of his shoulders, his firm grip.

She took a deep breath. And reminded herself that she was finished with men for the moment. Done, done, done.

Brian led her toward a station wagon that looked suspiciously like Liz's. He gave a wry smile. "I've borrowed Liz's car for the evening. I didn't think you'd appreciate vaulting into the truck when you're all dressed up."

Emma smiled in the darkness as they headed toward L'Etoile. Brian had thought of everything. This was going to be a wonderful evening.

Brian pulled into the parking lot of L'Etoile, and Emma was surprised to see how few spaces were left. The restaurant was bustling considering it was a Monday night. She looked around as they waited for the maitre d' to seat them. A table for six was filled with a group celebrating a birthday. She noticed a pile of wrapped gifts next to an older woman's chair. The private room off the main dining room was also filled, with businessmen in dark suits and ties staring at a pie chart.

The maitre d' led them to a table for two partially secluded by a giant fake fern. Emma quickly picked up her menu to hide her nervousness.

"I think such a grand occasion calls for a glass of champagne, don't you?" Brian peeked at her over the top of her raised menu.

Emma was startled. She'd been contemplating the relative merits of the duck versus the lamb. She liked them both but perhaps she should get something easier to eat? She didn't want to end up with a bird in her lap or sauce all over her dress. "Grand occasion?"

Brian's eyes twinkled. "Yes. The ditching of the pea-green shag. The closing of a chapter. The official end to the seventies. At least as they relate to Sweet Nothings." He spread his napkin in his lap. "Besides, we're almost done with the renovations, and that's something to celebrate as well."

The waiter appeared at Brian's elbow, and he sent him away with an order for two glasses of Moët & Chandon.

"You don't look very excited."

Emma shrugged. "I wish the police would figure out who killed Guy. Frankly, it's casting a shadow over everything."

"I know what you mean. Have you heard anything from that detective recently?"

Emma shook her head. "No. If he weren't so determined to blame it on me, perhaps he would get a little further."

The waiter glided over with their champagne and silently placed the two bubbling flutes on the table.

Brian lifted his glass and held it in the air toward Emma. "Cheers! Here's to you. You're looking especially lovely tonight."

Emma raised her glass and clinked it with Brian's. "Thank you." She knew her face was getting red, and she hoped Brian wouldn't notice in the dim light.

She quickly turned back to the subject at hand. "It seems to me that between us we should be able to figure this murder out ourselves."

Brian took a sip of his champagne. "I'm going to see if I can track down anyone else who might have been at that poker game Angel's boyfriend claimed to be at."

"According to Kate, it's quite possible Angel wasn't home that night, either. But it sounded like it was some kind of regular thing. Maybe Tom was counting on her not being there when he decided to murder Guy?" Emma shivered. She would never get used to the idea of murder, never.

"And maybe," she said, watching the bubbles in her glass jostle each other to the top, "it's something else all together, and we'll never figure it out. I know Chuck Reilly doesn't have any evidence to link me to the crime, but still . . . I keep hearing the prison door clanging shut." Emma laughed humorlessly.

They looked up to see the waiter hovering near their table, pad and pencil in hand. They placed their orders and watched as he headed toward the kitchen.

There was a momentary awkward silence, but then Brian mentioned having run into one of their former teachers and soon they were reminiscing about their days at Henry County High. Brian regaled Emma with the tale of the time his entire English class had gotten up and moved to the empty classroom next door, and it had taken Mrs. Mulberry ten minutes to notice it.

"It wasn't until she went into the desk drawer, and her glasses weren't there that she realized we had switched rooms."

Their laughter was interrupted by their waiter with their order—chicken *francese* for Emma. She knew the chicken would be boneless breasts sautéed in butter and lemon— easy to cut and easy to eat. She peered over at Brian's dish. He'd opted for the osso bucco. She loved osso bucco but was afraid to have to deal with dissecting bony veal shanks swimming in a plate of soupy sauce. She could just imagine her white silk dress after two or three bites of that!

Brian obviously wasn't as nervous as she was. Maybe he didn't really mean this to be a date, and all she really was to him was his kid sister's best friend. She watched as he deftly separated the meat from the smooth, round marrow bones.

Of course a couple of dots of sauce wouldn't show on his dark blazer.

"Are you planning on staying in Paris after you and your aunt open Sweet Nothings?"

Emma hesitated. She hadn't thought it through yet. She'd always assumed she'd stay long enough to get Aunt Arabella's shop on its feet and then she'd head back to New York to resume her career. She glanced up at Brian. Now she wasn't at all sure that that was what she wanted.

Emma fiddled with her spoon. "I'm not sure. What about you?" she asked, hoping to turn the conversation away from her.

"Oh, I'm staying here. I'm launching my own firm and plan to specialize in renovating older homes. Besides, there's nothing for me to go back to in Nashville. But I'd rather talk about you, Amy." Brian glanced up, a stricken look on his face. "Emma. I'm so sorry, I meant to say Emma."

Before Emma could say anything, the waiter arrived with the dessert menu. Brian insisted they share a chocolate molten lava cake, L'Etoile's signature confection, but Emma had lost her appetite.

Brian had paid the check and they were lingering over coffee when his elbow caught his cup and sent rivulets of coffee splashing across the white tablecloth. Emma jumped up as the brown puddle got closer to her edge of the table.

"I'm so sorry." Brian jumped up, too, and began dabbing at the mess with his napkin. "Liz always says, you can dress me up, but you can't take me anywhere." Emma noticed that his face had turned a dark, dusky red. So, Brian wasn't as cool as he made himself out to be.

Suddenly the whole thing struck Emma as unbearably funny, and she began to giggle. Brian glanced up, surprised. Then he began to smile, and he, too, began to giggle. Soon they were both convulsed with laughter.

"Let's blow this place before they realize the mess we've

made," Brian said breathlessly, wiping his eyes with the back of his hand.

He grabbed Emma's hand. "Come on. Let's get out while the going's good."

They bolted through the front door of L'Etoile, and into the close, damp night air. Brian kept hold of Emma's hand as they made their way toward his car, still dissolving every now and then into fits of giggles.

Brian beeped the car doors open and reached for the passenger-side handle. He looked down at Emma and their eyes locked. Suddenly she didn't feel like laughing anymore. Her heart hit warp speed as she stared into Brian's blue eyes. For one endless moment she thought he was going to kiss her, but instead, he let out a deep exhale and opened the car door with a flourish.

"Madame, your coach awaits."

Emma plastered a smile on her face as she slid into the darkened car. She didn't want to admit, even to herself, that she was deeply disappointed. She wasn't sure, but had she closed her eyes in anticipation of Brian's kiss? She closed her eyes now—in embarrassment. What an idiot she was! Brian just didn't see her as girlfriend material. Besides, who was Amy? Was she the one who was really on Brian's mind?

Brian slid into the driver's seat, and Emma could feel her face burning in the darkness. To cover her discomfort, she dug around in her purse and pulled out her phone. She'd turned it to vibrate during dinner and needed to check her messages.

There were two—one from her mother in Florida, and one from an unknown number. Emma pressed some buttons and held the phone to her ear.

She was startled when she heard Nikki's voice come through her BlackBerry.

"Hi, Emma? Call me." The disembodied voice sounded strange in the darkness of the car. "You know that earring you found? I know whose it is. And I think it leads to Guy's murderer."

"What!" Emma exclaimed suddenly.

"What is it?" Brian glanced at her quickly before returning his gaze to the darkened road in front of them.

"That was Nikki." Emma relayed the message.

"She actually said that?" Brian pulled over to the shoulder of the road. "She thinks she knows who murdered Guy?"

"Not exactly. But she seems to think this earring is going to lead us to the murderer. She wants me to call her back so we can arrange to meet."

"Well, you're not going alone." Brian looked up and down the road before making a swift U-turn to take them away from town, back toward the Beauchamp Hotel and Spa. "Call her and tell her we're on the way."

THE quiet, soothing atmosphere of the Beau was at odds with the rapid beating of Emma's heart. She focused on the trickling water spilling over the rock wall supporting the front counter. She tried some yoga breathing—in, out, in, out. Her heart continued to beat at her breastbone like a prisoner trying to escape a cell.

Brian looked cool, calm and collected, but Emma could see the pulse beating in his temple, and the minute, jerky movements of his jaw as he clenched and unclenched it.

A different woman was behind the counter tonight, although she was wearing the same uniform of white tunic and black yoga pants.

She smiled broadly as Brian approached the desk.

"Welcome to the Beauchamp Hotel and Spa," she said by rote, but the warmth directed at Brian seemed real.

Brian explained that one of their guests had called and was expecting them.

The desk clerk smiled, picked up the house phone and dialed the number of Nikki's room. She listened intently then placed the receiver in its cradle.

"I'm sorry, but there's no answer. Miss St. Clair does not appear to be in her room."

Brian smacked himself on the forehead as if suddenly remembering something. "Sorry! She did say she was about to jump in the shower and that she'd leave the door open for us."

The woman's forehead creased into a frown. "I really shouldn't . . ."

Brian gave her his most winning smile. "Would it be all right if we just went up and checked to see if the door is open? If not, we'll come right back down and wait until she answers her phone."

The woman shrugged and looked around. "I'm really not supposed to, but . . ." She jerked her head toward the elevators. "It can't really do any harm."

Brian and Emma turned and started to head toward the elevators.

"If the door isn't open . . ." the woman called after them.

"Don't worry." Brian gave her another big smile. "We'll come right back down and wait."

THE corridor was as quiet as it was the last time they visited, the plush carpeting swallowing the sounds of their footsteps.

"Do you think Nikki is really out?" Emma whispered as they rounded the corner toward her room.

"Don't know," Brian admitted. He glanced at his watch. "It's kind of late to be out and about in Paris, Tennessee. The sidewalks get pulled in pretty early around here." He grinned ruefully. "More likely she *is* in the shower or just didn't get to the phone on time. Fingers crossed." He held up his hand.

The bulb in the sconce opposite Room 251 was burned out, making the hallway especially dark and shadowy. Brian peered at the room numbers closely.

"This is it." He raised his hand and rapped on the door. He turned to Emma in surprise. "It's open."

Emma started toward the open door to Nikki's room, but Brian held up a hand.

"Let me go first."

Emma shivered. "Okay." She was more than happy to let Brian be the one to enter the room. She didn't know why, but she had the awful feeling that this wasn't going to be good.

The living area of Nikki's suite was messy but empty. A stack of crumpled newspapers threatened to tip off the coffee table, and a film of cigarette ash smudged the thick glass surface. Emma was shocked to see several cigarette butts half buried in the lush pile carpeting. The crystal bowl Nikki had been using as an ashtray was missing.

"Nikki?" Brian called.

Emma tagged behind as Brian went around the corner of the suite and peered into the kitchen. An empty container of expensive bottled water stood in the sink.

"Shall we look in the bedroom?"

Emma was reluctant, although she didn't know why. "Shouldn't she have heard us by now? Maybe she went out and accidentally left the door open."

"Let's hope you're right." Brian's face was grim. "Something doesn't seem right to me."

Emma silently agreed with him. Brian peered into the bedroom, but it, too, appeared to be empty. Emma breathed a sigh of relief. The bed had been turned down, and an orchid and a sachet of chamomile tea had been left on the pillow.

Brian gestured toward them. "Classy."

"I guess she really isn't here." Emma started backing toward the door.

"There's still the bathroom."

Emma's heart sank. She did *not* want to look in there.

Brian's broad back blocked the entrance to the bath. Emma couldn't see around him, but she heard the strangled noise he made as he backed swiftly out of the room.

Emma got only a glimpse of the scene, but she didn't need more than that to know that Nikki was dead. The missing crystal bowl was on the floor beside her head, and Emma was pretty sure it would turn out to be the weapon that put that sickening dent in Nikki's skull.

Chapter 12

EMMA was perched on the edge of the sofa when the police arrived. Brian offered to bring her some water, but Emma thought that the less they touched in the suite, the better. They heard the soft ping of the elevator and braced themselves.

Chuck Reilly was the first one into the room. Emma groaned when she saw him. He stopped short when he saw her.

"Not you again," he said. "You attract trouble like honey attracts flies."

Emma didn't bother to dignify that with a comment. She clenched her hands in her lap and gritted her teeth to keep them from chattering. She didn't want Chuck Reilly to know how scared she was.

She caught sight of Brian out of the corner of her eye and saw him stiffen. Chuck ignored him and barged into the bathroom. He came back out seconds later.

"Now that's a crying shame," Chuck declared, jerking his head toward the bathroom.

The line from a poem Emma remembered reading in high school ran through her head; "any man's death diminishes me." Its meaning was becoming increasingly clear.

"You know what I'd like to know?" Chuck stood over Emma and stared down at her.

She had the urge to jump to her feet, but she fought it. "What?"

"I'd like to know why you keep showing up at the scene of the crime? You're like some kind of modern day Typhoid Mary."

Emma saw Brian's jaw clench, followed quickly by his fists.

"Now, wait a—"

Emma gave a loud, fake laugh in an attempt to diffuse the tension. "Very funny, Chuck."

Chuck pulled his notebook from his back pocket and put on a serious expression. "You two," he looked from Emma to Brian and then back again, "want to tell me what you're doing here?" He gestured toward the door. "How'd you get in, for starters?"

"We came to see Nikki." Emma's words tumbled out and over each other in her haste to explain herself. "Brian went to knock, and we discovered the door was already open."

Chuck glanced at Brian.

"It's the truth."

"Yeah? How about this? How about Nikki was alive when you got here, and she let you into the room?"

"No!" This time Emma did jump up from her seat.

Chuck held up a hand to silence her. "And then you," he pointed at Emma, "got all riled up again and clonked her on the head with that crystal bowl. Just like you clobbered your ex-boyfriend with that walking stick. Same modus operandi both times." He grinned. "That's cop speak for same murder method, in case you didn't know."

Emma felt like steam was rising from her head, and she was surprised that clouds of it weren't coming out her ears. How dare Chuck treat her like this.

"I'll have you know, Chuck Reilly—" She was interrupted by a knock on the door.

Chuck gave a sly smile. "The rest of the team must be here to help process the scene. Let's see what they have to say."

He made it sound like a threat.

EMMA could hear her teeth chattering in the silence of the car as Brian drove them back to town. She couldn't believe what had just happened. It was bad enough that Guy was dead . . . but now Nikki, too? Not that she was at all close to Nikki, but murder? It was incomprehensible as far as she was concerned.

"I hate the thought of your being alone in that apartment tonight," Brian said as he pulled up in back of Sweet Nothings. "I could sleep on the couch."

Emma felt her heart turn over, and a lump formed in her throat. She looked at Brian in the shadows of the car. She'd known him almost all her life. And, she realized, she'd had a crush on him for almost as long.

"Thanks." She dared to put her hand over his. "I'll be fine."

Brian didn't look convinced. "You know if anything happened to you—"

"I know," Emma interrupted. "Liz would never forgive you."

She laughed and Brian joined in.

"You're right. Liz would kill me!" Brian's expression

softened. "As I said." He squeezed Emma's hand. "I'd never forgive myself."

"I'll be fine," Emma said with more enthusiasm than she felt. "Besides, can you imagine what the town gossips would say if they saw your car parked outside my apartment all night?"

Brian frowned. "I hadn't thought of that." He was quiet for a moment. "But you do have my phone number. Just in case."

"I have it on speed dial," Emma admitted.

EMMA glanced at her alarm clock. One o'clock in the morning. She'd been tossing and turning for two hours. She sighed, flipped on the light and slipped out of bed. Perhaps a few relaxing yoga poses would help.

She knelt on the floor, leaned back on her heels and folded forward into child's pose. She tried to focus on her breathing, but her thoughts continued to intrude. Her mind was playing a kaleidoscope of murder scenes—first Guy's, then Nikki's. Perhaps a more active restorative pose would be the answer. She stretched into downward facing dog, feeling the pleasant pull in her calves and hamstrings.

She had to concentrate a little harder to hold the pose, and slowly the intruding thoughts swirled toward the back of her mind. She finished with legs up the wall pose, finally falling into an uneasy sleep, dreaming about someone named Amy. When she woke up two hours later, she was surprised to find herself on the floor. She crawled back into bed, pulled up the covers and quickly dozed off again.

The next morning Emma felt as if she had a hangover, although she'd had only a little champagne the night before. She tossed a handful of strawberries, an almost too-ripe banana and the last bit of a container of Greek yogurt into the blender. She didn't really feel like eating, but she thought she could stomach a smoothie.

She wanted to get down to Sweet Nothings early. The renovations were almost finished, and a team was coming to put down the new carpet. As soon as that was done, she could begin arranging the stock. The shipment from New York had already come in and needed to be unpacked.

And they still had to organize the grand opening. She'd tentatively decided on a date and had already arranged for some newspaper ads in the local paper. She needed to find some girls willing to model the fashions. It wouldn't be a traditional fashion show with a runway—Sweet Nothings was way too small to accommodate something like that. But she envisioned girls dressed in the vintage pieces circulating among the crowd, showing off the best of Arabella's collection.

They would serve some sparkling wine and juice and fancy little hors d'oeuvres and canapés. Emma had a meeting with the caterer later that day.

EMMA enjoyed being all alone in the Sweet Nothings shop. She looked around at Brian's new, glass-fronted white cabinets, the yummy pastel pink paint, the black-and-white toile accents, and felt a glow of satisfaction. It was all coming together just as she had envisioned it.

Except for the murders of Guy and Nikki, of course. She couldn't have envisioned them in a million years.

Emma realized with a start that once the renovation was over, Brian would no longer be around all day. He'd already lined up his next job—a huge project redoing one of the oldest homes in Paris. The owners had been very impressed with his portfolio and the work he had done in Nashville and planned to spare no expense in returning their home to its former glory. Brian was obviously excited about the project. Emma sighed. Things just wouldn't be the same without seeing him every day.

She headed toward the back room where Brian had stacked the boxes from the shipment of lingerie from Monique Berthole. Emma dragged one of the cartons out to the front of the shop and ripped off the packing tape. There was an inner box containing tissue-wrapped bits of silk and lace. Emma's breath caught in her throat when she saw the beautiful array of colors and felt the softness of the fabric. She was organizing the camisoles and panties by size when someone knocked on the front door of Sweet Nothings.

Emma started toward the door and then hesitated. She realized she was all alone in the shop. What if it was the killer? She crept to the door quietly, inched one of the blind slats to the side and peered out. Then she threw open the door.

"Kate!" Emma felt terrible. Somehow she had managed to forget all about Kate! Bless Sylvia for taking care of her.

"Oh my God, Emma." Kate's words ran all together coming out, "OhmyGodEmma." "I just heard about Nikki. It was on the news." Her eyes looked enormous behind her tortoise-framed glasses. "Oh, Emma, this is terrible."

Emma embraced her friend. "I know. I never really liked Nikki, but murder?" Emma shuddered.

Kate drew back but kept her hands on Emma's shoulders. "I know what you mean. The only time I ever came close to liking Nikki was when I found out she'd taken in the feral kittens Guy had found lurking around the garbage cans outside his studio. Still, we have to find out who did these horrible things."

"I know." Emma nodded. She felt tears pressing against the back of her eyelids. She'd been trying so hard to be brave, but now, with Kate here, she felt her resolve slipping. "I just wish I knew what to do." Emma grabbed a tissue from the box on the counter and blew her nose. "I'd like to know what Angel is up to on those nights when she disappears."

"Do you think it has something to do with the murders?" Kate pushed her glasses up her nose with her index finger.

"I'm not sure. I'm thinking it's more likely Tom Mulligan took advantage of her absence to . . . to . . . murder Guy." Emma's voice trailed off and her last words were nearly swallowed up.

"Can we follow her?" Kate's face brightened.

"I've kind of been thinking about that," Emma admitted.

"But what do we do? Sit around and wait to see if she goes out?"

Emma shook her head. "Brian should be able to find out what night Tom's poker game is. I'll give him a call."

Emma pulled her cell phone from her pocket and pressed the button for Brian. Kate gave her a slightly quizzical look, and Emma was a little embarrassed to be caught with Brian's number on speed dial. She was about to offer up some plausible explanation when Brian answered.

Emma explained about Tom and Angel and the poker game and was surprised that Brian sounded a little . . . disappointed? Had he thought she was calling just to call? The possibility gave her a warm glow as she snapped her phone shut.

She started to relay the conversation to Kate when they were interrupted by rabid and intense scratching at the front door.

"That would be Pierre," Emma said, and smiled ruefully. "He's taken half the paint off the door already with his pawing at it."

"It's the perfect opportunity to repaint."

Emma paused. She hadn't thought of that. "Great idea. The door's been white forever, but we could have a slightly deeper shade of pink than we have in here." She gestured toward the walls that Brian had recently painted.

The door opened and Pierre rushed in. He gave Emma a

quick greeting then hurried over to Kate, sniffing and snorting and dancing rings around her, his ears twitching furiously.

"Oh, my goodness, I just heard the news!" Arabella declared as she burst through the door. "Darling, Emma, are you all right?"

"Just fine." Emma reassured her. "It was . . . horrible . . . but I'm fine."

"Who on earth would have done a thing like that?" Arabella shook her head. "Things like this just never used to happen in Paris." She took off her rain hat and shook it out. "I'll make us a nice cup of coffee. I'm sure that will make us all feel better."

Emma wasn't so sure that the recuperative powers of caffeine were up to such a tall order, but she knew that keeping busy would be more beneficial for Arabella than sitting around twiddling her thumbs idly.

Arabella had just finished pouring the last cup when there was a knock on the door.

What now? Emma wondered. She peered through the glass. Les was standing outside the shop, his head ducked against the rain. Emma quickly opened the door.

"Is Arabella all right? I just heard about the murder out at the Beau. What is Paris coming to?"

"I'm fine." Arabella put down her cup and started to get up. "Would you like some coffee, Les?"

He shook his head. "No, thanks. I've got a bit of heartburn. Had to take my antacid this morning." He placed a hand on his chest.

"Emma and Brian are the ones who found the body of that model at the Beau."

Les gasped. "Oh my dear," he said to Emma, "there are some things a lady should not have to see." He put a hand on Emma's arm. "Are you sure you're okay?"

Emma nodded. "A little shaky, but I'll be fine."

Les patted her hand reassuringly. "If you need someone to talk to, just remember, I'm right across the street. I've seen my share of the world's sins." He shuddered. "I can't imagine who would do something like that."

"The two murders have to be connected," Arabella said firmly. "This isn't some random crime spree."

"I still worry about you gals being alone here in the shop." Les frowned. "Be sure to keep the door locked."

"Oh, we do, don't worry." Arabella gave Les's arm a squeeze. "You're a dear to be so concerned about us."

"A Southern gentleman would do no less. Besides, you're two of my favorite ladies." Les's eyes twinkled. "And now I'd best be getting back to the shop. I just wanted to check on you two."

EMMA was standing on a stepladder, dusting the insides of the cabinets—having barely shut the door behind Les—when she noticed the front door of Sweet Nothings ease open. She sighed. She must have forgotten to lock it, and it seemed that people were oblivious to the large *Closed* sign hung out front.

A woman entered quietly—she was older, with permed, white, close-cropped hair. Her navy slacks looked like the type with an elastic waist, and her white blouse had a sailor collar in back.

She cleared her throat and looked up at Emma. "Is Arabella around?"

Emma sighed and made her way back down the stepladder. She was almost finished with the cabinets, another few minutes . . . But there was nothing she could do about it now.

"I think Arabella is in the back. Let me go get her." Emma ran a hand through her hair and brushed ineffectually at the front of her top where sawdust clung tenaciously.

But before Emma could turn around, Arabella came out from the stockroom.

"Is someone here?" She looked at Emma, then turned her head slightly and caught sight of the woman. "Sally!" She turned back toward Emma. "Emma, this is Sally Dixon."

Emma held out her hand, and Sally took it between both of hers and gave it a squeeze. "So nice to meet you. Arabella has told me so much about you."

Emma smiled. She was getting used to hearing that phrase wherever she went.

"Did you hear that Francis Salerno is in town?" Sally's cheeks flushed slightly.

"He's already been here," Arabella said, and Emma noted her slightly superior tone.

"Really?" Sally wagged a finger at Arabella. "Just you remember, I knew him first."

Arabella and Sally laughed. Emma looked from one to the other of them.

"Sally knew Francis when she lived in Jackson," Arabella explained. "She and his wife were very good friends."

Sally nodded. "We were both in the Ladies Auxiliary Sewing Circle and First Baptist Church Choir."

"It's really so sad," Arabella said.

"Yes. Cancer is a terrible disease. She was only sixty." Sally shook her head. "You wouldn't believe how many women brought Francis casseroles after Grace's death. Throwing themselves at him shamelessly." She rolled her eyes. "No wonder he never did remarry."

"I'm willing to bet your friend Sally was one of the casserole bringers," Emma said softly as Arabella closed the door on Sally's retreating back a few minutes later.

"I'm sure she was." Arabella laughed. "Her famous shepherd's pie, no doubt. Well he *is* good-looking, don't you think?"

"Yes. He looks like that actor, what's his name?"

"Tom Selleck. I used to love him in *Magnum P.I.*" Arabella glanced at Emma. "That was before your time, dear."

"There's such a thing as reruns, you know." Emma smiled. "But just don't forget," she added, wagging her finger at Arabella the way Sally had done, "she knew him first."

KATE had offered to help out at Sweet Nothings, and Emma was happy to take her up on it. Kate twisted her long hair into a knot, secured it with a pencil, and got down to business. Emma knew she was very organized—she had to be to deal with Guy who, while wildly creative, was immune to mundane things like schedules and appointments.

A prolonged fit of coughing heralded the arrival of Sylvia Brodsky later that morning. She had on heavy, dangling earrings that stretched her thin earlobes almost to her shoulders. They swayed as she bumped her oxygen tank over the threshold and parked it in the corner.

She looked around, nodding her head in what Emma hoped was appreciation.

"You done a lot with the place, Arabella."

Arabella smiled. "Actually, it was pretty much all Emma's doing."

"And Brian's," Emma added to be fair. After all, Brian had done all of the really hard work—she'd just had the vision.

"So when's the big opening? Everyone is talking about it. When they're not talking about the two murders, of course. Shame about that model. Who on earth could have had it in for her?"

"I don't know," Emma said, and shuddered.

Emma quickly turned her attention to the second carton in the shipment of lingerie from Monique and was relieved to note that Sylvia and Arabella had moved behind the counter and were going through one of the drawers. The less said about the two murders, the better, in her opinion. She was bending over the box when she had the feeling someone was watching her. Arabella and Sylvia had retreated to the back room, and Kate was facing the opposite direction, so unless she had eyes in back of her head, she definitely wasn't looking at Emma. Still, the feeling persisted. Emma glanced over her shoulder. Someone was peering through the front window of Sweet Nothings. It wasn't the first time. Everyone in Paris was curious about what they were doing.

Emma was about to turn around when the woman motioned at her.

Emma sighed. She really wanted to finish unpacking her box and get the items sorted. But it didn't pay to ignore a potential customer. She twisted the lock on the door and cracked it open.

"Yes? Can I help you?"

The woman standing there looked vaguely familiar. She was wearing white cotton pants and a sleeveless, fitted black T-shirt, and both showed her figure to great advantage. Her diamond studs were the size of headlights, and Emma wondered how she could lift her arm considering the weight of the gold bracelet encircling it.

Suddenly Emma recognized her. It was Deirdre Porter.

Chapter 13

ARABELLA glided forward swiftly. "Deirdre." She motioned to Emma to open the door wider. "Please come in."

Deirdre lifted her chin in the air and breezed past Emma. *Well, fiddle dee dee*, Emma thought to herself.

"Are you open yet?" Deirdre looked around the shop.

"Not quite. We're having a grand opening soon." Arabella smiled. "What do you think?"

"It's lovely." Deirdre looked around at the new cabinets, furniture and paint job. "Perfectly lovely." She smiled.

"Well, thank goodness," Sylvia muttered under her breath, and Emma shot her a conspiratorial smile.

"Can we help you with anything?" Arabella tilted her head and smiled. "We're closed, but we do have some stock in—"

"Oh, no," Deirdre shook her head, and her long hair whipped back and forth. "I just wanted to see what you were up to." She walked toward one of the glass-fronted cabinets and glanced inside. "These things are lovely though."

Sylvia was watching her keenly, and Emma wondered what she was thinking.

Sylvia gave a long, drawn-out cough, and moved away from the counter where she had been leaning. She gave one final, deep, phlegmy rattle before speaking. "You're wearing the wrong size bra," she declared sizing up Deirdre's chest. "Do you have a tape measure?" She glanced at Arabella and then at Emma.

"I don't know." Arabella flapped her hands and began opening drawers.

"Call yourself a lingerie shop, and you don't have a tape measure?" Sylvia snorted.

"And just what do you know about fitting bras?" Arabella asked, hands on hips.

"Only spent thirty years as a fitter at Macy's," Sylvia spat out.

Meanwhile, Emma had unearthed a tape measure that had been coiled, like a snake, in the back of a drawer. "Will this do?" She held it out to Sylvia.

Deirdre's face had turned red, and Emma expected her to protest, but she let Sylvia wind the tape around her chest.

"Just what I thought." Sylvia glanced at the number on the measuring tape. "You're wearing a size that is way too small for you."

"Really?"

"Yup." Sylvia said economically. "You've been wearing a B when you're actually a D. No sense in hiding your light under a bushel. It was Warner's, you know, who first started using the A, B, C, D bra cup sizing."

Deirdre looked pleased. "I don't suppose . . . since you're not open . . . ?" She looked questioningly from Arabella to Emma and then back again.

Emma spoke first. "We have gotten in new stock as it turns out. A D you said?" She turned to Sylvia, who nodded.

"A 36," Sylvia added.

Emma rummaged through the drawer she'd just organized and passed Deirdre a handful of bits of silk.

Deirdre disappeared into one of the dressing rooms with Sylvia right on her tail.

She emerged fifteen minutes later with the entire handful of lingerie.

"I'll take these." She put them on the counter and turned toward Sylvia, who was taking a drag of oxygen from her tank. "Thanks for your help."

Sylvia flapped a hand in response. Emma noticed her color had become alarmingly gray.

Emma took the lingerie from Deirdre and arranged it on a piece of the pink tissue she'd recently ordered. She folded up everything carefully and slipped the package into a glazed white bag with *Sweet Nothings* written in bold, black script across the front.

"I don't suppose," Emma began, one eye on Deirdre, "that you'd be interested in modeling in our fashion show?"

Deirdre turned a very becoming shade of pink. "Me? I'd love to. What would I be modeling?"

Emma took one of the vintage peignoir sets from the cabinet and showed it to Deirdre.

Deirdre's eyes widened. "It's beautiful." She clapped her hands. "I'd love to model in your show."

"I didn't know you'd been a bra fitter!" Arabella said as soon as the door closed behind Deirdre Porter.

Sylvia shrugged. "We've all got our secrets, I guess." She began to laugh, but it quickly turned to a cough.

Arabella fiddled with the long strand of amber beads around her neck. "We could use a bra fitter. It would be by appointment only so you wouldn't have to work full-time."

"Are you offering me a job?" Sylvia took a last puff of oxygen. Her face had turned pinker, and her breathing was easier.

"I guess I am," Arabella said with a laugh.

"Well, then I'm accepting." Sylvia laughed and this time she managed not to cough.

"This has been a productive afternoon," Emma said as she slid the last pile of lingerie into a drawer. "We've got our first model for our fashion show, and Sweet Nothings now has its own bra fitter."

"And you just had your second sale in your newly renovated shop," Kate piped up.

"All we need now are those armoires," Emma finished.

AFTER a quick lunch at The Coffee Klatch, Emma got back to work. Liz had sent some preliminary designs for the Sweet Nothings web site, and Emma needed to go through them and begin making some decisions. But every time there was a noise outside Sweet Nothings, she stopped to listen. Not because she thought it might be the delivery of the armoires—she'd all but given up on them for the moment—but because she was hoping Brian would stop by. They'd had such a good time at dinner. At least until he'd confused her with someone named Amy. She felt her face get hot at the memory. She'd thought he was going to kiss her, and she'd tilted her face toward his. The heat in her cheeks reached Fahrenheit 450. She had to find out who this Amy was. And whether or not Emma had any chance at all with Brian.

Emma was trying to focus on the designs from Liz when she heard a noise at the door. Pierre sat up in his dog bed—his latest nap of the day interrupted—to twitch his ears and assess the possible danger of this latest occurrence. He began growling, quietly, but deep in his throat, then reached a crescendo and began to bark just as a knock sounded on the door. Emma paused. It couldn't be Brian. Pierre wouldn't be barking like that. Maybe the armoires had, at long last, arrived?

Emma opened the door to find two young men standing

there, a roll of carpeting balanced across their shoulders like a battering ram. They were all brisk efficiency and, with hardly a word spoken, laid the carpet out and began tacking it into place. Emma, Arabella and Kate watched from the back room as the Sweet Nothings shop was transformed.

"I love it!" Arabella clapped her hands.

"Me, too," Kate piped up. "Great choice, Emma."

Kate wandered over to the small rolltop desk that Arabella used when she was paying bills. "What's this?"

Kate held up the earring that Emma and Brian had found in the carpet.

Emma explained about it.

"It's lovely." Kate held it up to the light. "It's a beautiful aqua terra jasper stone."

"Is that what it is?" Emma joined Kate in examining the earring.

Kate nodded, then blushed. "I'm such a nerd. But I love jewelry." She put the earring back on Arabella's desk. "Too bad you didn't find the mate."

"Hey, anybody there?" One of the carpet layers stuck his head around the corner.

"Coming." Emma grabbed the checkbook from the desk drawer and hurried toward the door. She gasped when she saw Sweet Nothings. The carpet was perfect. Everything was perfect.

Without thinking, she reached for her phone to call Brian. He had to see how all his hard work had turned out.

The phone was ringing for the third time when Emma was struck by the realization that Brian might think she was *calling* him. She *was* calling him, obviously, but not in the way he might interpret it—the "I've got a crush on you and I want to hear your voice" kind of way.

She almost hung up the phone, but before she could make a move, Brian's smooth voice was coming over the line.

"Hello?"

"Brian," Emma said, hoping she didn't sound as breath-less as she felt.

"Emma," Brian said, and there was no mistaking the enthusiasm in his voice.

Emma felt her spirits rise but then remembered the mysterious Amy. She managed to make her voice sound perfectly cool and aloof.

"Brian, the carpet's been laid, and it's perfect. I thought you might want to come see how everything has turned out." Emma squeezed her eyes shut. Hopefully Brian wouldn't think—

"Is that an invitation?" Brian's deep chuckle made Emma go weak in the knees.

Emma cleared her throat, but her voice still came out too high. "I just thought if you have a minute . . ."

"Give me twenty and I'll be right over."

Emma hung up the phone wondering what Brian was more enthusiastic about—seeing the finished product at Sweet Nothings or seeing her again?

EMMA was surprised when she heard a knock twenty minutes later. Didn't Brian still have his key?

She pulled open the door. "Oh." Her face fell.

"You don't look very glad to see me." Chuck Reilly said as he walked past Emma.

Emma couldn't help it—she looked down at Chuck's feet. At his enormous black shoes. She just hoped he'd wiped them before coming in.

"Can I help you with something?" Emma tried to keep the disdain from her voice.

"Actually, yeah, you can." Chuck cracked the knuckles on his right hand, then his left.

Emma hoped it would be something quick and easy so Chuck would leave Sweet Nothings immediately.

"We've got all of Guy's stuff down at the station. The hotel wasn't going to let us keep it in the room any longer without charging for it." He let out a low whistle. "Expensive place, the Beau." He stuck his hands in his pockets. "We don't want to keep it anymore, either. Seeing as how you're the closest thing we got to next of kin . . ."

"Oh." The thought of going through Guy's things made Emma shudder. Hopefully everything would be in plastic bags, and she wouldn't have to see it. But what on earth would she do with it afterward?

Kate had come out from the back room and was watching Emma. "Why don't I go get it?"

"Would you?" Emma's sense of relief surprised her.

"And who are you?" Chuck looked Kate up and down.

"I am . . . I was . . . Guy's assistant. He has a sister in Montreal. I have her number and address at the office. I can send the things to her."

"Guess that'd be all right." Chuck grumbled.

Emma had been slowly edging Chuck toward the door, hoping he would get the subliminal message and leave. She actually had her hand on the doorknob when someone pushed the door open.

"Oh!" Emma jumped.

"Sorry, did I scare you?" Brian peered around the slight opening. "You did say it was okay to come over."

A slow, nasty smiled crossed Chuck's face. "Looks like you've already exchanged one boyfriend for another."

Emma desperately wanted to punch Chuck Reilly right in his big, fat mouth, but she kept her clenched fists at her sides. She felt her face grow hot with embarrassment. It was bad enough that Brian might have thought she'd *called* him, but now Chuck was trying to peg him as her boyfriend. The words *if only* flashed across Emma's mind, and she clenched her fists tighter.

Brian gave Chuck a look that would have wilted anyone else on the spot, but Chuck was too dense to comprehend it.

"Were you about to leave?" Brian held the door wider.

Chuck gave Emma one last sneer and finally disappeared through the open door.

"I'd like to . . ." Brian waved his clenched fist in the air.

"I feel the same way." Emma gave a small smile. Just being with Brian made her feel better.

"I'm going to go grab a coffee. Anyone want anything?" Kate slung her purse over her shoulder and headed toward the door.

"No, thanks," Emma and Brian chorused.

"Let's see that carpet." Brian said as soon as the door shut behind Kate. He grabbed Emma's hand and stepped back toward the window so they could take it all in.

While Brian admired the carpet and the finished renovations at Sweet Nothings, Emma tried desperately to ignore the feelings that the warmth of her hand in his stirred up.

"Everything looks wonderful." Brian turned toward Emma with a smile. "Your ideas were perfect."

"So was the execution." Emma smiled back.

Brian grabbed her around the waist and waltzed her across the newly carpeted floor. He stopped suddenly, and they were face-to-face, his arm around Emma's waist, her hand warm in his. They stood locked in place for several seconds.

Once again Emma thought he might kiss her, but this time she restrained herself from either tilting her face or closing her eyes. The moment passed, and Brian took a step backward, a slightly embarrassed look on his face.

"Guess I got carried away." He laughed and Emma joined him, although she didn't feel like laughing.

Brian's hand lingered in hers for another moment before he let go. He glanced at his watch quickly. "I'd better get back to work," he said but made no move to leave.

The jingle of the bell over the door sent them scurrying apart. Kate entered carrying a paper cup labeled *The Coffee Klatch*. She looked from Emma to Brian and back again.

"I was just going," Brian said, and Emma thought she noticed a slight flush to his face.

"Yes, Brian was just going," Emma repeated, slightly surprised to note how disappointed that made her feel.

BY early evening, the rain had stopped, and the last of the sun was peeking through the swiftly scattering clouds. Emma took a deep breath. The air smelled of rich, wet earth, flowers and greenery. She was on her way to Let Us Cater To You, which was just around the corner from Angel Cuts. Emma peered into the salon as she walked past. Angel was on the telephone at the front desk and waved as Emma went by. Emma felt slightly guilty knowing that she and Kate planned to follow Angel. She gave an extra big wave and smile, as if that would make up for it.

Let Us Cater To You was a sliver of a shop tucked between two larger stores. It had been there for as long as Emma could remember. The proprietor, Lucy Monroe, had started out working from home and eventually her business had grown to the point where she was able to open her own place.

Inside, the basic setup of the shop was the same, but Emma noticed that the color scheme had been freshened along with some of the accessories. A glass case still dominated the small space and was filled with gourmet-type sandwiches and bite-sized confections. Two wrought-iron café tables were wedged into the remainder of the floor area.

No one was behind the counter, so Emma pinged the bell that sat out on the top of it.

"Can I help you?" A woman came out of the back, wiping her hands on an apron. She had white hair teased into a bouffant on top of her head, and she sported huge diamond studs.

She stopped short when she saw Emma. "Emma!" She rushed forward, her arms held out for a big hug. "It's wonderful to see you again," she said, crushing Emma to her chest.

Emma hugged her back. "You, too, Aunt Lucy. It's been ages."

Lucy Monroe wasn't really Emma's aunt. She and Emma's mother had been best friends since kindergarten, and when Emma was born, Lucy had immediately been christened "Aunt Lucy."

Lucy gestured toward one of the café tables and pulled out the chair opposite Emma. She sighed. "Feels good to get off my feet whenever I can." She rotated her ankles clockwise, then counter-clockwise. She was wearing a hot pink silk blouse and slim-fitting beige silk trousers with a pair of comfy-looking clogs.

"It really is so good to see you." She reached across the table, took Emma's hands in hers and gave them a squeeze. "It's been far too long."

Emma couldn't help but notice the enormous diamond ring on the ring finger of Lucy's left hand.

She must have noticed Emma's gaze. She waggled her fingers in front of Emma. "Like it?"

Emma nodded, somewhat speechless.

Lucy laughed. "Cubic zirconia. These, too." She pointed to the diamond studs in her ears. "Doesn't hurt to have everyone think that Harry, he's Mr. Lucy number five, is rolling in money. Keeps everyone's mouth shut. This way they figure I married him for his dough. Reality is that I just happened to like the guy. We get along, know what I mean?" She winked at Emma.

Emma smiled. Lucy had never had much luck with men.

Emma's mother always said it was because she was taken
in by their looks and married them before having the time
to learn that their beauty was truly only skin deep. Fortunately, Lucy was a strong woman and had always been perfectly capable of taking care of herself.

"Not like that Angel Roy," Lucy jerked her head in the
direction of Angel's shop. "It may have taken me five times
to get it right, but I finally did. She keeps stepping out with
the same sort over and over again."

Emma hoped Lucy was right and that this Harry fellow
would turn out to be different from the other men who had
drifted in and out of Lucy's life.

"Of course our little Angel is up to something herself,
just can't figure out what it is," she drawled on, her voice as
sweet and thick as honey. "Wednesdays and Thursdays like
clockwork. Now, I happen to know that her current squeeze
has a poker game on Thursdays and works late on Wednesdays." She looked at Emma and laughed. "You probably
think I'm a horrible old Miss Nosy Pants, sticking my nose
in other people's business."

Emma shook her head.

"This is a small town, and in small towns we do mind
each other's business, for better or for worse. Take old Mr.
Whimple. If his near neighbor, Miss Marshall, hadn't
noticed his mail piling up and called the police, well, would
anyone have ever found him before it was too late? He'd
fallen in the bathroom and was wedged between the bathtub
and the vanity, unable to get up!"

Emma was about to express her amazement, but Lucy
continued on.

"Shame about your young man being killed in your shop
like that. You must be devastated. Have the police arrested
anyone yet? By the time our little local paper reports on
anything, the news is months old."

"The police seem to think it was an intruder who did it,"

Emma said with her fingers crossed behind her back. The police had said no such thing. "You didn't happen to see anyone that night . . ."

"A Thursday, wasn't it?" Lucy scratched her head, then began to nod. "Yes, I was in the shop that night. Friday I was catering a big bridal shower—I was making the cheese straws. You can't get married, engaged or baptized in Paris without my famous cheese straws! I did them for your christening, you know, and your graduation. Next, I suppose it will be for your wedding." She looked at Emma coyly.

Emma just smiled.

"I don't know why, but the cheese straws I'd made earlier in the day just didn't taste right to me. That's the last time I buy butter from Meat Mart, I can tell you." She took a deep breath. "Anyway, I happened to look out the window, and someone was walking past. Didn't recognize who at first, so I went over to the window to get a closer look. It was Angel, right on schedule. And right behind her comes Tom Mulligan. It's a wonder they didn't run into each other! And both of them looking like they couldn't get away from there fast enough."

Aha, Emma thought. Further confirmation that both Angel and her boyfriend were out and about the night Guy was killed. She would definitely have to follow Angel to see what she was up to. Maybe there was another suitor in the picture and maybe he killed Guy?

"Anyway, enough about that. Tell me about this grand opening you and Arabella are planning. Do you want me to do my cheese straws?"

Emma surfaced from her thoughts to find that Lucy had finally started discussing the menu for their grand opening.

"I promise not to get the butter from Meat Mart this time." Lucy shuddered. "I'll stick to buying my meat there. It's excellent, by the way." She tapped Emma lightly on the arm.

"I thought we could have a selection of hors d'oeuvres . . ."

Lucy laughed suddenly. "Hors d'oeuvres," she repeated. "My grandma used to call them horses' ovaries. Can you imagine? She didn't have any use for fancy language." She slipped off her right clog and began massaging her foot. "I can do you a real nice spread. Believe me, no one will leave hungry. And," she tapped the glass case next to her. "A selection of pastries to finish. It's what the French call the piece of least resistance. At least I think so." She swung her foot, her clog bobbing back and forth from her toes.

Emma nodded. Her mother had assured her she could trust Lucy to do a good job, so she wasn't worried about the menu.

At least not too much.

Chapter 14

"I wish I could go with you."

It was Wednesday evening, and Emma and Arabella were sitting on Arabella's porch after another long day at the shop—Emma curled up on the swing, and Arabella stretched out on a chaise longue. A pitcher of homemade lemonade was within easy reach.

"Why don't you? You're more than welcome." Emma struggled upright and poured herself seconds of the lemonade.

Arabella looked slightly flustered, and her hands fluttered around her face like moths. "I have an . . . er . . . previous engagement."

"Aha." Emma pounced. "With Les?"

"No." Arabella hesitated. "It's with Francis, actually."

"Aren't you risking Sally Dixon's ire?"

Arabella laughed. "I figure if Sally had any chance with Francis at all, he'd be asking her out to dinner instead of me."

"Some things never change, I guess." Emma sipped her lemonade and licked the delicious tartness off her lips.

"That's for sure." Arabella pushed the swing, and it rocked gently back and forth. "I remember when your grandmother was in that assisted living place over on the other side of town. There were hordes of women to one poor man. And it was the same thing. Just like junior high school all over again." Arabella put down her empty glass. "I guess I'd better be getting ready."

"Where are you going?

"He's taking me to L'Etoile," Arabella said and blushed.

"Ooooh, fancy."

Arabella quickly changed the subject. "Do you want to borrow my car tonight? Francis is picking me up so I won't need it."

Emma shook her head. "Kate is borrowing Sylvia's car. We thought your Mini might be too recognizable. Same thing with Liz's bright red station wagon." Emma peered around the corner of the porch. "They both should be here any minute now."

"Well, I'm going to go in, then, and perform my ablutions, as my mother used to say."

Emma looked blank.

"My toilette?" Arabella proferred. "No?" She shook her head. "I guess I'm older than I thought. Or," she said with a smile at Emma, "I've become too wrapped up in the vintage world." She paused. "I'm going to go freshen up."

Arabella started toward the door, then stopped. "What on earth is that?"

"I don't know." Emma listened as the screeching got louder and closer.

They both stood at the edge of the porch and stared as Sylvia's Cadillac lurched into view.

Arabella shook her head. "You should be very inconspicuous in that."

"I don't know what's wrong with the car," Kate said as she walked up the front steps to Arabella's house. The hair around her forehead was damp and curling, and her cheeks were flushed. "Are you ready?" She glanced at her watch.

"Yes, but I asked Liz to come, too. She should be along any minute now."

Kate's face took on a strange expression, but then she smiled and it was gone. "Great."

"There she is," Emma said as a Subaru station wagon pulled up in back of Sylvia's car.

Liz beeped the locks and came bounding up the steps. "I hope I'm not late," she said breathlessly. "I wanted to get the kids fed before I left so Matt wouldn't have to."

"We're just about to go. Let me just grab my purse." Emma turned back toward the swing where she'd draped her bag over the arm. "Do you want me to drive?"

Emma heard a thud, followed by a thunk, followed by a cross between a squeal and a scream. She turned around to see Kate sprawled at the bottom of the porch stairs, rubbing her head.

"Are you okay?" Emma and Liz clattered down the steps quickly and rushed to her side.

"I think so." Kate shifted experimentally. "Nothing broken, at least." She wobbled to her feet. "Oh." She put a hand to her head.

"What's the matter?"

"Nothing. Just feeling a little dizzy." She sat down abruptly on the top step.

Liz frowned. "That doesn't sound good. Maybe we should get you to a doctor." She turned toward Emma, and Emma nodded.

"No, no," Kate protested. "I'll be fine." She put a hand to her head. "I think. Besides, we'd better leave soon or we'll miss Angel."

"Maybe you should stay here." Emma put a hand out.

"No! I don't want to miss this." Kate grabbed Emma's hand and scrambled to her feet. She groaned and put out a hand to steady herself.

"You're staying here," Emma declared firmly. "Aunt Arabella won't mind. We'll pick you up on the way back and fill you in on all the details."

Kate looked like she was going to cry. Emma gave her a quick hug, palmed the keys to the Caddy and went around to the driver's side. Liz opened the passenger door, and they both got in and waved to a disconsolate-looking Kate as they pulled away from the curb.

WASHINGTON Street was almost deserted by the time they got there. Shops were dark and the sidewalks were empty, except for Let Us Cater To You where a single bulb burned toward the back of the store. Emma glanced over quickly, catching a quick glimpse of Aunt Lucy.

Emma pulled up to the curb. "What time is it?"

Liz glanced at her watch. "Just about time. Angel should be along any minute now."

They heard a door slam and a car came around the corner from the back where the parking lots were. It was Angel driving her fire-engine-red Turbo Trans Am. Nothing inconspicuous about that car. She'd be a cinch to follow.

Angel rounded the corner with tires squealing. Emma threw the Cadillac into gear, but something was obviously wrong because it lurched three times before slowly picking up speed. By the time the speedometer reached the speed limit, Angel's red sports car was a blur in the distance.

"Hurry, she's getting away."

"I'm trying." Emma hit the gas, but nothing much happened other than that the squealing increased to epic proportions. She prayed Angel would hit a light, and the Caddy would be able to catch up.

Luck was on their side. When they got to the corner, three cars were idling at the red light. Angel was up front, and Emma could sense her impatience to get going. When the light changed Angel shot forward and quickly put distance between herself and the other cars. Emma coaxed the Caddy up to maximum speed, which hovered around the forty-five-mile-per-hour mark. Unfortunately, Angel's Trans Am was merely warming up at that speed.

Emma did her best, but at one point she lost sight of Angel all together.

"I don't see her, do you?" She glanced at Liz.

Liz craned her head, her eyes focused on the window. "I'm afraid I don't see her either."

"Maybe we should go back? We can try another night."

"No, wait." Liz grabbed Emma's arm. "Look." She pointed out the window. "I'm sure I saw a flash of red."

"If you say so." Emma put pedal to the medal and the Caddy obliged by eking out an extra ten miles per hour. It was enough. Within a couple of minutes, Angel was within view.

"Where on earth is she going, do you think?"

"I have no idea," Liz said, grabbing the door handle as the Cadillac picked up speed.

Angel slowed, and Emma was able to ease up on the gas, although the Caddy continued to squeal like a pig at the slaughter. Angel pulled into the driveway of a large, beige brick, lit up building.

"Look," Liz pointed to a large sign with *Tennessee Technology Center* written on it in large, black letters.

"What?" Emma was so startled she momentarily took her foot off the gas, and the Caddy rumbled to a stop. "What is Angel doing *here*?"

"Maybe she's seeing one of the teachers?" Liz stared out the window.

"Could she be a student? People of all ages go back to school—they're not all teenagers."

"True." Liz admitted. She turned toward Emma. "But Angel?"

Emma shrugged her shoulders. Three or four more cars pulled into the lot, swerving around Emma and zooming into parking spaces. Emma eased up on the gas and began to move forward. Angel was getting out of her car with what looked like books under her arm. Emma was more confused than ever.

There was a space five cars beyond where Angel had parked the Trans Am. Emma thought she'd park there and follow Angel on foot. As the Caddy approached the space, Emma gently tapped the brake. Nothing. She tried again.

"Where are you going?" Liz asked in alarm. "Don't you think you should park?"

The Caddy not only sailed on past the empty parking space but began to pick up speed. Emma applied the brake in earnest. Still nothing.

"Stop, Emma. Stop."

"I'm trying." Emma stomped the brake again.

Her heart sped up in time to the Caddy's speedometer. "I don't know what's wrong." She stomped the brake as hard as she could, sending it to the floor.

Nothing.

Emma began to panic in earnest. The row of cars went by in a blur, and pedestrians jumped out of the way, their mouths open in alarm. She stomped the brake again and again.

"I think the gas pedal is stuck or something."

Liz quickly unbuckled her seat belt. "Let me see if I can fix it." She slid half off her seat and leaned forward, sweeping a hand under the gas pedal.

Emma, meanwhile, continued trying to steer around

obstacles in her path—a girl in skinny jeans and a cropped T-shirt, a dark blue SUV that hung out of its space by several inches, a row of gnarly looking bushes alongside the sidewalk. The blur through her windshield sped up like a film strip out of control. She had to do something.

But what?

Liz sat back in her seat and refastened her belt. "I can't fix it. I don't know what's wrong." She looked out the window. "Maybe you should drive onto the lawn? That might slow us down."

Emma aimed Sylvia's Caddy toward the grass. She pictured Liz and herself jumping out of their seats like in old cowboy movies where people jettisoned themselves from runaway stagecoaches.

The Caddy bumped over the curb and started across the lawn. Emma's teeth knocked together as the car negotiated the rutted terrain. She clung to the steering wheel for dear life, not so much steering the car as aiming it around obstacles in its path. Liz held onto the sissy strap, and Emma could see how white her face had become in the glow of the passing lamps. The back of Emma's dress was soaked, and her hands were slippery on the wheel. She kept the brake pressed to the floor, but it wasn't slowing her progression across the lawn of the Tennessee Technology Center.

Emma glanced in her rearview mirror to see several dozen people running after her and the Caddy. She thought she saw Angel in the crowd, moving awkwardly in her high-heeled sandals. She'd managed to follow Angel all right, but whether she lived to find out what Angel was doing at the Tennessee Technology Center was another story.

Suddenly, a dark shape loomed in the distance. Another tree. Liz partially stifled a scream, and Emma gritted her teeth and prepared to swerve around it. People were still walking across the lawn, laughing, talking and joking, unaware that a runaway Cadillac was on the loose. Emma fought the urge to close her eyes as she narrowly missed a couple strolling arm-in-arm, locked in a tight embrace.

The tree almost filled her window when she jerked the wheel to avoid it. Too late she saw a fellow in a T-shirt and baseball cap standing in her path.

"Emma, watch out!" Liz screamed.

This time Emma did close her eyes. She winced as something thudded against her windshield and then crashed to the ground, rolling behind her. A sob caught in her throat, and she sent up a prayer for help. Surely there was some way to stop this wretched car.

Emma yanked on the emergency brake, and the car slowed slightly, the tires churning more heavily through the turf. A row of bushes bordered the edge of the lawn, and they were coming closer with each passing second. The road beyond was empty at the moment, but there was no guarantee it would stay that way. It was now or never.

Emma got a good grip on the wheel and angled the car so that the first bushes in the row hit it toward the side. Branches slapped against the windshield, and twigs, leaves and bits of bark slithered down the hood of the car. Emma hit the next bush and the next. The needle on the speedometer dropped to thirty miles per hour, then twenty-five miles per hour. Finally she came to the last bush. The lawn sloped slightly upward just beyond it. The Caddy smacked the bush, bending and breaking dozens of branches, then hit the incline and sputtered to a stop.

Chapter 15

AS soon as the car rocked to a stop, Emma scrabbled for the door handle.

"Where are you going?" Liz asked.

"I have to get help," Emma gasped. She had to go back and get help for whoever it was she had hit. She thought it was the guy in the baseball cap, but she wasn't sure. She just prayed there was still hope. If they got the paramedics there on time . . .

Emma's hands were shaking so badly, she couldn't grasp the car door handle. Suddenly, the door was yanked open, and someone stuck his head inside the car.

"You ladies okay?" The man smiled at them.

Emma looked around and saw that the crowd that had been chasing the Caddy had caught up with her.

"We're fine. But we have to check on that man. The one in the baseball cap." She babbled incoherently. "I didn't mean to hit him."

The guy laughed, and Emma suddenly realized that he

was wearing a baseball cap. Was he the same young guy who . . .

He stuck out a hand and helped her from the car. "Come on." He waited as Liz scrambled from the passenger seat then led them back over the grass, toward where Emma thought she'd run him down.

"See?" He motioned toward a trail of decaying food, discarded paper and fruit and vegetable peels that littered the lawn in a wide swathe.

"What?" Emma swayed, and the young man put out a hand to steady her. "I hit someone. I know I did." She began to cry softly.

He shook his head. "You hit a trash bag. I was carrying it, and when I saw you coming toward me, I freaked and tossed it in the air. It hit your windshield and exploded." He indicated the debris.

Now Emma's legs really began to give way. She hadn't hit anyone! No one was injured or dead. Everything was going to be okay.

"Emma! What on earth are you doing?" Angel caught up to them. The twist in her hair was slightly askew, and perspiration gleamed on her upper lip. She glared at Liz.

"I . . . I . . ." Emma stammered.

Angel glanced at the young man in the cap. "It's okay. I'll make sure they get home. Don't you worry your little head about a thing."

Angel began moving Emma and Liz away from the crowd, which had started to disperse.

"Just what on earth did you two think you were doing?" Angel hissed as soon as they were out of earshot of the other students.

Emma flashed back to her dear, departed Uncle Maxwell. He always said, "When you know you're wrong, take the offense."

"Well, I could ask you the same thing," Emma said trying

to sound firm despite the shakiness in her voice. "What are you doing here?"

"Uh-uh. I asked you first." Angel took Emma and Liz by the arm and guided them toward her Trans Am.

"We were just driving along when the brakes failed." Emma tried to inject a note of indignation into her tone, but her voice insisted on quivering like a bowl of jelly.

"And you just happened to be driving across the parking lot of the Tennessee Tech Center." Angel's lips snapped shut into a firm line. "And you just happened to be following me since we left town. Honestly!" She shook her head, and her twist wobbled perilously, her high-heeled sandals slapping the macadam angrily. "Did you seriously think I couldn't hear you coming in that . . . that . . . ridiculous car? Isn't that Sylvia's car, by the way?"

"Yes."

"Piece of junk, if you ask me. Why she paid to have it shipped down here, I'll never know." She turned and looked at Emma and Liz, then stopped suddenly. Her voice softened. "You've had a bad fright. Really bad. You're both as white as a sheet after it's been bleached and hung in the sun."

"It was . . . scary." Emma admitted. A sob rose in her throat.

Liz merely nodded mutely.

"Come on. Let's get you back. You need a hefty shot of some good old Tennessee whiskey. That'll fix you right up. Then you can tell me all about why you've been following me tonight. Okay?'

Emma and Liz nodded weakly and allowed Angel to tuck them into her car.

"What about Sylvia's car?" Emma jerked and tried to look out the back window toward where she'd abandoned the Caddy.

"Tom will come get it later. And he can have a look at those brakes of hers. She probably forgot to top off her brake fluid. Lord knows how long it's been since someone looked under the hood of that relic."

"Can I ask you a question?" Emma's voice came out more timidly than she'd intended.

"Depends." Angel flipped on her blinker and exited the parking lot onto Wilson Street.

"Fair enough." Emma nodded. "I was just wondering what you were doing here tonight? At the Tennessee Tech Center, I mean."

Angel threw back her head and laughed. "I've been seeing one of the professors. We don't want his wife to know, so I've been pretending to take his class in business information systems. Even been doing the homework and taking all the exams so that it looks real legit. And I show up for class Wednesdays and Thursdays regular, as clockwork. So far the poor woman doesn't have a clue."

Emma inhaled sharply; then she realized that Angel was playing with her. "You're taking classes."

"Yes. And what of it? Am I the only one in town not allowed to better herself?" They had turned onto Washington Street and were nearing Angel Cuts salon.

"Isn't the shop doing well?" It was always full whenever Emma walked past.

"Yes. And that's just the point." Angel's head swiveled and she looked Emma right in the eye. "I'm hoping to expand. And in order to do that, there are a few things I need to understand first." She gestured toward the stack of textbooks balanced on the console between them. "That's why I'm taking some business classes. Don't want to make any mistakes and ruin everything I've worked for so far."

"Oh." Emma felt terribly small. Here she'd been thinking Angel was having an affair, and she'd actually been doing something extremely worthwhile.

But that didn't let Tom Mulligan off the hook. And, if he were the killer, she'd better not let him anywhere near Sylvia's

Caddy. Because it suddenly struck Emma that someone could have tampered with Sylvia's brakes. And who would know more about cars than Tom Mulligan? She shot Liz a look. It would be a piece of cake for him to do whatever was necessary to render the brakes useless.

She shuddered. Who knew what he might do next? They'd been lucky this time, but their luck might not last. Perhaps she'd better leave the investigating to the police.

Chuck Reilly's sneering face came to mind. Then again, perhaps she'd better keep investigating. She'd just have to be a lot more careful.

"OH, my goodness, Emma, Liz, what happened?" Kate cried as she leapt off Arabella's porch and ran toward Emma.

"We're okay. Just kind of shaken up." Emma waved to Angel, and Angel waved back then pulled away from the curb.

Liz collapsed onto the porch swing, her head propped against the backrest.

"You both look terrible." Kate swiveled toward the street. "Did Sylvia's car break down?"

Emma shuddered. "It was horrible. Something happened to her brakes, and I couldn't stop, and I thought I'd hit someone, and it was just horrible." Emma concluded with a sob.

"I think you need to sit down, too." Kate started to lead Emma toward the swing.

"What about your head? Are you okay?" Liz said without lifting her head from the back of the swing.

"I'm fine. Got a bit of a goose egg, that's all." Kate touched a hand to the back of her head and winced. "Arabella left a pitcher of sweet tea in the refrigerator. Why don't I pour us a couple of glasses?"

"Sounds good to me." Emma sank onto the swing next

to Liz. "Add a shot of whiskey," she called over her shoulder. She'd decided to take Angel's advice.

Maybe it would stop the shaking in her hands.

EMMA found herself automatically glancing at the front window of Sweet Nothings the next morning, but so far there hadn't been any more threatening notes. But the stakes had been raised—first the note on their window, then the threatening phone call and now an attempt at what could have resulted in . . . murder.

Emma waved to Bitsy, who was hurrying down the other side of the street, and pushed open the door. The fresh smell of new paint and recently laid carpet greeted her. She took a deep breath and looked around. Everything was coming together just as she'd envisioned it. The carpet was perfect, the paint was just the right color, the touches of black-and-white toile added a bit of elegance without being too stuffy looking. Now all they needed were those armoires. She would call the company again and find out what was going on.

Someone knocked sharply on the front door. Emma listened but didn't hear any scratching, so it wasn't Arabella. Perhaps it was Brian? Her spirits lifted. She yanked open the door and, when she saw who was standing there, had to stop herself from slamming it shut again.

"Can I come in?" Chuck put one of his large paws against the door and pushed.

Did she have any choice? She shrugged and walked toward the display counter. She'd feel better having something between herself and Chuck Reilly. Chuck leaned on the glass and spread out his thick, spatulate fingers. Emma couldn't help staring at them. She shivered.

"What do you want?"

"Me? Nothing." Chuck feigned indifference. "I thought

maybe you'd like to know what I just found out." He smiled, but his blue eyes were cold.

This isn't going to be good, Emma thought. She just knew it. She tried to keep her expression calm and neutral. "What?"

"We got the report on the murder weapon back from the TBI. You know, the walking stick that killed your lover boy."

Emma felt heat rising to her face but reminded herself to be calm. Chuck was trying to get the better of her, and she wasn't going to let him.

"Yes?"

"It was covered in prints." Chuck paused and pointed at Emma. "Yours."

"I told you." Emma could hear the exasperation in her voice and tried hard to tone it down. "I had handled the walking stick before. When I brought it to Aunt Arabella to use after she twisted her ankle."

"Really?" Chuck began a slow and agonizing examination of his fingernails. "If I were you, I'd consider lawyering up. They say Sullivan and Doyle over on the next block are pretty good."

WHEN Brian arrived five minutes later he found Emma alone, her face red and tear-stained, and a pile of crumpled tissues on the counter.

"What's wrong?" He crossed the floor of Sweet Nothings in three strides.

Emma could feel her face brighten at the sight of him. She tried to keep the proverbial stiff upper lip, but Brian's presence melted her like a pat of butter on a hot griddle. She burst into tears again and spilled everything—Chuck's visit, the ride in Sylvia's car the night before, how she'd thought she'd actually run someone over and possibly killed him. She tried to stop herself, but when Brian put his arms around her and pulled her close, she couldn't help it. The floodgates opened and all of the stress of the last week splashed out unhampered.

She was vaguely aware of Brian murmuring soothing words into her hair, and she tried to pull herself together. But it was hard. Being within the circle of Brian's arms made her feel so safe and secure. She didn't ever want to leave.

They heard a key in the lock of the front door, and they drew apart as if scalded. Arabella bustled in, with Pierre at her heels, stopping short at the sight of the two of them.

"Am I interrupting something?" She asked eagerly.

"No," Brian and Emma choroused emphatically.

"You've been crying." Arabella rushed forward and took Emma's hands in hers. "What's wrong?"

Emma told her about Chuck's visit.

"I think it's high time we made a complaint about the behavior of Sergeant Chuck Reilly. He has really gotten out of hand. I'm going to speak with Francis about it. I know the TBI tries to keep out of the way of the local boys unless absolutely necessary, but this is ridiculous." Arabella's forehead creased with concern.

"No!" Emma protested. "It might make him even worse." She shuddered. "If that's possible."

"Chuck should start doing his job—protecting innocent citizens, not persecuting them. He should be investigating who tampered with Sylvia's brakes." Brian slammed his fist into the palm of his other hand.

"We don't know for sure that they've been tampered with—"

"What?" Arabella's hand flew to her throat, and her face paled. "Someone tampered with Sylvia's brakes? But you," she said, looking at Emma, "drove her car yesterday . . ."

"Emma and Liz could have been killed!"

Emma nodded. "I wasn't going to tell you about it since everything turned out okay." She glanced at Brian and was pleased to see he looked as contrite as a boy caught with his hand in the cookie jar.

"Thank goodness for that." Arabella sank into one of the toile Louis XIV chairs. "Tell me what happened." She fixed Emma with her bright blue stare.

"How was your date with Francis?"

"Are you trying to change the subject?" Arabella smiled at her niece. "It was a wonderful evening, actually."

"You're blushing."

"No, I'm not." Arabella insisted as her face continued to pink up. "First tell me about Sylvia's car and the brakes. Then I'll tell you everything you want to know about my date with Francis."

"OKAY," Emma said later, after Brian had left and she and Arabella were alone, "now I want to hear all about your evening with Francis."

"My, my, you are like a dog with a bone," Arabella said, but she smiled to take any sting out of her words.

"Well?" Emma raised her brows.

Arabella sank into the chair next to the counter. "It was a lovely evening. It was almost as if we were old friends. The conversation just . . . flowed."

"What about Les?"

Arabella shrugged, but Emma did notice she looked slightly chagrined. "I like Les."

"But?"

"Are you reading my mind?" Arabella laughed. "Yes, there is a but. I'm afraid Les is slightly more . . . serious . . . about our relationship than I am. Believe it or not, we dated briefly in high school, but Les graduated two years ahead of me and was drafted into the army." Arabella was quiet for a moment, and Emma noticed the shadows that crossed her face. "He was sent to Vietnam. When he came home," she shrugged, "like so many other young men, he was never quite the same again. He tried various careers, even moved out to California at one point, but he couldn't escape the things he'd seen and that haunted him day and night. He came back to Paris eventually and opened his own store, but that didn't quite work out either. Finally he took the job at The Toggery, and it seems to suit him. He's been there ever since." She turned toward Emma suddenly. "It's not that I don't care about him. I do. But I'm not ready to take on the responsibility."

Emma nodded her understanding.

"Meanwhile, we continue to go out and, while I appreciate his company, I'm afraid nothing more will ever come of it."

"And Francis? He seems to be more your type."

Arabella gave a grin that Emma could only describe as wicked. "I keep telling myself I don't want to get involved in a long-distance romance—Francis does spend most of his time in Jackson—but on the other hand . . ."

Arabella didn't have to finish the sentence. Emma knew exactly what she meant.

There was a loud thump against the front door of Sweet Nothings. Emma listened. Had someone knocked? She hesitated, then made her way toward the door and slowly opened it. She peered around the edge. No one was there.

She glanced down. A brown-paper parcel lay on the black mat. That was strange. The mailman had already come, and the UPS delivery woman always knocked and came in to shoot the breeze and enjoy a glass of Arabella's sweet tea.

Emma picked up the box and brought it inside. There was no return address. There was no address at all. Just *Sweet Nothings* scrawled across the front in black marker. Odd. Maybe it was from one of the local shopkeepers and Arabella was expecting it.

"Aunt Arabella?"

"Yes, dear?"

"I found this outside on the mat." Emma held the box out. "Is this from one of your suitors?" She smiled.

"Let me see." Arabella settled her glasses on her nose and stared at the strange package. "The writing doesn't look familiar, I'm afraid." She shrugged. "Should we open it?" She looked at Emma with her eyebrows raised.

"Why not?" Emma looked around. "I'll get the scissors."

"Never mind, it's just tape." Arabella slipped her finger under a flap of the paper and loosened it. She did the same on the other side and whipped the brown wrapping off.

Underneath was a glossy white box. There was nothing written on top, and the two longer sides were taped shut. Arabella slit the tape and took off the lid. A cloud of delicate pink tissue paper puffed out. She and Emma exchanged glances.

"Whatever it is," Arabella said, "it must be expensive to warrant such wrapping." She peeled back the layers of tissue and gasped.

"What is it?" Emma peered over her shoulder.

"Oh" was all Arabella could say for a moment. Her fingers floated reverently above the silk garment folded into the box. "It's a Michelene—early or perhaps mid-1940s, although I can't say for sure until I get it out of the box."

"Is it very valuable?" The pink peignoir looked exquisite, but so did so many of the pieces Arabella had shown her.

Arabella nodded. "Yes. And also quite hard to come by. It looks to be in excellent condition."

"Shall we take it out?"

"Of course." Arabella put the box down on the counter, grasped the garment by the shoulders and lifted it out. She found herself holding the top six inches of what once must have been an exquisite negligee. The rest had been cut into strips no wider than an inch. Arabella dropped the piece of silk. "Who would do something like this?" She jerked toward Emma, knocking the box to the floor.

Ribbons of silk floated this way and that like airborne confetti.

Emma thought she saw something amidst the pink strips of fabric. She knelt down and teased out a piece of paper. It was white, and looked like something torn off a cheap pad. Emma picked it up by its edges.

On it was written a word in bold black strokes. Just one word.

A very naughty word. One that was only socially acceptable when referring to female dogs.

Chapter 16

"WHO would do such a thing?" Arabella said over her shoulder. She grabbed a wooden spoon from a blue and white enamelware pitcher she used as a container for her kitchen utensils and stirred a quarter of a cup of honey into the mixture in her ceramic bowl.

Emma noticed Arabella's hand shake slightly. She suspected that the mysterious package had unnerved Arabella more than she was willing to admit. When Arabella had invited her to dinner, she had agreed immediately. She wanted to keep an eye on her.

Arabella reached for a canister marked *Flour* and scooped several cups into a brown paper bag. She then shook in some salt, pepper, a dash of green herbs and a smidge of something Emma didn't recognize.

"What's that?" Emma gestured toward the spice jar in Arabella's hand.

"My secret ingredient." Arabella smiled and handed Emma the container. "You have to promise not to tell anyone what it is. Especially Sally Dixon. She's been after my recipe for years."

Emma glanced at the label. "You put curry powder in your fried chicken?"

Arabella nodded as she shook the mixture in the bag. "Just a pinch. It gives real depth to the flavor."

"Well I doubt Sally Dixon would ever think of that."

Arabella pulled a tray of chicken pieces from the refrigerator.

"The package and that nasty note must be connected to Guy's murder somehow, don't you think? Someone knows we've been snooping, and they're getting nervous," Emma said.

"Do you think Angel sent it? She's the one you've been following."

"Not very successfully," Emma said with a laugh. "Besides we know what she was doing on Wednesday and Thursday nights—going to school."

"And I say, good for her." Arabella opened the oven door, and a blast of heat caught Emma around the knees. Arabella slid a cast-iron pan of corn bread into its depths and shut the door again. "But what about this Tom fellow?"

"Brian is still trying to find out whether or not he was at that poker game the night Guy was killed."

"If Chuck Reilly and the rest of the police department would do their job—" Arabella stopped. "I think that's the doorbell."

Pierre scrambled to his feet and made a mad dash for the front door, stopping midway and sliding the last five feet. He pounced at the door, barking furiously.

Emma slid down the hall right behind him. She remembered doing the same thing when she was little and Arabella would babysit her while her parents went out. It didn't happen often—Arabella was usually off someplace exotic herself—but Emma had always loved when her aunt was home.

Emma grabbed the handle and yanked it open.

Kate stood on the doorstep, a bottle of wine in her hands. Her light brown hair hung in limp strands on either side of her face, and her glasses were smudged and slightly askew.

"Come on in." Emma ushered Kate into Arabella's foyer. "You look like you could use a nice cold drink of something."

Kate followed Emma out to the kitchen, where Arabella was shaking the pieces of chicken in the flour mixture in her paper bag.

"I've brought a chilled sauvignon blanc." Kate handed the bottle to Emma. "We can open this if you like."

"Sounds good." Emma rummaged in the drawer next to the oven and pulled out the corkscrew. "How's your head? I still think I should have taken you to the doctor."

Kate touched the spot on her head experimentally. "It hardly hurts at all anymore. I'm fine. You need to stop worrying." She smiled at Emma.

"We've been discussing Guy's murder again." Emma stood on tiptoe and eased three wineglasses off the top shelf with her fingertips.

"Did you tell Kate about our mysterious package?" Arabella lowered a piece of chicken into the oil that was sizzling and spitting in a pan on the stove.

"What package?" Kate took a sip of her wine. "Mmmm, this is just what I needed."

"Rough day?"

Kate ducked her head, and a curtain of hair fell across her face. "I went to the police station today to pick up Guy's things." She looked up, and her eyes were brimming with tears. "It was sort of . . . difficult."

"I can imagine." Emma put her arms around Kate. "And I really appreciate you doing that so that I didn't have to."

Kate nodded. "When I saw his camera . . ." She made a gulping sound like a swallowed sob. "I can't believe he's gone." She finished finally. "The police gave me all his clothes and that gold chain he used to wear around his wrist." She looked at Emma. "I thought perhaps you ought to have it." She put down her glass and began to forage in the large leather satchel she always carried.

"Is that Guy's camera?" Emma pointed to the Nikon in Kate's bag.

"Yes. I'm not quite sure what to do with it."

"Are there any pictures on it?"

Kate found the chain and handed it to Emma. "Yes, there are. I think the card is almost full."

"Have you looked at them?"

"Oh, no, I wouldn't. I mean, they might be private or something." Kate blushed.

"I think we should look at them. Maybe there's a clue to his murder on there somewhere."

Kate shrugged. "You never know."

"That's a great idea, but right now, dinner is ready." Arabella put a platter of golden brown fried chicken on the table.

"And you haven't told me about that package." Kate tucked her napkin into her lap and took the basket of corn bread Arabella handed her.

Emma explained about the mysterious box, the destroyed negligee and the nasty note.

"Who would do something like that?" Kate said, echoing Arabella's previous sentiments. "Sending the note was bad enough, but destroying that vintage gown."

Arabella put down her fork. "That's the thing. Seeing that beautiful piece of lingerie . . . ruined . . . was more hurtful than anything."

"Do you think it's the murderer who sent it?" Kate chose a piece of chicken and put it on her plate.

"Who else?" Arabella buttered a piece of corn bread and took a bite.

"Could it have been someone who had a grudge against

you personally?" Emma pointed her fork at Arabella. "Cutting up that beautiful nightgown strikes me as being very spiteful."

"Oh, my gosh!" Arabella's hand flew to her mouth. "You don't think . . ."

"Les?" Emma concluded.

"But why?" Kate looked from one to the other, a puzzled expression on her face.

Arabella turned that becoming shade of pink again. "Well, you see, Les might have been a little . . . upset . . . with me. Because of Francis." Arabella finished vaguely.

"Francis?"

"Arabella's other suitor."

"Oh." Kate gave a somewhat mirthless laugh. "I can't seem to find one boyfriend, let alone two."

"They're not really boyfriends," Arabella protested. "But I suppose you could be right. Les might have been upset when he saw me at L'Etoile that night with Francis."

"He saw you!" Emma declared.

Arabella patted her lips with her napkin. "He was just leaving as we were going in. He'd taken his mother for her birthday dinner."

"And he didn't invite you?" Emma was appalled.

Arabella cleared her throat delicately. "It seems that his mother doesn't exactly approve of me. She's very suspect of the fact that I've traveled throughout Europe and have actually been to India and Asia."

"But Les is—"

"Old enough. You're right. But try telling him that."

Arabella changed the subject, and they chatted about a number of things for the next half hour until Arabella stood up and began collecting the empty plates. "Who's up for some dessert? I've made a fresh peach cobbler."

"I'm going to gain so much weight living here." Emma laughed and tugged at her waistband playfully.

"I think I've already gained five pounds," Kate confided. "Sylvia is continually plying me with food, and I can't resist."

They took plates of cobbler and cups of freshly brewed coffee out to the porch. The setting sun left rosy streaks across the pale sky, and a soft breeze ruffled the grass.

"I almost hate to think about going back to New York," Kate said, idly pushing the swing back and forth with one foot. "This is heaven."

Emma finished the last bite of her cobbler and put down her fork. She hated to destroy the relaxed mood. "Do you think we should take a look at Guy's camera now? Perhaps we'll find some answers. Like where Guy went the night he was killed. Nikki claims to have left him by nine o'clock. Did he go somewhere after that?" She sighed in exasperation.

"Fortunately, if Guy went somewhere, his camera went as well. I can't remember any time when he wasn't snapping away randomly," Kate concluded.

"I'd like to know how he got into Sweet Nothings that night." Arabella set down her coffee cup. "The police said it wasn't a forced entry."

"I think I might have the answer to that." Kate slipped off the swing. "Let me get my purse. And I'll take some dishes in while I'm at it."

Emma protested, but Kate insisted. They could hear the plates rattle as Kate put them in the sink, and her footsteps as she crossed the hall back toward the porch. She came out with her tan leather satchel slung over her shoulder.

Kate sat down and began to dig in her handbag. "Here." She pulled out a key that hung from a slightly worn-looking pink ribbon.

"That's our spare key." Arabella held out her hand. "We always keep it in the back room by the door."

"Guy must have taken it when he was at the shop." Emma leaned forward in her chair and looked at the key in

Arabella's hand. "But why? Why would he take the key? There was nothing to steal—"

"Guy wouldn't stoop to stealing," Kate declared indignantly.

"Maybe he thought it would get him into your apartment," Arabella suggested, turning to look at Emma and dangling the key in the air tantalizingly.

"Oh." Emma collapsed against the back of her chair. "I hadn't thought of that."

"He might have been afraid you wouldn't keep your date with him." Arabella pulled her braid over her shoulder and began to undo it.

"We did have a big fight once—I can't even remember now what it was about. But I refused to see Guy for several days—didn't answer his calls, wouldn't open my door when he came by. Of course the minute I relented and met him for coffee, it was all over. I couldn't stay mad. Not when he was being so charming." Emma smiled at the memory. "Taking the key was probably his insurance that he would be able to work his usual magic on me."

Arabella pulled her fingers through her hair and then began to coil it on top of her head. She twisted the elastic around the makeshift bun. "Maybe it's time we had a look at Guy's camera?"

They adjourned to the living room, a room Emma thought must once have been called a parlor—probably even the front parlor. The beautiful bay window was still there, with the deep window seat that just invited one to sit and spend lazy days watching the world go by. The fireplace was the centerpiece of the room, and Arabella had arranged the furniture—a huge overstuffed sofa and chair—in front of it. A carved wooden elephant from India held center stage on the coffee table, and a stone Buddha from Thailand had pride of place on the mantel.

Emma had brought along her laptop to show Arabella

some of Liz's web designs. She set it on the coffee table and powered it up while Kate fiddled with the Nikon.

"I can't get this thing out." Kate fumbled with the memory card, and Emma noticed that her hands were shaking.

Kate finally wrested the chip from the camera, and Emma hooked it up to her computer. She was about to click the mouse when Kate put out a hand.

"Maybe we shouldn't do this." Kate had a slick of perspiration on her upper lip. "Maybe we should give the camera to the police, and see what they think."

"The police had the camera." Arabella scooted her chair closer to the computer screen. "And, as far as we can tell, they didn't do a thing with it."

"True." Kate sank back into her seat. "I suppose we might as well go ahead then." She motioned toward the mouse in Emma's hand.

Emma pressed SLIDE SHOW and then PLAY and the first image appeared on the screen.

It was a New York street scene so alive and vibrant that Emma thought she could smell the car exhaust and hear the horns honking. A wave of nostalgia washed over her—for the city, for Guy, for all the dreams she used to have. How naïve she had been!

The picture changed, and there was a young girl in a black leather jacket posed against the red door of a brownstone on the corner of Perry Street. She wasn't a model— Guy liked to approach women on the street and ask if he could take their picture. He felt the resultant shots were more spontaneous and more genuine. If this photo was anything to go by, he was right.

"He certainly could take a good picture," Arabella said, and leaned closer to the screen.

The kaleidoscope of photos changed from New York City street scenes to rolling green hills and empty meadows. Emma's stomach tightened. They were getting closer to the more recent snaps. She was half afraid they wouldn't find anything useful, and half afraid they would.

Emma recognized Nikki in the next photo and felt her jaw clench. The setting looked familiar, but she couldn't quite place it. Nikki was peering out from between tall, ornamental grasses with only her face and a bare, bronzed arm and leg visible. With her cat eyes rimmed in black she looked like an exotic wild animal. Emma's mouse hovered over the NEXT button. There was something about the picture that was familiar. It came to her—it must have been taken outside the Beau Hotel, on the island covered with striped grasses. Now they were really close. Her stomach clenched another notch tighter. Maybe the next photograph would tell them . . . something.

The next picture was a shot of downtown Paris. Emma wondered if Guy had taken it when he first arrived. The following one zeroed in on the front of Sweet Nothings with its white awning and name in elegant black script. Paris's own Eiffel Tower filled the next photograph.

Arabella pointed at it. "That must have been when Angel took Guy on the tour of Paris."

Emma clicked to the next image. "Here she is posing in front of it." She leaned closer trying to see if there was anything to be discerned from the photograph.

"Angel photographs well, I'll give her that," Arabella said as she, too, leaned closer for a better look.

Following were several more pictures taken in and around Paris. Emma clicked through them with a sinking heart. It didn't look as if Guy's camera was going to reveal much of anything at all.

Emma almost clicked past the last slide, but something caught her eye, and she hit the back arrow.

"Who's that?" Arabella retrieved her glasses from the top of her head and settled them on her nose.

Emma studied the photograph. A stable door was in the

foreground, and a young couple embracing was in the background. The woman had on a crisp white shirt and jodhpurs that showed off her slim figure. The man had a cowboy hat pushed to the back of his head.

"Wait just a minute," Arabella declared, pointing at the photo. "I think I know who that is."

Emma had come to the same conclusion. And now she suspected she knew why Guy had been murdered.

He'd been up to something.

Blackmail, by the looks of it.

Chapter 17

"WHO is it?" Kate looked from Emma to Arabella and back again, her eyes huge behind her smudged lenses.

"If I'm not mistaken . . ." Arabella adjusted her glasses and peered more closely at the picture. She tapped a finger against the woman's image on the screen. "That's Deirdre Porter. And," she said, turning toward Emma and Kate, "that"—she tapped the computer screen again—"isn't Peyton Porter."

"Do you mean . . . ?" Kate's eyes got even bigger, and a slow flush rose from her neck to her cheeks to her forehead.

"Absolutely." Arabella nodded. "It looks like your friend Guy caught Mrs. Porter in a compromising position. A very compromising position, indeed."

"They've only got their arms around each other. It doesn't necessarily mean anything," Kate protested.

Arabella raised an eyebrow. "True. But I doubt Peyton Porter is going to like seeing his wife with her arm around Skip Clark. Especially since it was Skip Clark who tackled

Peyton during football practice and broke his arm. Peyton missed the big game when all the college scouts came looking." Arabella paused. "And even if Peyton can't muster some anger, his parents certainly will. Especially Marjorie Porter. She holds the purse strings in that family, and she's as tight as a tick. She's a Davenport. Her family made all their money from a special skin care lotion that they eventually sold to Revlon for a small fortune. They didn't make as much money as the Mitchums, of course. The Mitchums started the Paris Toilet company, which sold bleaching creams before they developed their famous antiperspirant. I think it's always stuck in Marjorie's craw that the Mitchum name is better known than that of the Davenports. She's not letting a dime of the hard-earned family fortune escape. If Deirdre embarrasses her son, she'll be out on the street without even the clothes on her back. And there's no use her looking to the Blackmores," Arabella turned toward Emma. "That's her family. Very well connected but without a dime to their name. Deirdre's great-great grandfather gambled and drank away all their money a long time ago." Arabella leaned back in her chair. "A friend of mine's daughter was at UT with Deirdre—same sorority I think. She told me all about it."

"And I did hear those two ladies talking that day at Angel Cuts," Emma said. "This isn't the first time someone's suggested there's something going on between Deirdre and her riding instructor."

Arabella nodded. "And Guy managed to get proof." She tapped the computer screen again. "Are there more pictures?"

"I don't think so." Emma hit the forward button, but the next photograph to appear was the first street scene of New York. They were back at the beginning again.

"Should we tell the police?" Kate worried her bottom lip with her teeth.

"I don't think it would do any good." Emma's shoulders slumped. "They seem determined to pin the crime on me."

"What if I mentioned it to Francis? And asked him to look into it for us?"

"He's already said he leaves most of the detecting to the local force."

"But perhaps, just this once—"

Emma stifled a sob and swiped at the tears that sprang to her eyes.

"Oh, sweetie," Arabella put her arm around her niece. "This changes the game, don't you think? Maybe Guy tried to blackmail Deirdre. And even if he didn't, just the existence of this photograph could have put his life in danger." She gave Emma a squeeze. She pointed to the young man on the screen. "If Skip is really crazy about Deirdre, who knows what he would do to protect her and her reputation."

Emma sniffed back her tears and straightened her shoulders. "You're right, Aunt Arabella. But I think we should look into it ourselves first before going to Francis. If we can present him with some hard facts . . ."

"Excellent idea." Arabella held up her hand for a fist bump. "What's that look for?"

"Nothing," Emma said as she joined Arabella and Kate in sealing their decision. "I didn't think you'd be up on the latest—"

Arabella sniffed. "I'm not that old, you know."

"ARE you open yet?"

Emma was unlocking the front door of Sweet Nothings the next morning when two young women approached her.

"Not yet, no. But our grand opening is next week. If you don't mind waiting a second, I'll get you a card with all the information."

"That would be super." The taller girl giggled.

"We can't wait till you open," the other one said.

"How nice." Emma smiled.

"Yeah," the taller one said, cracking her gum. "We can't wait to see where that man was murdered."

They both giggled.

"But . . ." Emma got the door open and went inside to grab some postcards off the counter. "Here." She handed one to each of the girls.

"Thanks." They chorused as they flounced on down the street.

Great, Emma thought. She'd been imagining Sweet Nothings becoming renowned for its beautiful vintage garments and innovative new stock, not becoming notorious as the site of a murder.

Would that entice people to the grand opening or repel them? she wondered.

Emma vowed to print the photo from Guy's memory card as soon as possible. That photograph changed everything. It might provide the clue that would solve this whole mess.

She would have to figure out a way to approach Deirdre. She suspected Arabella was right—Skip Clark probably had taken it upon himself to protect Deirdre. Perhaps he'd just meant to talk to Guy, but things had gotten out of hand. Maybe Nikki had put two and two together and had had to be eliminated as well? It's quite possible she had seen the photograph on Guy's camera herself.

Undoubtedly Skip had told Deirdre about it. Probably said he didn't want her to worry, things had been taken care of—not realizing that any sane person wouldn't condone murder no matter what. Was Deirdre tossing and turning at night not knowing what to do? If she turned in Skip, she'd be exposing their affair, but how could she feel the same about him knowing what he'd done? Maybe the slightest bit of pressure would get her talking. Or, better yet, a sympathetic ear. No doubt Deirdre was just dying to talk to someone.

A sharp bark heralded Pierre and Arabella's arrival. Pierre burst through the door with his usual enthusiasm and proceeded to circle the shop, sniffing furiously.

"What's he doing?" Emma watched as Pierre rounded the room for the second time.

"I think he hid his bone here somewhere yesterday." Arabella put her handbag behind the counter. "He's been looking for it everywhere."

Just then Pierre backed out from behind the counter triumphantly dragging a half-chewed rawhide bone. He carried it to his dog bed and nestled in for a good gnaw.

"Thank goodness he's happy now. He was driving me crazy," Arabella said.

Emma told her about the two girls who had stopped by earlier.

Arabella sighed. "I know. Whenever I go to Angel Cuts or Meat Mart everyone stops talking the minute I walk in. I do hope this doesn't hurt business."

"I think curiosity will bring people out." Emma opened one of the drawers. "And when they see these beautiful things, they'll buy."

"I do hope you're right."

THE sign Emma had ordered arrived later that morning. It announced their grand opening and fashion show in script that matched the Sweet Nothings canopy.

"That should get everyone's attention." Arabella stood back and admired it.

"Now to get it into the window."

"Be careful." Arabella followed behind Emma, making sure the corner of the sign didn't hit anything. "Maybe we should get some help?"

Emma looked over her shoulder, one eyebrow raised. "By help, do you mean Brian?"

Arabella looked sheepish. "Well, it is nice having him around."

It certainly is, Emma thought. Every time the phone rang, she hoped—But Brian was busy, she knew that. That project outside of town was huge.

"If you can hold the sign while I step into the window . . ." Emma pulled herself up and turned toward Arabella. "I can take it now." Emma carefully maneuvered the sign into the small space. She centered it and turned back to Arabella. "If you can push the mannequin a little closer . . ."

Emma indicated the mannequin she'd dressed in a sky blue chiffon and lace Ro-Vel nightgown and peignoir set from the sixties. She planned to put it in the window along with the sign.

"Fingers crossed. Let's hope this generates some buzz," Emma said.

"Honey, all we have to do is announce we're serving hors d'oeuvres and we'll have the whole town lined up outside."

A couple of people stopped and watched as Emma corrected the positioning of the sign and angled the mannequin just so. Being perched in the window gave her a unique view of Washington Street. She caught sight of Les coming out of The Toggery and noticed him glance across the street at Sweet Nothings. He paused for a moment but then continued walking. He hadn't gotten far when Emma noticed Francis coming down the street.

"Uh-oh."

"What is it, dear?"

Emma poked her head back into the shop briefly. "Les is across the street." She glanced back over her shoulder. "And Francis is coming straight toward him. Les's face is getting all red."

"Oh, dear." Arabella put a foot on the window ledge. "Here, give me a hand."

"Are you sure—"

Arabella grasped Emma's hand and pulled herself up. "Yes, I'm sure. Stop fretting, dear, it will give you wrinkles."

They both turned to look out the window. Francis was obviously angling to go around Les, a noncommittal look on his face, when Les took a step forward and purposely bumped him.

Arabella's hand flew to her mouth. "Oh, dear. This is not going to end well."

Francis stopped in his tracks, the same bland look on his face, as if he expected Les to apologize and then move out of the way. Les was obviously having none of it. He balled his hands into fists and stood in front of Francis.

"Very brave of him, don't you think?" Emma indicated Les, who was dwarfed by Francis.

"Or very foolish." Arabella's nose was glued to the glass as she watched the scene unfold.

Francis stood with his arms crossed over his chest while Les made ineffectual jabbing motions with his fists. Finally, Francis put his hand on Les's shoulder, gently moved him out of the way and continued down the street.

They could see Les's mouth moving but couldn't hear what he was saying.

"Probably a good thing," Arabella commented sagely.

"And I thought small-town living was going to be dull."

Arabella laughed. "Good heavens, this place is positively seething with passions and secrets and I don't know what else."

Murder, Emma thought to herself. *That's what else.*

She helped Arabella out of the window and was about to jump down herself when she spied Sylvia Brodsky coming down the street, her oxygen tank on wheels bumping and swerving behind her. She appeared to be headed toward the front door of Sweet Nothings.

"Sylvia's coming," she said to Arabella.

Arabella pulled open the front door and stood aside as Sylvia maneuvered over the doorstep. Pierre gave her a perfunctory sniff and went back to his rawhide bone.

Sylvia paused and took several drafts of oxygen. She had a paisley scarf pulled down nearly to her eyebrows, gold hoops in her ears and a ring on each of her gnarled fingers. She looked like a cross between a pirate and one of the Rolling Stones.

"I've got something very important to tell you," she wheezed between breaths of oxygen.

"What?" Both Emma and Arabella stopped and stared at her.

"Danger," Sylvia eked out before beginning a prolonged and intense coughing fit.

Emma and Arabella looked at each other.

"Maybe a glass of water?" Arabella suggested.

"I'll get it." Emma flew into the back room and filled a glass with cold water. She didn't really believe in Sylvia's pronouncements, but, on the other hand, she couldn't quite dismiss them out of hand, either.

Sylvia waved the glass of water away and continued to wheeze and hack. Finally, the coughing spell sputtered to an end. Sylvia stood with her hands on her knees, panting slightly. She took a couple of hits of oxygen and straightened up, her hoop earrings swinging back and forth.

"I laid out the cards this morning. Well, I do it every morning, as you know. Can't start my day unless I know how it's going to turn out."

Arabella didn't say anything, but Emma noticed her raised eyebrows.

"First card I pull is the Moon. Can you believe it? Never before. Never. This was a first."

"What is the significance of the Moon card?" Arabella retrieved some glass cleaner from behind the counter and began to wipe down the countertops.

"Significance?" Sylvia sputtered, shaking her head. Her earrings swung so violently, Emma was afraid they might take flight.

"Deception!" Sylvia barked, her eyes darkening. "Hidden enemies!"

"And just what does that mean?" Arabella spritzed the counter with the cleanser and tore a new section of paper towels off the roll.

"It means . . ." Sylvia paused dramatically. "Someone is not who they say they are!" She pulled a tissue from her sleeve and blew her nose with a loud honk. "Someone is trying to fool us." She shook a finger at Emma and Arabella. "And that friend of yours," she pointed at Emma, "had just walked into the room when I pulled the card." She finished triumphantly.

"Kate!"

Sylvia nodded. "What if she isn't who she says she is?"

"But I know Kate," Emma protested. "I've known her for a couple of years. She's a perfectly nice, normal—"

"Okay, so maybe it's not Kate. But someone is deceiving us. The cards said so!"

"Far be it from me to argue with the cards." Arabella rolled her eyes.

"The murderer," Emma said. "The murderer is certainly deceiving us."

Chapter 18

"WHO'S thirsty?" Arabella bustled out of the back room with a pitcher of lemonade and a plate of cookies.

Sylvia was perched on a stool helping fold stock, and Emma was sorting through the negligees and peignoirs in the glass-fronted cupboards.

"None for me, thanks." Sylvia waved Arabella's plate away. "I've kind of lost my appetite lately."

Arabella paused. "Why? What's the matter?"

Sylvia shrugged, and her earrings bobbed back and forth. "The kids want to put me in one of those assisted living places. They're trying to say I'm not safe living on my own anymore." She threw her hands up. "Just because of a little fire!"

"What fire?"

"It wasn't anything. Just some smoke. I left the teakettle on the stove a little too long. I was watching something on the television and forgot all about it. Someone saw the smoke and called the fire department." Sylvia shook her head.

"That could happen to anyone," Emma said, remembering the time the wind had blown her curtains into a lit candle. Guy had thrown his glass of wine at the flames. A very nice Château Lafite Rothschild Guy had brought to celebrate . . . something. Emma could no longer remember what. She tried to swallow the memory past the lump in her throat.

"I've heard those assisted living places are actually rather nice," Arabella said, biting the end off one of the sugar cookies. "There are all sorts of activities, and you get all your food prepared for you."

Sylvia snorted. "Yeah, and everyone is wearing a diaper and the place smells like you-know-what. No thanks. The only way they're getting me in one of those places is feet first." She grabbed another item from the puddle of garments on the counter and began to fold the white lace teddy.

"I can't decide what to put on the mannequin." Emma took out a Lucie Ann gown and held it up to the dummy.

"That's nice, but what about that baby-doll set I picked up last week at that estate sale outside of Memphis? What could be more appropriately Southern than a nice baby-doll nightgown?" Arabella opened one of the cupboards, pushed several hangers aside and pulled out a short pink chiffon confection with matching panties.

"It's darling!" Emma said. "But why *baby doll* I wonder? Isn't it the same as a shortie nightgown?"

Arabella shook her head. "They're meant to be a little . . ." She lowered her voice. "Sexier than the typical shorties."

"But why is it called a baby doll?" Emma looked from Arabella to Sylvia.

"It comes from that movie." Sylvia folded a pair of panties and added them to the stack on the counter. "The one with Eli Wallach in it. He was so handsome back then."

Arabella nodded. "And Karl Malden as the husband. It took place somewhere in Mississippi."

Emma looked from one to the other, confused.

"It was called *Baby Doll*," Arabella explained. "That's what Karl Malden called his teenaged bride."

"Carroll Baker," Sylvia supplied.

"You're right. And she was always prancing around in a nightgown like this."

"Driving the men crazy." Sylvia snorted.

"After the movie, everyone began calling these baby dolls. I think it came out sometime in the mid-fifties." Arabella looked over her shoulder at Sylvia.

Sylvia nodded. "1956 if I'm not mistaken."

"It's perfect then." Emma gently pulled the nightgown over the mannequin's head.

Sylvia glanced at her watch. "Looks like I gotta go. Tom said my car would be ready this afternoon."

"Your car?" Emma spun around. "You took it to Tom to be repaired?" Emma and Arabella exchanged glances.

"Why not? Everyone goes there. He said I had a hole in some line or other that caused the brake fluid to leak out."

"A hole!" Arabella declared as soon as the door closed behind Sylvia's oxygen tank.

"A hole that he might have put there himself." Emma added.

"And now we'll never know. It's too late to go to the police about it. The repair has been done, and the evidence is gone."

"But now that we've found that picture on Guy's camera . . . maybe Tom really didn't have anything to do with the murder."

"True. And Angel didn't, either."

"I'd like to know if Deirdre knew about that photograph." Emma fluffed the chiffon nightgown to its full advantage. "Or if Skip did."

"Deirdre's the one with the money. Or access to it. I'm betting Guy went to her if he tried to blackmail anybody."

"Guess I'll have to pay a visit to Mrs. Peyton Porter." Emma gave the fabric a final fluff.

Arabella raised her brows.

"I've invited her to model at our grand opening. That ought to serve as a pretext for ringing her bell."

As Emma moved the dressed mannequin into position, she had a thought.

Had they unknowingly picked a murderer to model in Sweet Nothings's first fashion show?

"A jeweler?" Bitsy wrinkled her nose.

Emma had stopped by Sprinkles on her way to work Saturday morning. The idea had come to her last night—Nikki had called to say she knew who the earring that was found in the Sweet Nothings carpet had belonged to, and before Emma and Brian could talk to her, she was dead.

Emma was standing in front of the cupcake counter at Sprinkles, trying to decide between German chocolate and banana cream pie. The heavenly scent of vanilla filled the shop, nearly making her swoon. She was leaning toward the chocolate, but the banana cream looked equally delicious.

"We found this earring at Sweet Nothings." Emma fished the earring she'd wrapped in some pink Sweet Nothings tissue paper out of her purse, unwrapped it and held it across the counter toward Bitsy. "Someone lost it at the shop, and we're wondering if any of the jewelers in town sold it. It's possible they might have kept a record of who bought it." Emma had decided to leave out the part about how the earring just might have belonged to Guy's killer.

"It's certainly a pretty little piece."

Emma pointed at a cupcake in the display case. "I guess I'll have the German chocolate."

"There's Moon over on North Market," Bitsy said as she placed Emma's cupcake in a bag. "And The Gold Nook near the shopping center."

"Are they real upscale sorts of places?"

"If it's upscale you're after, then try The French Jewel. It's just beyond the Paris Antique Market."

THE windows of The French Jewel sparkled with expensive-looking diamond, ruby and sapphire pieces. Emma paused for a moment to admire the gems gleaming on their black velvet background before pushing open the door.

A bell tinkled somewhere in the back of the shop, and a woman glided through the doorway.

"May I help you?"

She was wearing a plain black dress, the simplicity of which gave it an almost severe air. A pair of half glasses dangled from a chain around her neck, and her dark hair was sleeked into a smooth chignon.

Emma fumbled in her purse and pulled out the tissue-wrapped bundle. She unwrapped the earring and held it toward the saleswoman.

"I'm wondering if you can tell me anything about this earring."

"What do you want to know?" The woman settled her glasses on her nose and held up the earring.

"Is it valuable?"

"Valuable?" The woman raised her eyebrows and gave a slight sniff. "It's a very pretty piece, but I'm afraid it's not worth all that much. The stone," she said, pausing to indicate the blue green bead with the tip of her finger, "is an aqua terra jasper."

Emma remembered Kate calling the stone that. It looked as if she was right.

"It's quite attractive, but also quite common, I'm afraid."

The way she said it led Emma to suspect she'd said that to many customers before her.

"I found it on the floor of my aunt's shop," Emma explained. "Sweet Nothings," she gestured toward the window, "the lingerie shop down the street."

The woman handed back the earring, and Emma rewrapped it in the crinkled tissue.

"It looks as if one of our customers must have dropped it. We were thinking it might belong to Deirdre Porter . . ." Emma let the name hang in the air, holding her breath, hoping the woman would take the bait.

"Mrs. Porter is a customer of ours. If the earring does belong to her, she didn't get it here. Frankly, this is hardly her style." She pointed at the bundle of tissue Emma was about to put back in her purse.

"That's what I thought, but my aunt—"

"I've sold Mrs. Porter a number of important pieces." She looked around as if checking to see if anyone were listening, then leaned over the counter toward Emma. "For their first anniversary, Mr. and Mrs. Porter came in and chose a magnificent set of South Sea pearls."

Emma thought she had seen Deirdre around town in those. Magnificent was certainly the word for them. She couldn't begin to imagine how much they cost! No wonder the saleswoman had sneered at the pathetic little earring Emma showed her.

The saleswoman lowered her voice even more and leaned even closer to Emma. Her dangling glasses hit the counter with a clink, and she put a hand on them to still them. "Of course, I think they may have hit some . . . hard times." Her voice dropped so low, Emma could barely hear her.

"Really? Why do you say that?" Emma inched as close to the counter as she could get.

The bell tinkled, heralding the opening of the front door. If Emma had been the type to swear, she probably would have let loose with a stream of blue-tinged words right then. Just when the saleswoman was about to tell her something useful! It was all she could do to keep from slamming her fist onto the counter.

The new arrivals were a young couple in jeans and T-shirts. They had their arms around each other and were giggling.

Emma groaned inwardly. How long were they going to take, and could she stall long enough until they left? And would the saleslady be willing to talk, or had the moment passed? She studied a case of David Yurman jewelry, trying to kill time. The pieces were lovely, but not really her style, and certainly not within her budget.

Emma moved on to a display of watches. She glanced over her shoulder to where the saleslady was talking to the young couple. She'd pulled out a velvet pad and placed it on the counter along with several diamond engagement rings. The girl was trying one on, holding her hand up and admiring the gem. Emma couldn't help but notice that her nails were bitten to the quick.

They were talking, but Emma couldn't hear what they were saying. The saleswoman put the rings back in the case and replaced the velvet pad under the counter.

The couple finally left, the girl looking over her shoulder at the case of diamond rings.

The saleslady glided over to where Emma was standing and pretending to admire several gold link bracelets. She gestured toward the door. "I suggested The Gold Nook. I think the prices are a little more in line with their budget."

Emma nodded, wondering how she could turn the conversation back to Deirdre Porter.

"Is there anything else I can help you with?" The saleswoman raised her thin, penciled brows inquiringly.

Emma stuttered. "No, no . . ." She had to think of a way to bring the conversation back to the Porters. "We're planning a fashion show for our grand reopening at Sweet Nothings."

The saleslady looked unimpressed.

"We've invited Deirdre Porter to model in it."

"I guess they do need the money, then," the saleslady said in a low voice.

Emma was about to correct her and inform her that it wasn't a paying gig when her brain finally kicked into gear, and she bit her tongue.

"I guess we all have to do what we have to do," she said instead.

The saleswoman nodded. "Well, she did get the money from that bracelet, of course. Quite a bit, actually."

"Really?" Emma leaned closer over the counter.

"It was the one Mr. Porter purchased for her wedding gift. A beautiful sapphire and diamond piece. She came in to see if we would buy it back!" Her eyes widened. "We always stand by our merchandise, of course, so the owner immediately wrote her a check."

"When was this?" Emma asked, trying to look blasé although her heart was beating double-time.

"Last week. I don't remember the day, I'm afraid."

The bell tinkled again, and the front door opened. The saleslady turned toward the new arrivals, and Emma took the opportunity to slip out the door.

EMMA all but skipped down the sidewalk. Finally, they had a lead. A solid, concrete, *something* to pin a case on lead. Deirdre Porter had sold an important bracelet to The French Jewel. The kind of piece she would have been expected to keep forever and ultimately hand down to her children and her grandchildren. But instead she had sold it. She must have needed money desperately to do that. And what else could she have needed money for but to pay off a blackmailer? In this case, most likely Guy who had caught her and her riding instructor, Skip Clark, in a compromising position in living color. Well, not living color exactly, more like pixels or dpi or whatever digital photos were called. But it was one thing to have townspeople whispering and speculating, and quite another to have a photograph that proved you'd been playing around. It would end her marriage to Peyton Porter, heir to a considerable fortune.

When Emma got to Sweet Nothings, the front door was locked and the lights had been turned off. She used her key and pushed open the door. Arabella had left a note propped on the counter: "Off to Memphis for a huge estate sale. Let's hope I get lucky. Love, Aunt Arabella."

Emma felt deflated. Here she had all this great news to share, and there was no one to share it with. She glanced at the front window of Sweet Nothings and noticed someone standing there. Still, the knock on the door startled her.

Emma twisted the lock and eased open the door just far enough to allow her to stick her head out. Brian was standing on the doormat.

She felt the grin that immediately spread across her face and tried desperately to reclaim some semblance of cool. But it was all she could do to keep from throwing her arms around Brian and locking him in a giant bear hug.

"Can I convince you to take a few minutes off to go to The Coffee Klatch for a cold drink?"

THE Coffee Klatch was quiet—in that lull between the end of the lunch crowd and the beginning of the late afternoon crowd looking for a pick-me-up. Brian ordered an iced tea and Emma, a lemonade.

Sun slanting in the front window turned the highlights in Brian's dark hair to gold. Emma felt her heart catch in her throat, and she had to remind herself that there was another woman . . . a woman named Amy.

Emma wanted to blurt out her news as soon as the waitress turned her back on their table, but she tried to control her excitement.

Obviously, Brian could sense her impatience. "Well?" he said with a bemused look on his face.

"Well!" Emma nearly smacked her lips in her excitement. "I went to The French Jewel, and guess what?" She didn't wait for Brian to answer. "Deirdre Porter—"

"Whoa." Brian held up a hand. "Why did you go to The French Jewel?"

Emma closed her eyes and took a deep breath. "Okay. Remember that earring we found when we were tearing out the carpet at Sweet Nothings?"

Brian nodded and leaned back as the waitress slid a sweating glass of iced tea in front of him.

"I started to wonder if it might have belonged to Deirdre Porter."

"Deirdre Porter?"

Emma realized she hadn't told Brian about the picture they'd found on Guy's camera, and she needed to backtrack.

"Wow," Brian said when Emma finished. "So it looks like Deirdre and her riding instructor have something going on. Something they don't want anyone else to find out about." He twirled his straw around and around his glass. "But how does that earring we found play into this?"

"I'm not sure." Emma admitted. "I was wondering if whoever killed Guy dropped that earring that night. If there'd been any sort of struggle, the earring might have come loose." Emma fiddled with the saltshaker on the table. "Or sometimes when a woman is nervous, she'll play with her earring and accidentally dislodge it."

"Like that?" Brian pointed to the saltshaker that Emma was twirling between her hands and grinned.

Emma stopped abruptly. "Exactly." She leaned across the table. "Unfortunately, the saleswoman at The French Jewel didn't think it was the sort of piece Deirdre would wear. But she did admit that Deirdre, or, rather *Mrs. Porter* . . ." Emma imitated the woman's drawn out, snooty tones and was pleased when Brian laughed. "Sold back a very special diamond and sapphire bracelet her husband had given her as a wedding present."

Brian whistled. "Not very nice of her, I admit. But maybe she didn't like it?"

Emma shook her head. "No. Even if she hated it, a woman wouldn't return a gift like that. Too much sentimental value." She took a sip of her lemonade. "She'd keep it and wear it once in awhile to please him. No, I think she wanted . . . needed . . . the money."

"But aren't they rich? That BMW I've seen her driving around in must have cost a pretty penny."

"Yes. But if Deirdre is paying off a blackmailer, she can hardly just write a check or ask her husband for some pocket money. From what I understand, Peyton controls the purse strings. Or rather, his mama does."

"So our murderer is either Deirdre Porter, Skip Clark . . ." Brian took a last sip of his iced tea and pushed the glass to the side. "Or the mysterious owner of that lost earring."

Emma nodded. "I'm not sure what to do next. But I would like to see how Deirdre reacts when she sees that photograph Guy took."

Chapter 19

EMMA clicked a few last keys on her laptop, hit save, then print. She watched as the piece of paper slid slowly out of the printer. She held it up. Not bad. She'd managed to find some vintage clip art that gave the notice some eye-catching appeal.

She would tape the notice to the front window of Sweet Nothings under the grand opening banner. It was a call for volunteers to model in their opening day fashion show. She hoped at least a few of the young girls in town would be interested. They couldn't afford to pay anything, but she'd picked out a few pieces of new lingerie as a thank-you for the models.

Emma retrieved a roll of tape from behind the counter and climbed into the window to tack up her notice. She centered it carefully and secured it with several pieces of tape. Satisfied, she jumped down and went outside to admire her handiwork.

She was standing on the sidewalk, staring at the front

window of Sweet Nothings, when she sensed someone coming up behind her and turned to see Lucy standing there.

Lucy gave Emma a quick squeeze. "It looks just wonderful. I must take a picture and send it to your mother. Is she coming up for the grand opening?"

"Unfortunately not. Dad is having knee replacement surgery, and she has to be there to take care of him."

"That's too bad." Lucy frowned and looked at her watch. "Good Lord, look at the time. I've got to get a batch of cheese straws in the oven for Jessamyn Crocker's daughter's christening party this afternoon. If I'd've known that catering was going to be a seven day a week job, I'd have chosen some other profession." She tapped Emma on the arm. "But what are you doing here on a Sunday?"

"I just can't stay away, I guess." Emma smiled. "The sooner we're up and running, the sooner Aunt Arabella can bring in some money."

"She's lucky to have you." Lucy gave Emma another hug. "I'll see you later, honey."

Emma waved to Lucy and went back inside. She was about to close the door when she heard a bark heralding Arabella and Pierre's arrival.

Emma grinned and held the door open. "How was your day in Memphis?"

Arabella snorted and two spots of color formed high on her cheeks. She made a noise that sounded suspiciously like a growl to Emma.

"It was a huge estate sale," Arabella began as she put her purse behind the counter. "Run by one of those big la-di-da companies that make a fortune out of that sort of thing."

"Were the things overpriced?"

"The prices were absurd," Arabella said. Her head shook, and the hair coiled on top of it quivered. "And, even worse, they thought they could take advantage of their buyers." She slapped the counter with her open palm. "Well, they made a mistake in trying to put something over on me. What did they think we were, a bunch of rubes from the country?" Before Emma could answer, she went on. "There was a very pretty blue gown, cut on the bias, with some interesting details. They told me it was definitely vintage, circa 1935. I'm surprised they didn't try to tell me Jean Harlow once wore it in a movie," Arabella fumed.

Emma made sympathetic noises.

"As if I can't tell a vintage gown from a . . . a . . . piece of nothing that would be sold at Walmart."

Emma's eyes widened. She'd never seen Arabella so incensed before. "How did you know it wasn't—"

Arabella waved a dismissive hand. "It was easy. Only an amateur would have been fooled." She leaned over the counter toward Emma. "I turned the garment inside out, which I always do. I like to check the seams and see if any of the original labels are intact. That's when I saw it!"

"Saw what?" Emma's voice dropped to nearly a whisper.

"The care label!" Arabella finished triumphantly. "Can you imagine? There was a care label on the garment!"

Emma raised her brows. "But what—"

Arabella took a deep breath. "Care labels weren't put on clothes until after 1971. There's no way that gown was made in the thirties!" She finished triumphantly. "Honestly, what kind of a fool did they think I was? I gave that saleswoman a piece of my mind." Arabella clenched her fist, and Pierre growled in sympathy.

"I'm guessing you didn't buy anything then." Emma bent down and picked a microscopic piece of fuzz off the carpet.

Arabella shook her head. "No. But I did learn something very interesting. Very interesting, indeed."

"What?" Emma flicked the imaginary speck of dust into the wastebasket.

The bright spots of color flamed even brighter on

Arabella's cheeks. "Do you remember that package that was sent to me? With the negligee cut to bits?"

Emma nodded. How could she forget? She thought about it all the time. Dreamt about it even, wondering if the murderer had had a hand in it.

"I got to talking to one of the gals working the sale. She'd been at a similar one in Jackson a week or two ago. And she just happened to remember chatting with a customer there who said she was from Paris, Tennessee. I guess it struck her, the town being called Paris."

"Talk about a small world!" Emma exclaimed.

Arabella nodded, and the color in her cheeks deepened. "Well, it seems that this mysterious woman from Paris purchased a negligee—a lovely pink Michelene." Arabella paused looking very pleased with herself. "I managed to persuade her to check her sales records, and the buyer was none other than one Sally Dixon from La Tour Eiffel Antiques of little old Paris, Tennessee."

"Wow."

"Indeed." Arabella sniffed. She looked thoughtful. "I guess she did feel quite proprietary about Francis after all."

"What is going on between you and Francis?" Emma asked, a slight hint of amusement in her tone.

Arabella wagged her finger at her niece. "Don't you worry about a thing, missy. Francis has been the perfect Southern gentleman." And with that Arabella turned her back on Emma and the discussion.

IT wasn't exactly an audition for Victoria's Secret, Emma thought when she saw the girls lined up the next morning waiting to get into Sweet Nothings. But they'd attracted a decent crowd. She excused her way through the ones standing in front of the door, and opened the shop.

She felt the surge of warm bodies press against her back

and turned around. She checked her watch, and held up her hand. "Thank you so much for coming. We've got fifteen minutes until ten o'clock, and I'll have to ask you all to wait patiently until then. There are a few things I need to do before I open the doors."

An impatient murmur ran through the crowd, but the women obligingly backed away from the door.

Emma slipped inside Sweet Nothings and closed and locked the door behind her with a sigh. She tucked her purse under the front counter and hurried into the back room to put on some coffee and heat hot water for her morning cup of green tea.

She was setting out pads of paper and a supply of pens when she heard the rattle of keys at the front door. Arabella burst in, her hair threatening to topple from its perch on top of her head, and her cotton wrap askew. She'd tucked Pierre under her arm protectively, and he squirmed, trying to get loose.

"It's a madhouse out there." Arabella turned to shut the door behind her, when someone put their hand against it and pushed.

Arabella started to push back but then peered around the edge. "Sylvia! You'd better get inside."

Sylvia sidled through the opening and pulled out a handkerchief to wipe her brow. Arabella started to close the door.

"Hold on a sec." Sylvia maneuvered her oxygen tank through the opening and parked it against the wall. "Who are all those people?" She looked from Emma to Arabella and back again. "They can't all be here for the fashion show?"

Before Emma could answer, there was another knock on the door. She opened it and Kate entered, breathless. Her glasses were crooked, and a hunk of hair had escaped her ponytail. "I can't believe how many women are out there. I went to park the car and when I turned the corner I saw them all. I thought it was some kind of protest." She wiped her upper lip with the edge of her sleeve.

"It seems that all of Paris is interested in modeling in our fashion show," Arabella commented dryly.

"It's great for publicity," Emma said. "At least they know we exist."

Emma was headed toward the counter when fierce pounding on the door stopped her in her tracks.

"What on earth?" Arabella moved toward the door, but Emma stopped her.

"Let me get it. You're liable to be run over if everyone tries to crowd into the shop at once."

Emma eased the door open a chink and peered around the edge.

"What on earth is going on out there?" It was Bitsy with a bakery box in her hand. "I've brought you some cupcakes." She held the box toward Emma.

Emma widened the crack, and Bitsy slipped through.

"You've certainly attracted a crowd," Bitsy said as she straightened her top and tidied her hair. "I imagine that bodes well for your opening."

"Let's just hope people buy." Kate looked wistfully at the negligee displayed on the mannequin.

Sylvia cleared her throat and gave a small cough. "They will if we know how to sell. And honey, if I learned one thing in all those years at Macy's, it's how to sell." Sylvia moved behind the counter and settled in as if she were a ship coming into its home berth at last.

Emma undid the string on Bitsy's box. The cupcakes nestled inside had pink frosting and *Sweet Nothings* scrawled across the tops in white icing. "These look delicious!"

Bitsy smiled. "They're something of a bribe." She smiled shyly. "I'm hoping you all will let me model in your fashion show. This is just about the most exciting thing that's ever happened in Paris," she confided. "Aside from the murders, of course." Her face darkened.

"We'd love to have you." Emma looked at Arabella, who smiled and shook her head.

"I think it's time." Sylvia called from behind the counter, pointing at the ornate, gilt clock on the wall.

"Okay, brace yourselves!" Arabella shouted as she looked at her watch. "Two minutes till blast off."

Emma stood by the door with her hand on the knob, and they all counted down the last ten seconds as if it were New Year's Eve in Times Square.

As the countdown struck one, Emma opened the door with a flourish and stood aside as the women spilled into the shop. The girls ranged in size from model-tall to barely five feet and from beanpoles to so curvaceous that anything they put on would automatically look R-rated. But at least they had shown up.

It soon became obvious that the women had been as attracted by the opportunity to see the scene of a murder as they were by the chance to model in a fashion show. Emma heard Guy's name murmured under various women's breaths at least two dozen times. And she'd lost count of how many times she saw someone pointing at a nonexistent spot on the rug and whispering in a friend's ear. It wasn't exactly the publicity she'd planned for Sweet Nothings, but she would take what she could get.

Sylvia forged her way through the crowd, like a ship cleaving water, and went to stand next to Emma.

"So, what's the drill? How are we going to handle this crowd?"

Emma hadn't counted on so many people. She wasn't sure what to do. She looked at Sylvia helplessly.

Sylvia patted her on the shoulder briskly. "Leave it to me." She took a hit of her oxygen, tucked the tank back in the corner and gave an earsplitting whistle.

The cacophony of chattering female voices slowly ground to a halt.

"Thank you." Sylvia smiled at the women assembled in front of her. "If you will, take a sheet of paper from the pads we've put out"—she indicated the tablets Emma had arranged on the counter earlier—"and fill out your name, address, telephone number and size." She emphasized the last word. "Then please bring the paper to me, Emma or Miss Arabella." She pointed to each of them in turn.

Arabella had just bustled out from the back room with two pitchers of sweet tea and a tottering stack of paper cups. She smiled hesitantly at the assembled crowd. Arabella put her tray down on the counter and hurried over to where Sylvia was holding court behind the counter. "What are we supposed to do?"

"Check to make sure they've put down their name and contact information, and then check the size. I'm betting ninety percent of them are going to lie in one direction or the other." Sylvia sniffed knowingly. "Then make a notation as to your best guess of their actual size, and whether or not you want them in the show. Later we'll call back the ones who are possibilities."

Arabella nodded and the bun on top of her head wobbled precariously. Emma got into position beside her with Sylvia on the other side.

The first woman to approach Emma was a quiet, tiny, rather timid-looking brunette. She had short, curly hair that would look adorable with a ribbon threaded through it. Emma made a notation that she'd be perfect for one of the baby-doll negligees they'd collected. One of them was quite small and ought to fit her perfectly.

A very statuesque blonde turned away from the counter after chatting with Arabella. Arabella leaned toward Emma. "She's perfect for the red Miss Elaine nightgown. She'll fill it out like nobody's business."

The crowd was thinning slightly when the front door opened. Emma was surprised to see Deirdre Porter poke her head around the edge. She sidled into the room and started toward the counter. She was wearing a silk sundress that bared her smoothly bronzed arms and legs, and her hair was caught in a loose ponytail at the nape of her neck. She was going to make a gorgeous model, Emma thought. They would have to pick something extra special for her.

Deirdre approached the counter and squared her shoulders. A strange look crossed her face, and Emma wondered if Mrs. Porter wasn't quite as confident as she would have everyone believe.

Arabella bustled over and greeted Deirdre effusively. Emma knew she didn't really like Deirdre, but Emma could read her aunt's face and it basically said, "Whatever's good for business."

Bitsy, who had been hovering nearby, whispered to Emma. "Well, well, well. Just look who's here."

Arabella put her arm around Deirdre's shoulders and led her over to the glass-fronted cabinets. She opened a door and began showing Deirdre some of the contents.

Emma edged her way through the crowd toward them. A woman grabbed Emma's arm and stopped her.

"I can't wear one of them real flimsy nightgowns. Billy Bob wouldn't like it." She shook her head, and her blond beehive bobbed back and forth. "Billy Bob wouldn't like it at all."

"I know Billy Bob myself, and she's right," Bitsy came up behind Emma. "He'd have her in a burka if we did that sort of thing here."

Emma reassured the woman that no one would be forced to model anything they were uncomfortable in. The blonde nodded, satisfied, and moved away.

The floor was packed, and Emma felt a trickle of perspiration wend its way down her spine. The beginnings of a headache hammered behind her brow, and she wondered if she could sneak into the back room for some aspirin and a cold drink. She felt a moment of panic as she looked around at the crowd. How was she going to pull this whole thing together?

"Don't look so scared, kid. Everything's going to turn out fine." Sylvia came up behind Emma and put a hand on her shoulder.

"I hope so." Emma couldn't help but notice two women pointing at the floor and whispering in each other's ear. "Sometimes I worry that the only thing Sweet Nothings will ever be known as is the site of a murder!"

Sylvia gave a bark of laughter that segued into a rumbling cough. "This isn't New York, kid. People are going to be telling this story for a long time. But I've got faith in Sweet Nothings, and I've got faith in you." She thumped Emma on the back.

Emma smiled wanly. It was nice to know that someone believed in her.

"When you get a chance, Lucy is here from Let Us Cater To You." Bitsy grabbed Emma by the arm and pointed toward the stockroom. "I gave her a seat in the back and made sure she had a glass of cold, sweet tea."

"Thanks." Emma began to maneuver her way toward the back room.

She tried to get around two women, but they were so deep in conversation they didn't hear her murmured "excuse me."

"I heard he just up and left," the tall brunette, her eyes as wide as saucers, said to the other one.

In spite of herself, Emma sidled closer. Who were they talking about?

The shorter one, with dark curls and cherry red lipstick, nodded and lowered her voice. "Charlotte said she saw him toss three suitcases into the back of his car, although how he managed to get them into that little sports car he drives, I don't know."

The other one looked skeptical. "What on earth was Charlotte doing way over there?"

"You know she started that dog walking business, and I guess one of her customers lives on the same street as the Porters, although just a ways down. They've got a standard poodle, and Charlotte says she's the devil to walk."

At the sound of the Porters' name, Emma leaned in even closer.

"Mama said right away she didn't think it would last. He only married her on account of Marcie breaking up with him their senior year at UT."

The shorter one nodded in agreement. "They was together all of high school and then college. It about broke his heart in two. Next thing you know he's bringing this new girl home. Deirdre." She said the name with a sneer.

Emma heard someone give a tiny cry and looked up to see Deirdre Porter staring at them with a stricken look on her face. Before Emma could move, Deirdre had elbowed her way through the crowd to the door. Everyone turned to look as she slammed the door loudly in back of her.

Chapter 20

"WE should go after her, don't you think?" Arabella collapsed into a chair, kicked off her left shoe and rubbed her foot.

"Definitely." Sylvia swiveled in the desk chair opposite.

Arabella gave her a withering look. "It might be overwhelming if we all go," she said pointedly.

"We'd need a parade permit," Kate quipped. She was perched on one end of the desk, and Emma on the other.

Bitsy had already left to go back to her shop.

"I think it would be better if just Emma and I went."

"That's fine with me." Kate twirled a piece of hair around her finger. "I don't like confrontations." She shuddered.

Emma swung her leg back and forth and then in circles. All the chattering women had gone home, and Sweet Nothings was blessedly quiet. She'd written a check for the deposit to Lucy Monroe and the catering, and she had left, too. "Maybe we should just leave Deirdre alone for the moment?" She looked from Arabella to Sylvia. "She seemed pretty upset."

"All the more reason to go and make sure she's okay."

"But if we show her the photograph now, she's only going to get more upset . . ."

"It's better to strike while she's vulnerable, distasteful as that may seem. We're more likely to get the truth out of her."

"I suppose."

"Emma and I can pick up a box of candy at The Taffy Pull."

Emma was doubtful. She straightened the edges of a pile of papers on the desk. "Maybe it would be better if we take what we've found to the police? Let them handle it?"

Arabella peered at Emma over her half glasses. "Two words," she said. "Chuck Reilly."

Emma laughed. "You're right. I guess we're going to have to handle this ourselves." She hopped off the desk. "Ready?"

DEIRDRE and Peyton Porter lived in a new development of houses just outside of town. Emma was surprised that with their money they hadn't bought one of the grand old homes in need of fixing up. But perhaps that wouldn't have been Deirdre's idea of grand. Perhaps Deirdre was more interested in granite countertops, double sinks and spa tubs than owning a piece of history.

The development was named Arbor Woods, an inapt description since the developer had razed almost all of the trees that had once shaded the acreage. They drove slowly down the street, craning their necks to see the house numbers. Each home looked bigger than the next, and Emma wasn't surprised to see that the Porters' home was the biggest of them all.

"Would you look at that?" Arabella leaned out the car window and glanced up at the part-Georgian, part-Victorian wonder that loomed over them. "It has everything but a moat."

"I don't know about that." Emma pointed toward the front door. "Looks like that little bridge crosses over some kind of man-made creek."

Arabella squinted. "You know, I think you're right. This place really is something."

The triple garage was made to look like a stable block, and they could see Deirdre's red sports car pulled in front of the far door.

"I don't know about you, but I'm feeling slightly nervous," Emma said as the approached the double oak doors. She lifted the enormous brass knocker, and tapped it tentatively. They heard the clang echoing inside the house.

Emma half expected a maid to answer the door, but Deirdre opened it herself. Her face looked red, as if she'd just scrubbed it, and the hair around her face was damp. She looked startled when she saw them.

Emma handed her the box of chocolates. "I'm sorry, but something seemed to have upset you at Sweet Nothings. We feel really badly about it."

"It's not your fault." Deirdre opened the door wider and motioned for them to enter.

The foyer was two stories tall with a nearly blinding crystal chandelier hanging from the ceiling. The foyer itself was large enough to hold a small party and was dominated by a sweeping circular staircase that rose to a second floor balcony. Emma could see the dining room to the left, with a table that could hold twenty people, and a cavernous living room to the right.

They followed Deirdre down the hall and into a smaller room made cozy with red paint and book-lined walls. A comfortable sofa and two chairs were arranged in front of a large, flat screen television. A magazine lay open on the coffee table.

Arabella and Emma perched on the edge of the sofa while Deirdre curled up in one of the chairs, one leg tucked under her and her arms crossed defensively over her chest.

Emma felt heat rushing to her face. She had no idea how to begin. She hated the thought of upsetting Deirdre even more, but how else was she going to solve Guy's and Nikki's murders? She looked at Arabella out of the corner of her eye and noticed she looked equally uncomfortable. Her hands were folded in her lap, and she was kneading her fingers like bread dough.

"Women can be so catty." Deirdre picked up the decorative cushion on the chair and hugged it to her chest. "They don't care who they hurt with their gossiping tongues." She hid her face in the cushion momentarily. "Especially if you're pretty. Then they hate you for it and want to make you pay."

Emma cleared her throat and managed to find her voice. "So none of it was true? About Peyton leaving?"

Deirdre raised her chin. "He's on a business trip. He'll be home in three days."

Emma saw the shadow that crossed Deirdre's face. Deirdre wasn't being completely truthful. Perhaps Peyton really was on a business trip—but had he left in anger after a fight?

"So everything is okay between you and Peyton?"

"Of course. Why shouldn't it be?" Deirdre plucked at some loose strings on the pillow.

"I thought perhaps he might have seen this." Emma pulled the photograph Guy had taken from her purse. She glanced at it again.

"What's that?" Deirdre's back immediately stiffened.

Emma passed her the picture.

Deirdre held it by the edges as if it were radioactive. She didn't say anything at first, and Emma couldn't read the expression on her face. Finally, she turned the photo over, glanced at the back, which was blank, and tossed it back at Emma.

Deirdre gave a bark of laughter. "So Skip put his arm around me and some sneak photographer thought it was a Kodak moment." She threw the pillow on the floor. "My horse had just thrown me, and I was upset. Skip was trying to comfort me. Any law against that?" She stared at Emma, her face white except for two bright red patches high on her cheekbones.

"I'm guessing your husband wouldn't be very happy to see that," Emma ventured, brandishing the photograph. She felt Arabella stiffen beside her.

"Well, he's not going to see it, is he? Unless you're planning on showing it to him." Deirdre's eyes bored into Emma's.

She was already in up to her neck, Emma thought. She might as well go all the way. She took a deep breath, like a swimmer about to plunge into deep water, and said, "Something tells me Peyton might have already seen this photograph."

Deirdre arched one carefully plucked brow. "Really?" She drew the word out in full Southern drawl. "Did you show it to him?"

Emma jumped. That wasn't the response she had expected.

"Of course not!" Arabella protested. "We would never do that. I hope you realize that. We're simply trying to get to the bottom of things."

"Like whether I'm cheating on my husband?" Deirdre sprang from her seat and went to lean on the fireplace mantle.

"I could care less about that," Emma said. "What I'm trying to find out is who killed Guy Richard and why."

"And you think that picture has something to do with it?"

"I think Guy was trying to use it for blackmail, and it backfired."

"You think I killed him?" Deirdre laughed, and this time she sounded genuinely amused.

"Not you, necessarily. But I do think he tried to black-mail you."

Deirdre plunked down in the chair again and leaned back with her legs crossed. "And what on earth gave you that idea?"

"The fact that you seem to be in need of money."

"What!" Deirdre swept an arm around the room. "You've got to be kidding."

"Then why did you try to sell the diamond and sapphire bracelet your husband gave you for a wedding gift?"

Deirdre's jaw literally dropped. "How . . . how did you know about that?" She stuttered. She jumped to her feet. "Have you been going around asking questions about me? How dare you!"

She picked up the photograph Emma had placed on the coffee table halfway between them. She looked at it for a long minute then tore it in half and threw down the pieces. She glared at Emma and Arabella. "Now I think it's time our little visit was over."

"Do you think she'll still be willing to model in our fashion show?" Emma said as the door slammed in back of them so hard the pots of pink geraniums by the entrance jumped.

Arabella glanced over her shoulder. "I think that's our answer."

ARABELLA, Emma and Liz were curled up on the sofa in Arabella's living room watching a DVD of Bette Davis in *All About Eve*. The movie made Emma wish she'd known New York City in the fifties. Everything looked so sophisticated. Although she was having trouble keeping her mind on the movie and off of Guy's and Nikki's murders. How were they going to find out if Guy had tried to blackmail Deirdre?

"Maybe Guy didn't approach Deirdre first!" Emma exclaimed suddenly.

The others jumped.

"What do you mean?" Arabella pressed the PAUSE button on the remote.

"Maybe Guy showed the photograph to Skip, and he told Deirdre about it. Maybe he even suggested she sell her jewelry to pay the money Guy demanded."

"Even if Guy didn't go to Skip, Skip would certainly know about it. Probably the first thing Deirdre did was run to him. That's what I would do," Arabella said.

"You might be right." Liz reached for another tortilla chip and dipped it into the bowl of Arabella's homemade salsa. "Are you going to go talk to Skip now?"

Emma made a face. "I suppose I'll have to. I can't say I'm looking forward to it after that conversation with Deirdre."

"I'll go with you." Liz offered.

Emma grinned. "I'm not going to turn you down. I need all the moral support I can get."

EMMA realized she'd worn the wrong shoes as soon as she got out of the car at Skip Clark's farm the next morning. Her feet sank into the mud, and muck oozed up and over her sandals and between her toes. It sucked at her feet and squelched as she walked. She noticed Liz glancing at her.

"You'll get used to our country ways soon enough." Liz laughed.

Emma checked out Liz's shoes and noticed she'd chosen a pair of solid-soled clogs and had no trouble traversing the rutted road that led to the barn. If Emma was going to be visiting any more farms, she'd have to invest in a pair of those herself.

They reached the barn, eased open the door and peered

inside. The darkness was intense after the light of the day, and they both blinked furiously.

"I can't see anything, can you?" Emma rubbed her eyes.

"Not a thing." Liz leaned around the edge of the door. She turned toward Emma. "But I don't think anyone's in there. What would they be doing in the dark?"

"True." Emma let the door close. She surveyed the acres of dirt and patchy grass that surrounded them. Her legs were already speckled with mud, and the thought of walking across all that mire made her feel sick. But if they were going to talk to Skip Clark, they'd have to find him.

They started across the field in front of the barn. Every step threatened to suck the shoes off Emma's feet. She closed her eyes in misery and reminded herself of what she was after. If she didn't find out who killed Guy, the police would try to hang it on her. And even if they were unsuccessful, she knew enough about small towns to know that a cloud would hang over her forever. She could picture herself walking around with a cartoon-like bubble over her head with the words *suspected of murder* written inside in bold, black letters. And at the rate she was going, it looked like she would be living in Paris forever. Brian's face crossed her mind, and she felt a small smile tugging at her lips until she remembered Amy, whoever she was.

They hadn't gone far when the sound of horse's hooves pounding the earth was carried on the air toward them. A tuneless whistling reached them next and finally a speck of brown appeared on the horizon. The speck grew until they could see it was Skip Clark riding toward them.

He pulled up sharply alongside Emma and dismounted, throwing the reins over the horse's neck. The horse stood obligingly near, snorting and pawing the ground with its hooves.

"You gals looking to take some riding lessons?" Skip pushed his hat farther back on his head and smiled broadly.

Emma noticed not only how green his eyes were but also how alert and intelligent. Skip Clark was no fool, no matter how much dust clung to his boots.

"Not exactly." Emma hemmed, not sure where to begin.

He gave them both a long, appraising look. "So what can I do for you ladies then?" He crossed his arms over his chest, and Emma could see the muscles bulging under his T-shirt.

Emma looked at Liz, and Liz looked back at her. It reminded Emma of high school when she and Liz would get in some scrape or other, each praying the other would get them out of it. She decided not to beat around the bush. She pulled the photo Guy had taken from her pocket.

Skip looked at it and shrugged. "So?"

Emma closed her eyes as the heat rushed into her cheeks. *Keep cool*, she reminded herself. It was just like negotiating a better price for a new line of lingerie. She smiled at Skip. "I agree, it doesn't mean much by itself."

Liz looked at Emma with her mouth open in surprise.

"I'm sure there are plenty of innocent reasons why you might have put your arm around a married woman's shoulders."

Skip snorted. "You got that right. I'm the touchy-feely type despite my crusty exterior. So what of it?"

"I happen to know that Mrs. Porter," Emma began, and gestured toward the photo, "sold a very valuable and very sentimental piece of jewelry in order to get cash. You know what that says to me?"

"No, what?" Skip smiled and his eyes crinkled as if he were enjoying this.

"To me, it sounds like blackmail," Emma finished dramatically, like a lawyer summing up before the jury.

"Does it really?" Skip rocked back on his heels, the look of amusement still on his face.

"Why? What does it say to you?" Emma shot back defensively.

"To me . . ." Skip paused and slapped the horse on the rump affectionately. "It says she wanted to buy something and needed the money to do it."

"Really?" Emma couldn't keep the sarcasm out of her voice. She could picture Deirdre's enormous house with all its beautiful furniture, and the expensive little sports car parked out front. As if she had to worry about money!

"Yes, really." Skip's eyes danced, and Emma got the impression he was enjoying this.

He was a damned good-looking man, and he obviously knew it. But right now Emma found him merely infuriating. "What was this mysterious something she wanted to buy?"

"You seem to be pretty keen on playing detective. I think I'll let you figure that out for yourself," Skip said, infuriating Emma even more.

Chapter 21

"WHAT did you think of him?" Emma asked as they bounced back down the rutted road leading away from Skip Clark's barn.

"I thought he was kind of cute actually." Liz gave a last backward glance at the farm.

"He was. Is," Emma admitted. Her hands clenched on the steering wheel. "But so . . . so . . . annoying at the same time." She flipped on her blinker for a left turn. "I don't know what Deirdre sees in him."

"Do you think it's possible that she's really just taking riding lessons from him?" There was a note of amusement in Liz's voice.

Emma shook her head. "I hope not. Because if that's the case then she had no reason to murder Guy. And I'm back to square one on this."

Emma glanced out the window where a farmhouse stood in the midst of a manicured lawn that gave way to acres of cultivated fields. There were rockers out on the big wraparound, farm-style porch, and an American flag waved in the breeze from the pole in the center of the front lawn.

"That doesn't rule out Skip Clark though. Maybe Guy approached him with the photograph instead of Deirdre."

"Or, more likely, Deirdre wouldn't play along, and he had to go with plan B. Plan B being Skip Clark."

"If we could just put Guy at the farm, that would clinch things. But the place is in the middle of nowhere."

"I wonder if Skip has any help. You know, someone to give him a hand grooming the horses and mucking out the stalls. Maybe someone who gives lessons part of the time, too."

"Good point."

"And just maybe they were there when Guy came by with his photograph."

"Could be. But how will we find out?"

"I don't suppose we can just waltz up to Skip and ask him."

Liz laughed. "I'm pretty sure he wouldn't tell us."

"Yeah, and he'd enjoy every minute of not telling us." Emma eased on the brake as the light in front of them turned red. "But someone must know. We'll just have to ask more questions."

The very thought made Emma groan.

"WHAT did you find out?" Arabella asked the minute they opened the door to Sweet Nothings. She'd pulled a stool up to the counter and was busy addressing a stack of invitations to the Sweet Nothings grand opening. Emma looked at one and sighed in amazement. Arabella's handwriting was as beautiful as a calligrapher's. Emma's own rather decent penmanship began deteriorating in college when she was forced to take notes at warp speed, and it had disintegrated even further with the time she now spent on the computer.

She'd had the invitations printed at a shop in Jackson—an oversized postcard with a photograph of the awning outside the shop with *Sweet Nothings* scrawled in black script. It was one of the photos Guy had taken of the front of the store. Emma felt her heart lurch at the thought of Guy being gone forever. She found she was now remembering the good moments far more than the bad.

Liz began sticking stamps on the cards Arabella had finished. "We didn't have much luck," she responded glumly.

Emma nodded in agreement. "Skip Clark refused to tell us much of anything. But I got the feeling," she added, turning toward Liz for confirmation, "that he knew exactly what Deirdre needed the money for."

"Definitely," Liz agreed. "He seemed to think it was amusing to make us fish for it."

"What did you think of Skip Clark?" Arabella put the finishing touches on one of the invitations and added it to the stack. "His family has run that farm for generations, although I don't know much about Skip himself. I remember his mother had polio as a child and always walked with a limp."

Emma shook her head in amazement. Arabella was a walking treasure trove of information about Paris and its occupants. "He's very attractive," Emma admitted.

Liz looked up suddenly. "But not as attractive as Brian. I know he's my brother and all, but still . . ."

Emma laughed. "Don't worry. Brian has him beat hands down."

Liz looked relieved. "Do you think it's possible that Skip is the one who killed Guy? For Deirdre's sake?"

"He certainly looked capable of it," Emma said, recalling the sight of Skip's muscles rippling beneath his T-shirt.

"His mother is as sweet as can be despite all she's been through, but his father . . ." Arabella shook her head. "The Clark men are known for their temper."

"We need to find out if Guy approached Skip with the photograph. We're hoping maybe someone saw him. We need to find out if anyone helps out at the barn—you know, with the horses and stables. They might have seen something."

Arabella paused with her pen above the last invitation. "Maybe ask Mabel at The Coffee Klatch. She has a younger sister who's crazy about horses and runs in that circle. She might know."

"I feel the sudden urge for a cup of coffee coming on." Emma smiled and turned to Liz and Arabella. "Can I get you anything?"

A damp breeze was blowing, and Emma felt the shorter hairs around her face curling in the humidity. A handful of people were walking along the sidewalk, peering into windows before darting into the air-conditioned depths of Paris's various stores and boutiques. She waved to a burly, bald man with a waxed and pointed handlebar moustache. She recognized him as the owner of Leo's, the local barbershop.

She passed Meat Mart, and Willie Williams waved as she went by. He was always behind the counter whenever she went in for something. He was tall and skinny with a very prominent Adam's apple that bobbed up and down when he talked.

Emma felt a glow of satisfaction as she pushed open the door to The Coffee Klatch. She hadn't been back in Paris all that long, but she already felt at home.

She slipped inside the restaurant and stood for a moment, savoring the feel of the cool air on her skin. She looked around but didn't immediately see Mabel. She hesitated, but then the swinging doors to the kitchen opened, and Mabel backed out with a tray laden with cups of coffee and slices of various kinds of pie.

Emma wasn't at all hungry—her stomach was churning like the Atlantic Ocean during a hurricane—but she thought she'd have a better chance of chatting with Mabel if she ordered something. She slipped into a seat at a table for two and picked up the plastic-coated menu. She turned it over and scanned the desserts, but she wasn't in the mood for anything sweet. More like an order of fries.

A couple of minutes later, Mabel slid by and dropped a napkin-wrapped set of silverware on the table along with a sweating glass of water set on a scalloped paper doily.

"Help you?" Mabel held her pencil poised over her dog-eared order pad.

Emma smiled. "Just some fries, I think. And do you have any malt vinegar?" she asked as she handed Mabel the menu.

"Gotta check with the chef. You still want the fries regardless?"

"Sure." Emma nodded.

Mabel skittered away, and Emma mentally kicked herself. She'd have to seize the moment when Mabel came back with the order. She sat with her hands gripped in her lap, her eyes glued to the swinging door to the kitchen.

The doors opened and Mabel came out carrying a tray laden with burgers and sodas for a group of teens sitting near the window. Moments later, Emma saw straw wrappers shooting through the air like streamers as the kids erupted into fits of giggling. She remembered doing the exact same thing when she was their age. Right now that seemed like a million years ago.

Mabel came out from the kitchen once more, but this time she had a tray of food for two businessmen who were sitting together but were both conversing with someone else on their cell phones. No one else was waiting, and Emma hoped it would stay that way so Mabel would be inclined to linger and chat.

Finally the doors opened again, and Mabel emerged with a plate in one hand and a bottle in the other.

"Here you go." She slid the fries in front of Emma and plunked the bottle down next to them. "Chef managed to dig up some malt vinegar, although why anyone would want to put that on fries, I don't know. He said it was common in England, but I thought you were from these parts?"

Emma was encouraged by Mabel's chattiness. Maybe this wasn't going to be so difficult after all.

"Born and raised in Paris." Emma answered. "But an English friend introduced me to a splash of malt vinegar on my fries, and I discovered I liked it."

Mabel shuddered. "To each his own, I guess. Anything else I can get you?" She grabbed a sweating stainless pitcher of ice water off the waiter's station and refilled Emma's glass.

Emma shook her head, searching her frantic brain for a way to keep Mabel talking. Fortunately, Mabel must have heard her silent plea.

"You hear anything new on that murder in Miss Arabella's shop? I haven't seen nothing about it in the papers for days now."

"As far as I know, there isn't anything new. But Arabella and I have been doing some of our own sleuthing," Emma dropped her voice to a whisper. Just as she'd hoped, Mabel leaned in closer and got comfortable.

"I can't tell you everything," Emma paused and looked down at her plate. She didn't know all that much about marketing, but she did know a little something!

As she suspected, Mabel rose to the bait with a gasp and indrawn breath.

"I won't tell a soul, don't you worry about a thing."

Emma locked eyes with her. "Promise?"

Mabel nodded eagerly and slipped into the empty seat opposite Emma. She cast a nervous glance over her shoulder, toward the kitchen, but then turned her gaze back toward Emma.

"Well. I really shouldn't tell anyone this . . ." Emma paused for dramatic effect. "But I think Guy—he's the photographer who was killed—got a snapshot of someone doing something with someone they shouldn't," she finished enigmatically.

Mabel looked confused. "But who . . . where . . . how?"

"Do you know Deirdre Porter?"

Mabel tossed her head and gave a snort. "I sure do. Talk about putting on airs, as my mama used to say. May she rest in peace."

"Well." Emma paused again, her eyes on Mabel's. "It looks as if she might be having an affair with her riding instructor."

"Skip Clark?" Mabel said, disappointed. "Everyone in Paris knows about that. Not that I think there's anything to it, mind you. I can't see Skip being Deirdre's type or vice versa. Besides, there's too much money at stake. And Peyton isn't exactly hard to look at, if you get my drift."

Emma was taken aback. Was it really such common knowledge? In that case, wouldn't Deirdre and Skip just have laughed off Guy's blackmail attempts?

Emma straightened up. "But there's this photo . . ." Her voice dropped back to a whisper, and she was rewarded when Mabel leaned in closer. She was hooked.

"What I need to find out . . ." Emma looked over her shoulder suspiciously, "is whether anyone saw Guy at the barn showing the photo to Skip." She let her voice drop to a whisper once more. "That would really . . ." She paused again. "Clinch things."

"Oh," Mabel said, her voice very small, her mouth a round circle.

"Do you know if there's anyone who works at the

barn—you know, helping out with the riding lessons and mucking out the stables and such?"

Mabel leaned back in her chair and shook her head. "I don't want her to get mixed up in any murder. I told Mama I'd take care of her. Swore it on her deathbed, I did. And I'm not about to go against it now." She crossed her arms over her chest.

Emma held up a hand. "I would never want you to do anything you weren't comfortable with. I'm just wondering if anyone might have been at the barn when Guy showed up with the photo of Skip with his arm around Deirdre?"

Mabel gasped and put a hand to her mouth. "A photo? Like that?"

Emma nodded. She reached for a French fry, drizzled a bit of malt vinegar over it and popped it into her mouth. She chewed. And waited.

Mabel picked at her cuticles. "I don't suppose it would get her in trouble. Seeing as how she only works there." She put her thumb in her mouth and worried at the flesh alongside the nail.

Emma shook her head emphatically. "I don't want anyone to get into trouble. I just need to know if Guy went out to the farm and showed Skip the photo he took."

Mabel put her hands palms down on the table. "My little sister, Clary, is just crazy about horses. Can't get enough of them. She's willing to do anything just to be around them. Even if it means mucking out stalls." Mabel wrinkled her nose and made a face.

Emma wrinkled her own nose in sympathy. "I had a friend in elementary school who was like that."

"She took this job with Skip Clark," Mabel blurted out. "Lending a hand with things around the stables."

"Mabel!" The chef's voice cut across the low level of chatter that filled The Coffee Klatch.

Mabel jumped. "Go ask Clary. She's bound to know all about it."

"Wait!" Emma put out a hand. "What's her phone number?"

Mabel looked around before pulling her order pad from her pocket. She quickly scribbled a telephone number on the top sheet of paper and tore it off. "Here." She handed it to Emma. "You can reach her at this number. But, please," she turned to Emma with a pleading look in her eyes. "Don't get her in any trouble, okay?"

Emma picked at the remainder of her fries, but she wasn't at all hungry. She stared at the piece of paper Mabel had thrust at her and at the number scribbled on it. Her breath quickened. Was she getting closer to figuring out who had killed Guy?

She thought of Nikki, and her breath caught in her throat. Why kill Nikki? Was it out of fear that Nikki knew something? Had Guy confided in her? The thought made Emma's stomach churn. At one time she thought she was Guy's only confidante. Obviously, she'd been wrong. Dead wrong.

Emma shivered and pushed the plate of fries away. She'd call Clary as soon as she got back to the shop. With any luck she could meet with her right away and have the answers before night fell.

Chapter 22

EMMA put her key in the lock of the front door of Sweet Nothings, but before she could turn it, the door was flung open.

"I have a surprise for you!" Arabella cooed.

Emma jumped. "You scared me."

"Sorry, dear. I've just been so excited for you to get back so I could show you."

"Did you find another spectacular vintage piece?"

Arabella shook her head. "No. You'll have to come inside and see for yourself."

Emma followed behind her aunt, her curiosity definitely piqued.

"Voila!" Arabella pointed to either side of the shop triumphantly.

Even though Emma had been expecting them for weeks, she was still surprised to see two glazed white armoires tucked into the corners. The doors were propped open, and Arabella had already begun arranging stock on the shelves.

"They're gorgeous!" Emma stood and stared for a long moment. She didn't want to admit how many nights she'd tossed and turned worrying that the dimensions were going to be wrong, or that she had taken the measurements incorrectly, but they were perfect. Perfect!

"Do you like them?" Arabella asked anxiously when Emma remained silent.

"I'm speechless. They're perfect." Emma fingered the doors lovingly. "I was beginning to think they'd never get here." She opened one of the cupboards, pulled out a pink satin peignoir set and hung it from the door of one of the armoires. "What do you think?"

"Wonderful." Arabella clapped her hands. "It looks like milady has put out her gown preparatory to performing her bedtime toilette."

Emma giggled. "Did they have any trouble getting the armoires through the door?"

Arabella shook her head. "Not at all. As a matter of fact, Brian saw them and popped over to help. With the three of them working together, it was a breeze."

At the thought of having missed Brian, disappointment washed over Emma.

"Was Mabel any help?" Arabella fiddled with the heavy gold chain around her neck.

Emma retrieved the piece of paper from her pocket. "Yes. Her younger sister actually works for Skip Clark. She gave me her number." Emma dug in her handbag and pulled out her cell. "I'm going to call her right away."

Emma punched in the numbers and waited. The phone didn't ring, but an automated voice came on the line. Emma hung up, disappointed.

"Not home?" Arabella turned from where she was straightening the merchandise on the shelves of one of the armoires.

"Phone's been turned off." Emma's shoulders sagged.

"Oh, dear." Arabella shook out a white baby-doll night-gown and refolded it. "I think she lives in that trailer park over near the Henry County airport."

Emma straightened up. "I'll just have to go see her instead."

"I don't have the exact address . . ."

"There's bound to be an office of some sort. I'll see if they can tell me." Emma already had her purse in hand and was halfway out the door.

IN the end she didn't need any help finding Clary's trailer. It was at the end of a row of single-wides with a foot-high white picket fence surrounding a miniature lawn. A ceramic statue of a horse grazed on the tiny patch of grass, a toy saddle was slung over the fence and the front door knocker was a horseshoe. This had to be Clary's place.

Emma lifted the horseshoe and tapped it gently. She thought she heard music coming from inside the trailer and crossed her fingers. Hopefully that meant Clary was home.

The door was opened by a young girl in jeans and a blue T-shirt with *I ♥ Horses* on it in large white letters. She looked to be around eighteen.

"Clary?"

She nodded her head. "Yes. What can I do for you? If you're selling Avon or Mary Kay I can't afford any, and besides, I don't wear much in the way of makeup."

Freckles stood out across her nose and cheeks, her lashes were short and sandy, and her lips were pale.

"I'm not selling anything. I just wanted to talk to you. I'm Emma Taylor. I know your sister, Mabel."

"If that's the case, you might as well come in." She opened the door wider and stood back.

Emma stepped inside. The trailer was as neat as a pin. The equine theme continued throughout with a horse-head-patterned throw on the sofa, a lamp with a base in the shape of a mustang rearing on its hind legs and a cowboy hat slung on the coat tree.

"I've got some fresh sweet tea if you'd like." Clary indicated the refrigerator tucked in the corner of the tiny kitchen.

"Thanks. I'm fine." Emma perched on the sofa and Clary sat opposite her in an old wooden rocker. Everything was clean and neat and looked as if it came from yard sales or second hand stores.

"I can see you're very interested in horses." Emma indicated the horse-themed décor and the statement on Clary's shirt.

Clary nodded her head, and a big smile spread across her face. "I love 'em. All I've ever been interested in is riding. Used to go crazy in school waiting for the bell to ring so I could run over to the neighbor's and saddle up one of their old swaybacks." She poked at a small hole in her jeans. "I wasn't much for learning. Figured I'd get a job working with horses, and I did."

"I heard you work for Skip Clark at his place?"

Clary rocked the chair back and forth. "Even before that I was working for the neighbor after school and on weekends. I never minded how much manure I had to sling as long as I got to ride at the end of the day."

"But now you're working for—"

"Skip. I clean out the stalls, help with the lessons, stuff like that." She hugged herself as if she couldn't believe her great luck. "I love it. I can't imagine what it's like for those people stuck in an office all day or run off their feet at the mall."

Far from it being difficult to get Clary to talk, Emma mused, it was going to be touch and go as to whether or not she would be able to get a word in edgewise.

"Sprout's my favorite. He's Skip's newest horse. He's a great big quarter horse so the name Sprout is kind of funny, if you know what I mean. Do you ride? If you'd like to take lessons, we do that, too."

Clary paused briefly, and Emma jumped in. "Do adults take lessons or do you mostly have children?"

Clary thought for a moment. "It's mostly kids, but we do have some grown-ups, too," she said in a way that suggested to Emma she felt more akin to the children than the adults.

Emma had been brought up believing that lying was wrong, and even bending the truth a bit to suit one's own purposes never felt quite right to her. Nevertheless, she gritted her teeth, squeezed her eyes shut and said, "I think a friend of mine is taking lessons with Skip Clark. Her name is Deirdre Porter?" She let her voice go up at the end so that it sounded more like a question than a statement.

"Oh, Mrs. Porter." Clary's face lit up. "She's ever so nice. Gave me a pair of boots that she didn't want anymore, can you imagine? Genuine leather and ordered straight from some famous shop in Houston." She stuck out her feet so that Emma could admire them.

Emma made the appropriate noises while trying to decide where to steer the conversation next. She didn't want to put Clary in the position of having to defend Deirdre. She'd get a lot less information out of her that way.

"I guess Deirdre and Skip Clark are old friends," Emma hazarded, her fingers crossed again.

"Old friends? Oh, I didn't know that. That would explain—" She stopped abruptly and bit her lip.

"Explain?" Emma prompted.

"Nothing." Clary shook her head. "Just a feeling. Like maybe they knew each other in a past life or something." She giggled. "You must think I'm plain silly."

"Not at all." Emma smiled reassuringly. "Is there a Mrs. Clark?"

"Mrs. Clark?" Clary wrinkled her nose. "Oh, you mean like is Skip married?" She nodded her head. "Yes. She doesn't come around the stable much. I think she has a job in town. Least I see her leaving every morning around the same time. Just as I'm getting the feed ready for the horses."

How was she going to connect the dots for Clary, Emma wondered. Maybe she could sort of sidle into it.

She sighed dramatically. "People are so mean, don't you think?" She leaned closer to Clary.

"What do you mean?" Clary pushed the rocking chair back, away from Emma.

Emma sighed again. "People talk. And they say terrible things."

"What! You don't mean about Skip. He takes the best care of those horses anyone could. Pays for top quality feed, always got Doc Barber out there seeing to them even if it's no more than a strained muscle."

Emma was already shaking her head. "I don't mean about the horses. I mean about him and Deirdre Porter."

Clary stopped mid-rock. "What do you mean about him and Mrs. Porter? Why would they say anything?"

Emma lowered her voice. "They're saying that something is going on . . . between the two of them."

"Oh." Clary looked thunderstruck. "You mean like an affair? Like in the movies?"

"Yes." Emma sighed with relief. Finally she and Clary were on the same page. "What do you think?" She prompted.

Clary frowned, obviously giving it serious thought. "I don't know. Skip is friendly with everyone. He's just that way. Throwing his arm around you and giving you a hug now and then. It don't mean nothing. But I can see how someone else might see it different."

"Apparently someone took a picture of the two of them, and, as you said, they saw it different. They're trying to say that Skip and Deirdre are having an affair."

"That's just awful!" Clary's rocking increased furiously. "Why would they do that?"

"Some people just like to cause trouble."

"I suppose you're right. Is there anything we can do about it?"

Emma shrugged. "I don't know. I am trying to find out if anyone showed Skip that picture. It would have been a man with dark hair and eyes . . ." Emma sketched out a rough picture of Guy. "Skip would probably have been upset."

Clary nodded. "Especially seeing as how it's not true."

"Do you remember anyone like that coming around? I'm guessing Skip would have been furious afterward. You probably would have noticed something."

"Someone did come around one day. Couple of weeks ago, I'd say. I saw them walking together down toward the ring where we give lessons. I could tell, even from a distance, that Skip was upset. He shouted and threw something down on the ground. Even stepped on it with his boot and ground it into the dust."

"What about the other person? Did they get angry?"

"Nope. Just laughed."

"And it was a man? With dark hair?"

Clary looked confused. She began to shake her head. "No, no, it was a woman."

Chapter 23

"A woman!" Arabella exclaimed when Emma recounted her chat with Clary the next day.

Emma and Arabella were at the counter of O'Connell's Hardware Store. It hadn't changed a bit, Emma noticed, since she left Paris. It was tidier—that was obviously Brian's doing—but the same smell of sawdust, wood and grease mingled in the air. The wooden floors creaked and the glass-fronted cabinets were older than she was.

Brian thought one of the screws in the door of Emma's armoire was bent. It didn't seem to be doing any harm, but he was something of a perfectionist. He was behind the counter searching through a drawer in a row of dozens of similar drawers for the correct size.

"Got it." He held up a tiny piece of hardware, smiled and stuck it in his pocket. He leaned on the counter. "You say it was a *girl* who approached Skip with the photograph?"

The sleeves of his blue shirt were rolled up to his elbows,

and Emma noticed his skin was tanned a slightly darker shade than it had been just last week.

"It must have been Nikki doing Guy's dirty work, don't you think?" Arabella took a handkerchief from her purse and dabbed at her nose.

"I don't know." Emma looked at Brian, and their eyes met. She felt a hot flush creeping up her chest and looked down quickly. "It didn't sound like Nikki."

"How so?" Brian straightened a small Plexiglas holder of flyers advertising Bert's Mole Removal that sat out on the counter.

"Clary described her as ordinary. And that's hardly a word anyone would use in relation to Nikki."

"True." Arabella put her fingertips together. "What is this Clary like? A pretty girl? Into clothes and makeup and the like?"

Emma looked at her aunt curiously. "No, not at all. She's quite plain, and she's crazy about horses. She lives, breaths, eats and drinks them, by her own account."

"Do you think she would notice just how extraordinary Nikki is then? Probably the only thing she'd be inclined to notice would be her height."

"That's true. She did say the woman looked fairly tall." Emma smiled. "And she did say that if she were going to choose a horse for her it would be something called a quarter horse."

Brian smiled. "That's a good-sized horse. She must have been tall, then."

"So Nikki's the one who showed the blackmail photograph to Skip," Emma said. "But is Skip the one who acted on it by bashing Guy over the head?"

"It's beginning to look like that." Arabella tucked her handkerchief back in her purse.

"But what if . . ." Emma paused thinking the idea

through. "What if Guy wasn't the one resorting to blackmail?"

Arabella's and Brian's heads both swiveled in her direction.

Emma held up a hand. "What if Nikki found that photo on Guy's camera and decided to make use of it herself?"

"Why would she do something like that?" Brian took out a cloth and began to wipe down the counter.

"Maybe she needed money for something. Maybe she got into debt."

"But don't these girls rake in a fortune each day?" Brian said.

"They do. But their expenses are sky-high as well. Apartment rentals in New York City can be thousands per month."

Brian shuddered. "To live with all that dirt and exhaust and smog?"

Emma smiled. "There are compensations. Broadway, the symphony, some of the best restaurants in the world and amazing window-shopping at Christmastime."

"But surely this Nikki made thousands just for showing up." Arabella frowned. "What was she doing with it all?"

"Gambling?" Brian hazarded.

"Drugs?" Emma threw out. "It's epidemic among that crowd."

Arabella nodded. "I read a story on it in *People* magazine. Hard to imagine how those models keep their looks with all those late nights drinking and doing drugs."

"There's a reason the heroin chic look became so popular among magazine stylists," Emma quipped.

"She could have fallen prey to one of those unscrupulous investment advisors or stockbrokers," said Brian.

"Like one of those Ponzi schemes that have been in the news recently." Arabella tilted her head toward the wall-mounted telephone behind the counter. "Can you find out?

Call some people in New York and see what rumors there are?"

Emma let out a breath. No reason she couldn't call some people and at least chat. She'd been trying to avoid talking to her old friends. It stirred up longings for her life the way it used to be. But she was happy here in Paris with her aunt and Sweet Nothings, and she didn't want anything to ruin it.

Emma looked up to find Arabella and Brian both staring at her. "Sure," she blurted out. "I'll make a few phone calls.

As usual, her phone had fallen to the bottom of her purse. Emma dug it out and checked for missed calls or voice messages. Nothing. She clicked to the address book and began scanning the names. Who should she call? Tad Davito? He did Nikki's hair for several of the shoots she'd had with Guy. They always had their heads together when Nikki wasn't in front of the camera. Madeleine Montague? She did Nikki's makeup nine times out of ten. They often grabbed lunch together during breaks. She scrolled a little farther. Brigitta Sandstrom? If Nikki had a rival it was her. They'd started their careers around the same time and had been running neck and neck until recently when Brigitta scored a mega-millions contract with Blush Cosmetics. More than once Emma had heard Nikki ranting about the unfairness of it.

Emma thought for a minute. She needed to talk to someone levelheaded. Who didn't hold any grudges or have any complaints against Nikki. Brilliant, Kool-Aid red hair came into her mind—cut in an asymmetrical pixie with Bettie Page fringe. Frieda Strauss, booking agent at Top Model, Inc. She had no gripes with Nikki. Nikki made plenty of money for them and was completely professional when it came to showing up on time and being ready to strut her stuff.

Arabella looked in Emma's direction. "Don't mind me. I'm taking off."

"Are you okay?" Emma once again studied the dark circles under Arabella's eyes.

Arabella bristled. "I'm fine, dear. I just have . . . something to do, that's all."

Emma raised an eyebrow. "Something to do?"

"Never you mind." Arabella crossed her arms over her chest with a finality that made Emma smile. She knew when to stop asking questions.

Emma flipped open her phone and punched in Frieda's number.

TANTALIZING smells drifted down the stairs and curled under Emma's nose, leading her upwards. Sylvia and Kate had invited her for dinner in Sylvia's little apartment over The Taffy Pull. The scents of caramel and chocolate added interesting top notes to the odor of whatever it was that Sylvia was cooking.

"It smells heavenly," Emma exclaimed when Kate threw open the door.

"It is heavenly," Kate said. "It's Sylvia's famous goulash, and it's to die for."

Sylvia shuffled out of the kitchen, her chef's apron tied around a pair of black slacks and a colorful Indian tunic covered with brilliant embroidery and small mirrored discs. She gestured toward her feet.

"Pardon the slippers, but my ankles are swelling like crazy today. Must be the heat." She grabbed Emma's hand and pulled her toward the kitchen. "Come see what's on the stove."

Emma followed Sylvia into the tiny aisle kitchen where pots were bubbling and hissing on the stove. Sylvia lifted the lid of one of them, and the delicious steam wafted around Emma's face.

"It's my famous goulash." Sylvia replaced the lid. "But

first, let's have a drink." She opened the freezer door and brought out a bottle encased in ice.

Emma looked at it curiously. "What's that?"

"Vodka," Sylvia said, although she pronounced it "wodka."

Sylvia retrieved some tiny crystal glasses the size of shot glasses from the cupboard across from the stove and carefully filled each one. She handed one to Emma and one to Kate. She held hers up and proclaimed "*Nastrovia*," before downing the liquid in one gulp.

Emma and Kate approached their glasses with a little more caution. Emma took a sip and swore she could feel the liquid burning all the way down her throat and into the pit of her stomach. She put her glass down on the table and pushed it a safe distance away. She'd have to go easy on that stuff.

Sylvia took a platter from the refrigerator and shepherded them into the tiny living room, whose windows overlooked the square. An overstuffed burgundy sofa and two chairs dripped with lace doilies, and a curio cabinet was stuffed with nesting dolls, decorated Easter eggs and various icons. An elaborate silver samovar held pride of place on a gate-legged table. Emma wondered if Sylvia ever used it.

Sylvia put the platter on the coffee table. "Help yourself. An old, dear friend who works at Bloomingdale's just sent me a tin of caviar for my birthday. This is the perfect occasion to enjoy it." She beamed at Kate and Emma.

"Happy birthday," Emma and Kate chorused.

Sylvia turned slightly pink and waved a hand. "Go on. Enjoy."

Emma looked at the plate and hesitated.

"Go on." Sylvia made encouraging gestures. "First," she said, picking up a triangle of toast to demonstrate, "a dab of caviar." She waved the spoon at them. "And never, ever use a silver spoon. The caviar will tarnish it." She put a dollop of caviar on her cracker. "Then you add some chopped egg." She dipped into the pile of chopped hard-boiled whites and yolks. "A little onion adds some zest." She spooned a few pieces of onion onto the top of her bread. "And," she finished, picking up a lemon wedge encased in cheesecloth, "I like a tiny squeeze of lemon juice." She handed the toast to Emma.

Emma took a bite. It wasn't the first time she'd had caviar, but it was the first time she'd had it prepared like this. She closed her eyes. The sharp sea taste of the caviar blended with the pungent onion, tang of citrus and smooth blandness of egg. It was delicious.

Sylvia prepared another one and handed it to Kate.

"So. Tell me what's going on with this murder case you gals have been investigating."

Emma ventured another sip from her glass of vodka. This time she only wet her lips a bit. "We think Nikki was trying to blackmail Deirdre Porter."

"Really?" Kate looked startled.

"At first we thought it was Guy doing it. His camera was used to take the incriminating photograph." Emma paused for a moment. She doubted she'd ever used the word *incriminating* in a conversation before.

"But then why kill Guy if Nikki was the one who was blackmailing Deirdre?" Sylvia dabbed at her lips with a napkin, and Emma noticed she had toast crumbs and bits of egg clinging to the front of her blouse.

Emma's stomach descended as quickly as if she'd been in an airplane doing a nose dive. Why kill Guy indeed? She felt her theory crumbling around her. Obviously she wasn't exactly cut out to be a detective.

"Nikki." Kate mumbled around a mouthful of toast and caviar. "Sorry." She chewed for a second. "Maybe Nikki killed Guy?" She turned to Emma and Sylvia.

"Nikki?" Emma squeaked. "But why?"

"Maybe he found out what she was up to, and they got into a fight, and she clonked him over the head?"

Emma nodded enthusiastically. "That makes sense." She thought for a moment. "But then who killed Nikki?"

Sylvia shrugged as she loaded more caviar on a toast piece. "Maybe Nikki went ahead with the blackmail and"— she leveled a cocked finger at Emma— "Deirdre or her paramour went ahead with the murder.

"Come on." Sylvia stood up and swept them along with a flourish of her arm. "Dinner's ready."

She had a tiny table set up in the corner of the living room. It was draped in a white cloth with colorful embroidery along the edges, which matched the embroidery on the cloth napkins set beside each plate. Sylvia placed the steaming bowl of goulash in the middle of the table along with a smaller bowl of egg noodles. "Please, help yourselves." She gestured toward the food. "Eat."

Emma helped herself to a plate of egg noodles and spread some delicious smelling goulash on top. Her mind was whirling. Was it really possible that two killers were at work here—Nikki and Deirdre or Skip? It was inconceivable.

Emma spooned up a forkful of goulash, but she hardly tasted it with her mind going a mile a minute.

She was taking a second bite when her cell phone rang. "I'm so sorry," she jumped up. "I should have turned it off."

"Don't worry about it. Answer it. Maybe it's important." Sylvia filled her plate with noodles and stew.

"Hello?"

Frieda's familiar voice came over the line. Emma glanced at Sylvia but she motioned for Emma to go ahead.

Emma nodded apologetically to Sylvia and Kate, got up from the table and went over and perched on the edge of the rough velvet sofa. Frieda was never much for small talk, so Emma asked her straight out if she had any knowledge of Nikki's financial situation.

For several minutes, the only words Emma was able to interject into the conversation were "mmmhhmm" and "aha" mingled with the occasional "Really?"

Frieda's speech was crisp, succinct and firm. Emma got an immediate picture of her long lanky frame, short red hair and bright blue eyes.

"Really?" Emma said a final time before hanging up. She sat for a moment staring at her phone.

"What is it, darling?" Sylvia put her hand on Emma's arm.

Emma shook her head. "I'm so confused." She looked from Kate to Sylvia and back again.

Sylvia raised her bushy gray brows, and Kate tilted her head to the side.

"According to Frieda, and she got this straight from Nikki's financial advisor, Nikki had plenty of money. More than anyone could ever need."

Sylvia grunted, and Kate got as white as a sheet.

"It looks as if Nikki had no reason whatsoever to blackmail Deirdre or Skip."

Chapter 24

EMMA woke early with butterflies in her stomach. For a moment she couldn't imagine why. Then she remembered. The women they had picked for the grand opening fashion show were arriving for their rehearsal this morning. And the grand opening of Sweet Nothings itself was only two days away—whether they were ready or not! Emma ran through the ever-present checklist in her head. So far they were on track for a successful opening. As long as nothing happened between now and two days from now. She crossed her fingers.

Emma was glad she was up before her alarm. It gave her plenty of time to get ready for the day ahead. She dressed quickly and headed straight down to Sweet Nothings, a travel mug of green tea tucked in her bag. She paused with her key in the front door. She loved watching Washington Street slowly come to life. Mabel scurried past on the sidewalk across the street and waved. Les was right behind her, hurrying toward The Toggery where lights were already coming on. Emma felt a small warm glow of contentment form a ball in the pit of her stomach. She was really settling into life in Paris. Was this where she was meant to be?

Emma pushed open the door to Sweet Nothings and stood for a moment admiring the transformation the shop had undergone. Brian had done an amazing job. She pulled her cell phone from her purse and tucked the bag under the counter. She was about to drop the phone into her pocket when she noticed the message light was on. She checked and discovered she'd missed a call from Liz.

Suddenly a thought occurred to her, and she fished her cell from her pocket and punched in Liz's number.

Emma realized she'd go half crazy if she didn't find out who Brian's mysterious Amy was. And if anyone would know, it would be Liz.

THE Coffee Klatch was half filled with sleepy-eyed regulars downing bacon and eggs and glasses of orange juice. Waitresses moved sluggishly around the room, wielding pots of fresh, hot coffee. Liz was already seated at one of the tables when Emma got there.

Liz jumped up and they embraced quickly. Liz was already nursing a cup of coffee, and moments after Emma sat down, the waitress glided by and slid a cup and saucer onto the table in front of her. She held the coffeepot over it inquiringly.

Emma shook her head. "Could I have some green tea, please?"

The woman looked puzzled. Mabel, who was waiting on the table next to theirs, called over her shoulder. "Hank found a box of green tea bags. Should be on the counter next to the bin of sugar packets."

The waitress scurried away, and Emma picked up her menu and began fiddling with it. She wasn't planning on ordering anything, but she needed something to do with her hands. Now that she was here, seated across from Liz, she felt oddly reluctant to bring up the mysterious Amy. She wasn't sure she would like what she was going to hear.

"Okay, what gives?" Liz took her characteristic blunt approach.

"It's that obvious?" Emma leaned to one side as the waitress splashed hot water into her cup and plopped in a tea bag.

"Absolutely. You don't have much of a poker face, you know."

Emma laughed. "That's true." She dunked her tea bag repeatedly, watching as the water turned a pale green, avoiding Liz's questioning look.

"I'm guessing this has something to do with Brian?" Liz asked with a gentle smile.

Emma nodded. Better to get it over with—like ripping off a bandage quickly. "Who is Amy?"

"So that's what this is about."

"Brian called me Amy by mistake one day. He obviously didn't want to talk about her . . . whoever she is."

"His ex-fiancée," Liz said succinctly, before taking a sip of her coffee. She looked at Emma over the rim of her cup. "Notice I said ex."

"What happened?"

Liz put her cup down and sighed. "I have to be honest with you. None of us liked her all that much. She was very high-powered and ambitious. She was with a very prestigious law firm in Nashville and was determined to make partner. When Brian decided to come back to Paris after Dad's surgery, she dumped him."

"Oh." Emma felt a rush of conflicting emotions. She was glad that Brian was no longer engaged, but sad to hear that his heart had been broken. In spite of herself, she felt the beginnings of a smile tugging at the corners of her lips.

"He does like you, you know."

Emma ducked her head. "I'm afraid I'm just another kid sister to him."

Liz tilted her head, considering. "I think you're wrong. But you'll have to give him time. He's feeling pretty wounded after the way Amy treated him." Liz looked at Emma, a serious expression on her face. "But if you go back to New York, it's only going to break his heart again."

Emma shook her head. "I haven't decided about that yet." She felt a wave of sadness wash over her at the thought of giving up on the life in New York she'd dreamed about for so long. On the other hand, the thought of leaving Paris and Aunt Arabella, Liz and Brian and all the new people she'd met made her want to cry. She closed her eyes in frustration. Why did both options have to be mutually exclusive!

Emma noticed the worried expression on Liz's face and put her hand over her friend's. "Don't worry. I'm not going to hurt Brian. I like him too much for that." She'd almost said "love" but caught herself at the last moment. Even if she didn't have much of a poker face, there was still no need to wear her heart on her sleeve.

"I know that." Liz took a last gulp of her coffee. "I've got to run." She got up and put her arms around Emma. "I just know things are going to work out for the best."

Emma hugged her back. She wished she could believe Liz. If only the police would find out who was behind Guy's and Nikki's murders. Then Emma would be able to relax again.

THE door to Sweet Nothings had barely shut behind Emma when it opened again and Arabella walked in with Pierre. She unclipped his leash, and he immediately ran toward his dog bed, sniffing it thoroughly before climbing in and settling down for his first nap of the day.

"Land sakes, it's hot out there," Arabella declared,

waving a hand in front of her face. She took off the jacket to her white linen pants suit and hung it over a chair. Underneath, she had on a bright orange shell with a choker of coral beads at her neck.

"What time are these women supposed to arrive?"

Emma glanced at her watch. "Very soon. In ten minutes or so."

They both jumped when another knock sounded at the door. Emma hastened to open it, and Kate and Sylvia walked in. Sylvia was dressed to the nines in a purple sheath with a paisley shawl draped loosely over her shoulders. Shiny discs reflected from her earrings, which hung almost to her shoulders. She'd forgone her usual head scarf and had had her gray hair set in a sleek bob.

"Well, don't just stand there staring," she admonished Emma and Arabella.

"I must say, you clean up real good," Arabella commented dryly.

Sylvia cracked a smile. "Guess I've still got it." She took a last whiff from her oxygen tank and parked it behind the counter. "Now I've just got to prove it to the kids. My lease on the apartment is up next month, and they've made an appointment for a tour at that place over on the other side of town. Sunrise Hills, Sunset Hills, something like that. I figured I'd play nice and go along. But if they think I'm moving there . . ." She made a slicing gesture across her throat.

Kate giggled, took off her glasses and swiped a tissue across them. She was wearing her usual black, and Emma wondered whether she wasn't terribly hot in that getup. Her hair looked limp and shapeless, and she was visibly sweating.

"Hot enough for you?" Sylvia said as she got comfortable behind the counter.

"At least it doesn't smell," Emma answered, wrinkling her nose. "And it's not so crowded that you can't breathe."

"You're turning into a real country girl." Sylvia laughed, her laughter slowly turning to a nagging cough.

The first knock on the door came just as the clock ticked over to the hour. Emma opened it and stood aside as three women came in, laughing and chatting.

The door had almost closed behind them when it was pushed open again, and Bitsy strode in cradling a tower of white boxes tied with string. "I've brought you some cupcakes," she said, handing them to Sylvia who had rushed forward to help her.

"Lord, it is hot." One of the women stopped dead right beneath the ceiling fan, her face turned toward the breeze. "I could do with a big old glass of sweet tea right about now."

"Now that's one of the best ideas I've heard in a long time." Bitsy stuck out her hand. "I'm Bitsy. I run Sprinkles, the cupcake place around the corner."

"Ginger." The blonde took Bitsy's proffered hand.

Kate pushed off from the stool where she had been leaning. "I'll go get the tea. I know Arabella has a fresh pitcher all made up."

Before Kate could move, there was another knock on the door.

"I'll get it." Sylvia made for the front of the store. She pulled open the door, and several more women tumbled into the shop.

Emma had been up late creating lists and corresponding tags. Each garment was labeled with the model's name and hung in a dressing room. Each dressing room had a list of names taped to the door so the models would know where to find the item they would be wearing.

"Very organized, dear," Arabella said with admiration as she watched the women line up smoothly in front of each of the three dressing rooms.

Ginger was the first one dressed. While she was petite, she didn't lack for some really eye-catching curves, which the bias cut of the peach silk nightgown highlighted to perfection.

"Just call me Jean," she said, making her voice low and husky. "Jean Harlow." She circled in front of Emma and Arabella.

"I'd whistle, if I knew how," Arabella said.

Emma couldn't believe how the soft, silken fabric came to life on the human form.

"The French designer Madeleine Vionnet was a huge proponent of the bias cut," Arabella said, pointing to the gown. "You wouldn't be able to make the garment drape and stretch over the round contours of the female form if the fabric was cut on the straight grain. It has to be turned to an angle of forty-five degrees."

Emma watched Ginger transform from a very pretty but ordinary woman into a femme fatale thanks to a couple of yards of sensuous fabric. She really ought to rethink those old T-shirts she wore to bed every night. The idea of wearing one of these gowns for Brian streaked across her mind like a comet, and a flash of heat scorched her face. Arabella looked at her questioningly, and she fanned her face furiously.

"It is dreadfully hot, isn't it? Perhaps I'll go turn up the air conditioner."

Arabella nodded at her, but Emma didn't think she looked convinced. She escaped to the back room where she went to the sink and splashed some cold water on her face before returning to the showroom. Knowing that the mysterious Amy was no longer in the picture made Emma feel quite hopeful for the first time.

The girl with the short, curly hair who Emma had picked out earlier, emerged from the dressing room in one of the baby-doll nighties Arabella had scored from an estate sale in Jackson. It was perfect on her, Emma thought. Her face was youthful and innocent while her figure, though tiny, was every bit a woman's.

"We'd better bar the doors so that we don't get any men in here during the show," Sylvia said, wheezing.

"But aren't they supposed to be our best customers?" Emma tied a satin sash on Bitsy's gown. She'd been worried about finding a garment long enough for her, but Arabella had come up with something perfect.

"What you do is, you have special nights just for men. Right before Christmas and right before Valentine's Day. Close the shop to other customers. Give 'em something to drink and eat, and ka-ching!" Sylvia made the sound of a cash register.

Arabella and Emma looked at each other. "Brilliant!" they chorused.

Arabella patted Sylvia on the arm. "I don't know what we would do without you."

Sylvia smiled and the shadows behind her eyes momentarily lifted.

Finally, everyone was dressed in their assigned garment and lined up across the floor of Sweet Nothings. Emma straightened a strap here, retied a bow there. Emma, Arabella, Kate and Sylvia stood back to admire the lineup.

Emma glanced over her shoulder and saw several people had stopped to peer through the front window, their hands shadowing their eyes and their foreheads pressed to the glass.

She didn't want to give anyone a preview, especially not that boy on the end who didn't look to be much more than twelve years old. Emma climbed into the window, gave a sad smile as if to say "sorry," and pulled down the front shade. She heard groans and protests as the blind quickly obscured the view. At least people were interested and curious, she thought. Arabella's shop had stood on that same spot, unchanged, since the early 1970s. Until Emma got there, it had been covered in dust and some pretty heinous green shag carpeting. People hadn't stopped looking at it; they'd

stopped *seeing* it. Emma was grateful that they were now
sitting up and taking notice, even if that meant they were
trying to peer through the front window.

The women in the shop began chattering, quietly at first,
but then the sound of feminine voices rose to a crescendo.
Kate passed around glasses of Arabella's sweet tea, and
Emma watched carefully, terrified that someone would spill
something on one of the pieces.

One voice, a slightly nasal one with a native Southern
twang, rose above the others, cutting through the chatter
like a knife cuts through butter.

"I suppose that's where the murder took place."

Emma froze. Slowly, she inched her head around to scan
the crowd for the origin of the voice.

A tall brunette with dark eyes and a slash of crimson
lipstick stood pointing at the carpet with a long, blood-
red fingernail.

All other conversation died away as if someone had
sucked the oxygen from the room. Emma heard a couple of
gasps and a few "oh, dears." Some turned their heads away
politely.

The brunette was undeterred. "My husband was one of
the first people on the scene." Heads swiveled back in her
direction, curiosity getting the better of Southern manners.
"They still don't know for sure who done it, but the girlfriend's the most likely suspect. I heard he came down here
from New York just to go after her." She gave a high-pitched
laugh.

Emma tried to take consolation in the fact that if the
brunette was married to either Officer Flanagan or Kenny,
then she was married to a complete idiot, but it didn't help.
She knew her face was as flaming red as a chili pepper so
everyone in the entire room would know immediately that
she was "the girlfriend." Although in this case, it was more
like "the ex-girlfriend." She noticed Sylvia looking at her,

obviously concerned, and Emma forced herself to smile and make a devil-may-care gesture to reassure her. In reality, every fiber of her being wanted to walk over and throttle the wretched woman who'd brought up Guy's murder. That, however, would obviously not be good for business!

"I hope you all like cupcakes because I've brought some of my favorites." Bitsy's voice sang out, filling the awkward silence. "I've got red velvet, dark chocolate, lemon coconut and carrot."

Emma silently blessed Bitsy. The shrill ringing of the telephone sliced through the noise, and Emma didn't hesitate. She bolted for the back room, glad of the excuse to flee.

The phone was on the third ring, and she let it ring one more time while she caught her breath and composed herself, then she grabbed the receiver and held it to her ear.

"Hello? You've reached Sweet Nothings. How can I help you?" Emma was pleased at how calm and measured she'd managed to make her voice sound despite the fact that her chest was still rising up and down like a bellows.

"Who is this?" the voice on the other end demanded.

"It's Emma. Emma Taylor."

It was a woman calling. What did she want? The voice was vaguely familiar, but Emma couldn't place it.

"Emma, this is Deirdre Porter." She sounded apologetic, as if she remembered and regretted their last encounter and the way she'd slammed the door on them.

"Deirdre. Hi." Now Emma was really curious. Was Deirdre calling to tell her she was sorry to have missed the Sweet Nothings rehearsal?

"You know that picture you showed me?" Deirdre asked.

Emma was startled. That was the last thing she expected.

"Look at it again," Deirdre commanded. "Your friend Guy did not take that picture."

"What?"

"Just get the picture and look at it carefully. You'll see what I mean."

And she slammed down the phone.

"Who was that?" Kate stood in the doorway, her hand against the doorjamb.

How long had she been there? Emma wondered. She shook her head. "No one."

She didn't know why, but she had the feeling that she ought to keep the information from Deirdre to herself.

EMMA had arranged for Lucy to provide refreshments for the women who had shown up to model. Lucy had made a batch of delicate, crustless sandwiches—butter and cucumber, chicken salad and ham salad—and arranged them on silver platters with lace doilies and lavish swirls of curly parsley. The ladies oohed and aahed when they saw the feast spread out in front of them. The setup was complete with a huge crystal punch bowl, tiny white napkins with *Sweet Nothings* printed on them in black—a real splurge by Emma—and silver forks and white china plates. And now they would have Bitsy's cupcakes for dessert. Emma hoped the women would understand how much their help meant to her.

Emma ran around like a crazed sheep dog, rounding up all the garments for the opening and replacing the tags with the models' names. Her system would only work if she stayed organized and on top of things.

She kept thinking about Deirdre's phone call. She was dying to get out the photograph to see if she could spot whatever it was Deirdre was talking about, but there wouldn't be time until the ladies left. They seemed inclined to linger, and she noticed both Arabella and Sylvia behind the counter showing off some of the garments in the new lines. She supposed that was a good thing, but her curiosity was killing her.

Finally, they were closing the door on the last departing model, and the sounds of feminine chatter slowly faded down the street. Arabella groaned, sank into one of the armchairs, slid off her shoes and began to rub the balls of her feet. Sylvia was already collapsed in the other chair, her oxygen tank close by.

"I haven't been that busy since the day after Christmas in 1999," Sylvia said with satisfaction.

"Everything certainly went well. Let's hope that bodes good fortune for our opening." Arabella stuck her legs out and rotated her ankles.

Kate had retrieved the bottle of cleaner from behind the counter and was scrubbing at the mosaic of fingerprints on the glass. "I'm sure it's going to be wonderful. But I'm guessing you won't need me anymore when it's over, so I've booked my flight home."

"Oh!" Emma said. "Somehow I thought you'd be staying forever. But of course you have to get back to your life in the city."

Kate nodded. "There's a lot to do in relation to . . ." She hesitated. "Guy's estate."

Sylvia's face had taken on the look of a fallen soufflé. "I'm really going to miss having you around."

Emma thought she heard her sniff, but she wasn't sure.

"Guess I'll be going home." Sylvia struggled to her feet, leaning on the arms of the chair.

"Me, too," said Kate. "I should do some wash and then start packing."

"I'm right behind you." Arabella slipped on her shoes and got to her feet. "You need to get some rest, too." She pointed at Emma.

"I will. I'm going to have to get this place cleaned up before the big day." She looked around at the crumpled napkins scattered everywhere and the trail of crumbs across the new carpeting.

Emma waited while the others got their things together and left. For some reason, she didn't want to tell them about Deirdre's call and the photograph yet. Finally, the door shut behind Kate, and Emma locked it securely. She'd already kicked off her shoes, and she didn't want to know what she looked like. More than once she had run her hands through her hair in exasperation.

She had tucked the photograph and Guy's memory card into a cardboard mailer and put it in Arabella's desk drawer. Emma plopped into the swivel chair and eased open the drawer. A pad of paper had become stuck, the cardboard backing catching and keeping the drawer from opening. Emma eased her hand inside and managed to retrieve the pad and open the drawer.

The photograph should have been right on top, but she didn't see them. She sifted through the next layer, but there was still no sign of the bright yellow cardboard mailer. She methodically emptied the contents of the drawer, but finally she was down to the last piece of paper, and there was still no sign of them. Maybe Arabella had moved them? Emma opened the drawer on the right and started digging through it. Then the drawer on the left. The photograph wasn't there. Emma started to run her hands through her hair but then stopped. She'd likely already done enough damage in that department.

She couldn't remember moving the photos, but it was always possible she had done just that. She would check the apartment as soon as she closed up Sweet Nothings.

A rush of warm air greeted Emma when she pushed open the door to her apartment above Sweet Nothings. She dropped her handbag by the front door and went to turn up the air conditioner.

She'd made herself a pitcher of sweet tea, and it was waiting in the refrigerator. She poured a tall glass and held it to her neck, shivering slightly at the ice-cold contact. First stop, the small desk in the corner of her bedroom.

Five minutes later she'd emptied the contents of the small desk onto the floor—there wasn't all that much in the drawers, and the photograph was obviously not there, although she did run her hand under the top of each drawer just to be sure they hadn't become wedged. She checked the basket on the kitchen table where she corralled the mail, but no luck there, either. She hadn't tossed them on the coffee table or the end tables. They weren't on the bathroom or kitchen counters. This time Emma did run her hands through her hair. Where on earth could they have gone?

Emma decided to call Arabella. She dug her cell out of her purse and stood in front of the open refrigerator door as the phone rang once, twice. Arabella answered as Emma was popping the top off a container of blueberry yogurt.

Unfortunately, Arabella had no idea where the photograph was, either. She was certain she hadn't moved the envelope.

Emma hung up, puzzled.

Then she wondered if maybe Deirdre was right. The photograph did somehow contain proof that Guy hadn't shot it. Which meant someone else had used his camera.

And that someone was most likely the murderer.

Had they stolen the photograph right out from under her nose?

Chapter 25

EMMA glanced at the glowing face of her alarm clock. The numbers read 5:45 a.m. The last time she'd checked, it had said 3:55 a.m. and the time before that was 2:12 a.m. She pulled the pillow over her head and lay there, indecisive. Should she get up now, or try to catch another forty-five minutes of sleep? Right now, sleep seemed as elusive as a multi-million dollar lottery win. She ought to be tired—they'd worked till almost ten o'clock on Friday getting everything ready for today.

She swung her feet over the edge of the bed. She felt as stiff as if she'd run a marathon the day before, but it was from tossing and turning all night. She'd wanted to be especially well rested for the big day at Sweet Nothings, but it seemed that wasn't to be. She'd just have to fake it.

She showered and dressed quickly and filled a thermos with fresh green tea. She wanted to get down to Sweet Nothings early and do a last-minute check before everyone arrived.

* * *

EMMA put her key in the lock and pushed open the front door, her hand automatically reaching for the light switch. She hesitated when she realized that there was already a light on in the back room.

"Hello?" Emma called out tentatively.

A flashback to Guy's murder and then Nikki's made the hairs on the back of her neck bristle. The thought of calling Brian flashed through her mind, but her footsteps were already taking her toward the pool of light spilling through the doorway.

Emma peered around the edge, unconsciously braced for what she might find.

It was the last thing she'd expected to see. Arabella was sitting in the office chair, legs stretched out in front of her, chin to chest, fast asleep. Pierre was curled protectively at her feet, snoring softly. Emma glanced at her watch. It was barely past six thirty a.m. What time must Arabella have gotten there? Obviously she hadn't been able to sleep much, either.

Emma didn't want to frighten her so she went back out to the showroom and began making some gentle noises—opening and closing cupboards and drawers, rattling papers and whistling softly. Emma was giving a final tweak to the blue Ro-Vel gown on the mannequin when Arabella appeared in the doorway, yawning.

"I must have fallen asleep." She rubbed her eyes. "What are you doing here so early, dear? It's going to be a long day."

"Couldn't sleep." Emma took a sip of her tea. "I figured I might as well get the day started."

"I didn't sleep much, either," Arabella admitted. She looked thoughtful for a moment. She cleared her throat and put her hand on Emma's arm. "I don't know if I've told you or not, but your being here means the world to me. I couldn't have done it without you."

Emma felt sentimental tears pressing against the back of her lids. She dashed a hand across her eyes. "I wouldn't have missed it for the world."

"I have a little something for you." Arabella walked toward the back room. "Just a second."

She returned moments later with a small white box in her hand. She held it toward Emma. "I want you to have this. My mother gave it to me when I was around your age."

Emma took the tiny box. The silver script on the top had been worn away, but she could make out the word *jeweler*. She lifted the lid.

"Oh, it's lovely." She stared at the pin inside.

"It's vintage." Arabella smiled. "Pins aren't much in fashion these days, but I thought that would look lovely on you."

Emma fumbled with the clasp as she removed it from the box.

"It's made of platinum. They hardly ever use it anymore. Too expensive. My mother's brother made it for her. He was a jeweler."

Emma fastened the brooch to her dress and stood in front of the mirror to admire it. It was a spray of platinum flowers dotted with pearls and diamonds. "It's exquisite. I love it. Thank you so much." She hugged her aunt.

"I'm glad you like it."

They heard a slight tapping sound at the front door.

"I'll get it." Emma started toward the front of the store.

"I'll put some coffee on." Arabella turned toward the back room.

Emma opened the door to find Sylvia and Kate on the doorstep.

She noticed that the sky was getting darker toward the west. She crossed her fingers and said a quick prayer that any rain would hold off until later—much later. Preferably after they had all gone home and to bed.

Sylvia had had her hair done again and was wearing a simple black dress with a strand of pearls. Kate looked her usual self—charmingly disheveled in black pants, a black-and-white graphic T-shirt and high-heeled sandals. Her hair was clean and shiny, although her part was wildly askew and her bangs needed trimming.

Sylvia looked at Kate. "Give me your glasses. They've got a big smudge on them. It's a miracle you can see."

"They say that's not good for your eyes," Arabella added.

"I've got some lens cleaner in my purse." Kate began pawing through the contents of the big, squishy tote bag she called a purse. She shook her head. "I've got so much stuff in here. I really need to clean it out."

Sylvia gestured toward the wad of papers Kate had in her hand. "Do you need those? If you don't, you can throw them out and make a start."

Kate quickly glanced through the assortment of pages torn from various notebooks, restaurant receipts and other miscellaneous papers. "I don't really need any of these."

"There's a garbage can next to the desk." Arabella pointed toward the back room.

Kate had just disappeared into the back when there was a sharp rap on the front door. The brunette model was the first to arrive—the one who had had to bring up Guy's murder at the rehearsal. She looked sheepish when Emma opened the door. Emma still felt slightly irritated, but she plastered a smile on her face and acted as if she had forgotten the incident. The brunette quickly relaxed and began chatting with Sylvia about the time she'd spent a week in New York City seeing the sights.

From then on, the door opened and closed repeatedly as the rest of the models arrived. Bitsy came with her usual stack of bakery boxes filled with delectable cupcakes, and chatter soon filled Sweet Nothings as they nursed cups of coffee from Arabella's never-ending pot.

Emma glanced at her watch and decided it was time. She began shepherding the women toward the dressing rooms.

There was a thump at the front door, and Emma paused. It didn't sound like a knock—more like someone had hit the door. Best to check, she decided, as she eased the door open.

The young man standing there was nearly hidden behind a huge, tissue-wrapped bouquet. "Delivery," he mumbled around the flowers in his hands.

Emma couldn't imagine who had sent them flowers. She signed the delivery receipt and carried the vase to the counter. Her name was on the tiny white envelope tucked into the top of the bouquet of pink peonies.

She slid her finger under the flap, opened the envelope and eased out the card. *Wishing you the best on this special day, Brian,* was scrawled inside.

"Those must have cost a fortune!" Bitsy sighed as she admired the flowers.

Emma buried her nose in the velvet soft petals hoping to hide the blush that she could tell was coloring her face as pink as the flowers.

"I'm guessing it's your boyfriend who sent those."

Emma hesitated. "A friend, actually."

"Wish I had friends like that." Bitsy laughed and ran a hand through her hair.

Emma had just placed the vase of peonies on the counter when there was another thump against the front door. *What now*, she wondered?

"Yes?" She said as she swung the door open.

There was another delivery boy standing there hidden behind another gigantic floral arrangement. He dumped them into Emma's arms. "Delivery for you."

Emma eased the door closed with her foot and carried the flowers to the other side of the counter.

"Good heavens," Arabella exclaimed when she saw them. "It's beginning to look more like a florist in here than a lingerie shop. Who are they from?"

"I don't know. They're addressed to you." Emma retrieved the card from the heart of the dozen red roses.

"Really?" Arabella raised her eyebrows. "It's been way too long since someone has sent me any of these." She opened the card, and an array of emotions crossed her face. "Oh, dear." She put her hand to her chest.

Emma tried to peer over her shoulder.

"Here," Arabella handed her the card. "Read it."

Emma scanned the rather quaint penmanship. "*Wishing you a most successful opening. Regards, Les*," she read out loud.

"Indeed." Arabella rolled her eyes.

Emma handed her the card. "He's trying to get back into your good graces."

"Apparently." Arabella sniffed the flowers. "They are heavenly."

Women were coming out of the dressing rooms and mingling in front of the counter, admiring the two bouquets. Emma was collecting the used coffee cups when a third thump rattled the front door. She grabbed for the doorknob with one hand, the other clutching the three mugs by their handles.

"My goodness! Not more flowers." Emma said.

The delivery boy, who was wearing a yellow T-shirt that had *Francesca's Flowers* printed on it, grinned. "First time I ever heard anyone say that." He put the bouquet down on the doormat as he scrounged in his back pocket for the delivery slip.

Emma laughed. She signed the receipt and picked up the flowers.

"Good heavens!" Arabella said. "Another bouquet? These must be for you."

"I don't know who would have sent them." Emma poked around inside the tissue but didn't immediately find anything.

"Looks like they might have been sent anonymously."

"Whoever sent them has good taste." Arabella admired the arrangement of garden flowers.

Emma glanced down to see a small white square envelope lying on the floor. "Looks like I dropped the card." She quickly read the front. "And it looks like they're for you."

"Me?" Arabella said pointing to herself. "Who on earth . . ." She slid the card out and read it.

This time her face turned as pink as the peonies.

"Who's it from?" Emma prodded.

Arabella held the note to her chest. "They're from Francis. Can you imagine?"

Emma whistled softly. "Where shall we put them?"

"In the center between the other two, I think." Arabella quickly bustled off with the bouquet.

Emma looked at the flowers spaced out on the counter. They were just what Sweet Nothings needed for their opening day. She knew she was partial, but she thought Brian's bouquet was the nicest. She couldn't wait to thank him for it. She buried her nose in the flowers once more and sniffed the delicious scents.

"Should we get going?" Arabella asked. Emma noticed the frown between her brows and the shadows under her eyes.

Emma threw her arms around her aunt. "I just know this is going to be a success."

Arabella looked startled for a moment, but then her face relaxed. She kissed Emma on the cheek. "I agree one hundred percent."

Emma felt a warm glow of satisfaction that more than made up for any feelings she had about missing New York and her old life. This is where she belonged. She knew it now.

Emma was turning toward the counter when a terrible sound rent the air of Sweet Nothings. It was the sound of a garment ripping, and it was followed by a long, drawn-out feminine wail.

Chapter 26

ARABELLA grabbed her sewing bag and went running as fast as an EMT with a first-aid kit at the scene of an accident.

The woman who had introduced herself as Ginger tore open the black-and-white toile curtain to the dressing room and stood wailing loudly, her black lace Barbizon gown hugging her curves except where the seam had decided to separate into two pieces.

Arabella examined the hole the way a doctor might examine a wound. She furrowed her brow and checked the contents of her sewing kit.

"You're going to need to take it off," she told Ginger.

Tears were streaming down Ginger's face.

Arabella gave a hiss of impatience. "We'll get it fixed in no time. Don't you worry."

"I've so been looking forward to being in your fashion show," Ginger alternately cried and hiccoughed. "I didn't do nothing except pull the gown over my head."

"Don't worry about it," Arabella soothed as she threaded her needle with some black silk thread. "I'm sure I can fix it." She smiled reassuringly. "These old seams are fragile. It's not your fault."

"Honest, I've never worn anything as beautiful as this before," Ginger lamented. "My wedding gown wasn't even this special. I got it from the dry cleaner. Someone had taken it in to be preserved and never bothered to pick it up. He gave me a real deal on it seeing as how he never did get that spot near the hem out." She sniffed loudly.

Arabella gently urged her back into the dressing room and pulled the toile curtain closed. Moments later an arm, bearing the torn piece of lingerie, snaked its way through the part in the curtains.

Arabella grabbed the garment. "You just stay put. I'll have this fixed in no time."

Arabella retreated to the Louis XIV chair, perched her glasses on the end of her nose and set to work. Moments later, she'd stuck the repaired garment through the curtain, and Ginger reappeared clad in black lace and wearing a huge grin. She paused in front of the full-length beveled glass mirror to admire herself.

"Someone's at the back door," Kate called to Emma. "Do you want me to see who it is?"

"It's probably Lucy, the caterer, with the food."

Both Emma and Kate headed toward the back room. Lucy's small white van with *Let Us Cater To You* written on the side in rose-colored script, was backed up as close as she could get to the door. Lucy was waiting, holding a huge silver platter covered in plastic wrap.

"It's just starting to rain," she said as a plump drop splattered on the plastic covering the platter. "Let's get these things inside before we have a real deluge on our hands."

"Need some help?" Kate started toward the open doors to the van.

"Thanks." Lucy gestured with her chin toward a stack of boxes. "If you could bring in the napkins and silverware . . ." She glanced at Emma. "And we'll need the folding table and the linens."

"I'll get those."

Arabella was waiting anxiously by the back door. "Is it raining?" She stuck a hand out, palm up.

"It's just starting," Lucy said as she edged past the open door. "I think we're in for a real downpour."

Arabella's face darkened as she held the door open for Kate, with her armload of boxes, and Emma, who maneuvered her way through with the folding table. She trotted ahead of them, Pierre right on her heels, to the spot where they'd decided to set up the food. They didn't have a whole lot of room, so Lucy had chosen some of her smaller platters and planned to refill them with supplies kept in the refrigerated portion of her van.

Arabella, Emma and Kate hovered while Lucy whipped open the white tablecloth and adjusted it on the table, then arranged the platters of food and other supplies just so. Bitsy helped organize her cupcakes, and they all stood back to admire the impressive spread.

Emma felt her stomach growl at the sight of the homemade cheese straws and other goodies. She'd been too nervous to eat much more than a bite or two of yogurt for breakfast.

Lucy bustled out to the van and came back with another, smaller platter. This they set up in the back room for the models.

"One minute till time," Sylvia shouted above the chattering voices. "Places, everyone!"

Emma had organized things so that the models would

wait in the back room and make their appearance one by one, circulating through the salesroom in an ongoing loop. They'd each been given a card with information about their particular garment so they would be able to answer any of the customers' questions. Meanwhile, Sylvia was behind the counter ready to show off their new lines of merchandise, and Arabella and Emma were poised to greet people and generally make the customers feel at home.

Sylvia whistled and called loudly, "Countdown."

Again, they counted down as if it were New Year's Eve and the ball was about to drop, but this time the models joined in, giggling and jostling each other as they crowded into the back room.

Arabella pulled open the front door with a flourish and stood back, but no one was there. She stuck her head out of the door and looked up and down the sidewalk. Emma joined her.

"Not a soul," Emma called over her shoulder to Sylvia.

"It's early yet," Sylvia said to reassure them.

"Maybe when the rain lets up," Arabella added.

Emma's stomach clenched into a knot worthy of a sailor. If no one came, what would happen to Sweet Nothings and Arabella?

Everyone fell silent and listened as the clock ticked one minute past the hour, two minutes, three minutes. At the four-minute mark, Emma thought she would go crazy if she didn't do something—anything. She grabbed the bottle of glass cleaner and began cleaning the glass-fronted cabinets, even though they were already spotless.

At ten minutes past the hour, the front door slowly opened.

Everyone gave a collective sigh of relief. Sylvia straightened behind the counter, and Emma and Arabella began moving toward the door.

A woman stuck her head around the opening. Raindrops glistened in her white hair. She smiled apologetically. "Can you tell me where the hardware store is?"

Emma had to stifle a groan. She opened her mouth, but the words refused to come out. Fortunately Arabella had managed to keep her wits and she pointed the woman toward O'Connell's, catty-corner across the street.

Ginger stuck her head out of the back room. "You want us to come out now?"

Emma shook her head. "False alarm."

"Oh." Ginger looked as defeated as Emma felt. Emma glanced at the platters of food waiting temptingly on the table. Even the parsley garnishes were beginning to look tired.

Moments later the door opened again, and everyone snapped to attention.

"Hi," Liz called out, backing into the shop as she pulled her umbrella closed. "It's a monsoon out there." She turned around to see Emma, Arabella, Sylvia and Kate all staring at her. "What's the matter? Has something happened?"

"Nothing's happened," Emma said, her voice rising to a near wail. "No one's come by yet. No one at all."

Liz hurried over and put her arm around Emma. "It's pouring right now. As soon as the rain stops, I'm sure Sweet Nothings will be jam-packed."

"I hope so."

"Is there anything I can do?" Liz looked around the shop. "Everything looks just perfect." She moved toward the counter. "What beautiful flowers!" She stooped and sniffed the peonies.

"They're from Brian." Emma could feel her face getting red.

Liz raised her eyebrows. "Well! I didn't realize that brother of mine had such good taste." She put her arm around Emma. "If you're sure there's nothing I can do, I have to pick Ben up from his playdate. Although I'm sure Mimi could keep him longer if you need help . . ."

Emma shook her head. "We'll be fine."

Liz plucked her umbrella from the stand by the door and paused with her hand on the doorknob. "Call me later and let me know how it goes, okay?"

Emma nodded and went to stand behind the counter.

BY eleven a.m., Emma was biting her nails even though she'd never been in the habit of doing it before. The tea she'd drunk earlier felt like acid lining her stomach. If no one came to their grand opening, she would just die! She tried to think of what she might have done differently, but could think of nothing. They'd advertised, they'd created a dynamic window display, they'd sent out invitations. Her stomach contracted and she felt hot bile rise up her throat. Were people staying away because of the rain? Or because of the murder?

Arabella's smile had given way to a forlorn look that made Emma want to cry. She felt a deluge of tears pressing against her eyelids and threatening to spill out. She didn't want Arabella to see how upset she was so she ducked into the back room briefly.

A half an hour later, the door opened quietly, and everyone jumped. A woman entered, pulling off her rain hat. She smiled apologetically as drops of water scattered in an arc across the carpet. "Are you open?"

"Yes, yes, please come in." Arabella made a welcoming gesture.

The woman looked around nervously, and Emma turned her back trying not to stare and make her feel uncomfortable. Sylvia busied herself with something behind the counter, and Arabella stood back a respectful distance.

Ginger came out of the back room and looked around shyly. Emma suspected Kate, who was babysitting the models, had had to give her a bit of a shove to get her through the door.

The woman admired Ginger's black lace gown and soon she, Ginger and Arabella were chatting happily about vintage lingerie.

The bell over the front door gave a melodic tinkle, and the door opened to admit two women, each of whom was clutching a rather damp and dog-eared Sweet Nothings invitation card.

The first wave was followed by another and by the end of the hour, the shop was filled to capacity.

Emma overheard Arabella in conversation with a woman who was carrying what Emma was quite sure was a real Louis Vuitton handbag.

"Are you from around here?" She heard Arabella ask.

The woman shook her expensively coifed, highlighted and low-lighted head. "I'm from Memphis. But I read all about your little shop and just had to see it for myself."

Emma noticed her glance stray to the carpet, and she suspected she knew just what the woman had read about Sweet Nothings. She was relieved that the whole story of Guy's murder hadn't turned customers away. Quite the opposite. It seemed to be bringing them in. Emma shook her head. People could certainly be strange!

She glanced toward the counter where Sylvia gave her a thumbs-up. She noticed a lot of the women were leaving the shop with glossy black-and-white Sweet Nothings bags swinging from their arms. She crossed her fingers. Hopefully that meant lots of sales.

Emma edged her way into the back room. By now her stomach was complaining loudly about how empty she'd let it get. She grabbed a small plate and helped herself to some of the sandwiches Lucy had prepared. This time she'd done wraps filled with chicken, tuna and egg salads sliced into thin wedges. Emma took a bite of a chicken salad wrap and closed her eyes in appreciation. The chicken, which had been cooked to perfection, was mixed with homemade mayonnaise, sliced almonds and chopped watercress. Emma finished the piece and reached for a second one.

Pierre sat at Emma's feet, watching her longingly. Emma broke off a small chunk of chicken and gave it to him. "That's all you're getting," she warned him. "Arabella will never forgive me if you get a stomachache."

Pierre continued to worship at Emma's feet, but when he realized no more treats were forthcoming, he began a thorough sniffing of the floor to check for any crumbs or other dropped tidbits.

Emma washed her hands quickly and was about to head back to the salesroom when she heard a loud clang.

"Pierre!"

The dog had knocked over the wastebasket next to the desk and was sniffing the spilled contents. Emma righted the can and returned the various wadded up pieces of paper and torn envelopes.

Pierre had crawled under the desk and was worrying something between his paws.

"Pierre? What do you have?" Emma knelt down and stuck her head under the desk.

Pierre hung his head as if he knew he was being naughty. He put one paw over the scrunched up piece of paper he had contentedly been chewing.

Emma eased it out from under Pierre's paw and straightened up. She glanced at the paper quickly. It looked like an e-ticket. Had someone thrown it in the trash by mistake?

"Emma?" Emma turned as Arabella stuck her head around the door. "We need some help out here."

"Coming." Emma tossed the paper onto the desk. She'd look at it later.

BY six o'clock, Sylvia was packing pink, tissue-wrapped bundles into the shopping bags of their last two customers. Arabella had sent the models home several hours ago. All the vintage lingerie they'd been wearing was sold. All that remained was for it to be washed, checked once again for any necessary repairs and packed up for the ladies who would be picking it up next week.

Arabella was sprawled in one of the armchairs, her legs stretched out in front of her, shoes off. Pierre was on his back, snoring softly at her feet. Kate had claimed the chair on the other side of the room, and she, too, had kicked off her shoes.

Arabella let out a soft groan. "I can't remember when I've ever been so tired." She looked around the room at Emma, Kate and Sylvia. "Or so happy." She sighed.

Sylvia was busying herself with the cash register.

"Why don't you sit down for a minute?" Emma asked.

Sylvia shook her head, and her gray bob swung around her long, serious face. "I just want to total this up. See how we did."

Emma shrugged. If Sylvia didn't want to sit down, that was up to her. But she couldn't wait to get off her feet. She sank onto the toile love seat in front of the window.

"Are you ready for this?" Sylvia called.

All heads turned in her direction.

"The grand total is . . ."

Sylvia named a figure that was twice what Emma had hoped for and at least four times what she had actually expected.

Arabella clapped and gave a little squeal of excitement.

"And that's just our first day." Sylvia came out from behind the counter and plopped down next to Emma.

"I don't think we can expect every day to be like today." Arabella cautioned. "Still—"

"We really did do well," Emma said. She felt a glow of satisfaction warm her from the inside out. All the hard work had been worth it. Sweet Nothings was off and running.

"I don't know about the rest of you gals, but I say we all go home, soak our feet in some lavender salts and leave this mess until tomorrow morning." Arabella waved a hand toward the decimated food table and the wastebaskets overflowing with crumpled napkins.

"Sounds good to me." Sylvia took a long whiff of her oxygen and struggled to her feet. "You don't realize how tired you are until you sit down. I remember Saturdays at the store when we had our big sales—run off our feet from morning till night. Course I was younger then. And I'd stand on the subway all the way home to Brooklyn, and then walk the six blocks to my apartment. Didn't phase me a bit."

"Ah, but we're not young anymore." Arabella sighed.

"You got that straight. I'm going home," Sylvia said decisively. "What say we order one of those pizzas with everything on it?" She smiled at Kate.

Kate bounded to her feet. "Sounds totally yummy to me."

"Come on, kid, let's lock up and go soak our feet." Arabella pushed herself out of the chair and slipped on her shoes.

"You go ahead. I'm too wound up to sit still." Emma smiled. "I'll just clean up a bit first."

"Promise me you're not going to be here for hours on end." Arabella leveled a stern glance at Emma.

Emma shook her head. "Don't worry. I'm just going to get a few things out of the way, and then I've got an ice-cold bottle of pinot grigio waiting along with a lovely shrimp salad I had the foresight to order from Let Us Cater To You."

Arabella touched a finger to her head. "Brilliant girl. Brilliant. I shall make do with a boiled egg, some toast and a pot of strong tea."

Sylvia, Kate and Arabella trooped out the door, and Emma locked it behind them, breathing a sigh of relief. A comforting stillness settled over Sweet Nothings, and Emma stood there for a moment, savoring it.

Her glance strayed to the spot where Guy had been killed, and the moment was shattered. She shook herself and began to collect the wastebaskets, stuffing the overflowing mass of crumpled tissue down into the bins with her hands.

Emma glanced at the food table. The cheese straws were all gone, nothing but crumbs in their place. The platters, too, were empty, having been refilled several times during the course of the day. Emma plucked a decorative grape tomato off one of them and popped it into her mouth. She was starving. She ate another tomato and then a radish that had been carved to look like a flower.

Enough, she decided. She'd empty the trash and head back upstairs to her apartment and the dinner waiting for her. A shower first, she thought, and a change into something comfortable, then she'd take her glass of wine and plate of salad and sit in front of the television. The movie she'd rented from Netflix had arrived, with perfect timing, just that morning.

Small pleasures, she thought. It was something Arabella had taught her. Enjoy the moment, savor the little things. Sometimes they were the only thing you could count on, but they certainly made life worth living.

Emma opened the back door and a blanket of wet heat swatted her in the face. She staggered backward, sweating in the sudden onslaught of humidity. She'd empty the trash into the Dumpster, and then head up to her apartment. She could almost feel the cool, refreshing shower water washing over her already.

Emma balanced the first can on the edge of the Dumpster and tipped in the contents. Only three more to go. She was emptying the last bin when a flash of bright color caught her eye. It was the edge of an envelope sticking up out of the muddy and utilitarian colors of the rest of the trash.

Emma hesitated. She really wanted that shower and her glass of cold wine and her delicious shrimp salad. Instead, she stood on tiptoe, leaned over the morass of garbage, and reached for the brightly colored envelope. Her fingertips brushed the sharp corner, but she momentarily lost her balance and landed flat-footed, her hand now inches away from her quarry.

She tried again, arching up onto her toes and stretching as far as she could. Her fingers closed around the very edge of the envelope, and she slowly teased it out of the garbage packed into the Dumpster. Now she was able to get a better grasp on it and fastened her whole hand around it. Her calves were burning, and she eased back down to give them a rest. The envelope was probably nothing. Just some piece of junk mail or a colorful circular. But somehow Emma suspected that wasn't the case.

She was terrified of losing her grip on her precious find, and she leaned farther into the Dumpster, the sharp edge cutting into her midriff. As she eased the yellow envelope toward her, she realized it was the mailer she'd put Guy's memory card in along with the print she'd made of the photograph of Deirdre and Skip.

How on earth had it ended up in the Dumpster? she wondered. She grasped the envelope to her chest. She thought of Deirdre Porter and had a moment of panic. What if Deirdre had lied to her, and the photograph revealed nothing at all? Emma shook her head. She didn't believe that. She'd talked to Deirdre herself and had heard that note of desperation in her voice.

She was tempted to open the package right then and

there, but sweat dripped off her chin, and she smelled lamentably like rotting garbage.

Shower first.

Then she'd see if Deirdre had been pulling her leg.

Or not.

Chapter 27

EMMA tossed the envelope on the kitchen table and headed straight for the bathroom. She let the water get good and hot and then plunged underneath the stream. It felt heavenly. She luxuriated in the warmth as it soothed her tired and aching muscles. It wasn't until the water began to turn tepid that Emma switched off the taps and stepped out of the shower.

She heard her cell phone ringing. She'd tossed it on the sofa with her purse. She wrapped a towel around herself and went to answer it.

"Emma? It's Kate. I hope I'm not disturbing you."

"Not at all. I just got out of one of the best showers I've ever had in my life."

Kate's laugh came over the phone lines. "I know what you mean. Sylvia and I just finished our pizza, then I'm heading for the shower myself." She was quiet for a moment. "I just wanted to call to say good-bye. "

"What?"

"Not forever! But I've got an early flight out tomorrow morning. I've got a car picking me up at five a.m."

"Why so soon? I thought, hoped, you'd be able to stay a little longer." Emma opened the refrigerator and got out her bottle of wine. She stood on tiptoe and eased a glass off the shelf in the cupboard.

"I thought so, too. But I just found out that Guy's family is arriving in New York tomorrow night, and I'll need to be there. It looks like they're going to close down the business."

"Oh, no." Emma stared at the uncorked wine bottle helplessly. She didn't think she could hold her cell with her shoulder and deal with the wine at the same time. She'd have to wait.

"I do have a job interview, though." Kate's voice perked up. "I'm dying to tell you where, but I don't want to jinx it. I'll let you know right afterward."

"You'd better. I'll be waiting." Emma was relieved to hear that Kate was looking toward the future.

"I hate leaving while things are still so up in the air. Did you ever find out what Deirdre meant about the photograph?"

"Not yet." Emma ran her finger through the rivulet of water running down the side of the bottle. "But I did find the photo and the memory card. Someone threw them in the Dumpster. It was stupid of me not to have saved a copy on my computer."

She heard Kate's sharp intake of breath.

"No kidding! Have you checked the photo?"

"Not yet. But I'm going to."

They chatted for a few more minutes, and then Emma hung up the phone. She had a strange feeling in the pit of her stomach. It had been fun having Kate around. She thought for a minute. Fun wasn't really the right word. Kate had been a tenuous link to Guy and the past—when Emma was still living and working in New York and Guy was still alive.

Emma went to the refrigerator and retrieved the shrimp salad Lucy had prepared. It looked delicious, and she was starving. She started to reach for a plate in the cupboard but then changed her mind. Just this once, she was going to eat out of the container. She carried her salad and her wineglass to the kitchen table and plopped on a chair, one leg tucked under her. The envelope with the print of Guy's photograph was within arm's reach. Emma dug into her salad, savoring the first delicious, crisp bite, then spun the mailer toward her, and eased out the print.

Emma was still staring at it when she took the last bite of her salad and pushed the container aside. She couldn't imagine what it was Deirdre had noticed.

She looked at the picture again, turned it upside down, sideways and any other way she could think of. She was getting up to throw her empty salad container in the trash when something caught her eye. She should have noticed it right away.

The photograph taken of Deirdre and Skip had the date and time stamp on it. That was strange. Guy didn't normally bother with that. Emma examined the small white printing that established exactly when the picture was taken. Something about the date struck her as wrong.

She grabbed her cell phone from her purse and pulled up the calendar function. What she discovered sent her reeling backward a step.

Guy didn't take this photograph. He couldn't have.

The photo was taken several days after his murder at Sweet Nothings.

EMMA lay in bed in the dark staring at the ceiling. Waves of emotion washed over her. Guy's death had almost scabbed

over, but now she felt as if someone had unceremoniously
ripped off the bandage. She was extremely relieved that Guy
hadn't taken that photograph of Deirdre and Skip. That, in
turn, meant Guy hadn't blackmailed them. That wasn't how
she wanted to remember Guy. She was glad she hadn't been
completely wrong about him. Clary had been right—the
blackmailer was a woman after all. Nikki. It had to be.

Emma fell into an uneasy sleep plagued by strange
dreams that bordered on nightmares. She woke with a start
to find her legs helplessly tangled in the sheets, as if she'd
been wrestling with them during the night.

She lay in the dark for a moment, her heart pounding,
listening to the sounds around her. The birds were beginning
to chirp, which meant it was probably around five a.m. She
didn't think she was going to be able to sleep any longer.
The bed felt hot, rumpled and uncomfortable. She might as
well get up. Emma pulled on a pair of jeans and a T-shirt.
She would finish cleaning up the shop. Maybe the activity
would take her mind off of things.

The early morning air still had a hint of damp coolness
to it. All the storefronts were dark and shuttered, and the
streetlights were still on. Emma stood for a moment, her
keys in her hand, listening to the wakening birds and enjoying the stillness. The first streaks of daylight lightened the
sky and tinged it with color. For a moment she thought of
going for a walk, but then changed her mind and stuck her
key in the lock of the front door of Sweet Nothings.

She had done the major cleanup jobs already, but she
thought she'd run the vacuum, clean the counters and wipe
down the glass cabinet doors. She wanted everything to be
perfect for their first official day of business on Monday.

Emma unwound the vacuum cleaner cord, plugged it in
and turned it on. The burst of noise from the machine
sounded extra loud in the quiet shop. She ran it back and
forth across the new carpeting, trying not to think.

The carpet done, Emma stowed the vacuum in the closet and went into the back room for some cleaning supplies. She passed Arabella's desk and noticed the crumpled piece of paper she'd tossed on top the day before. She started to throw it in the wastebasket, but then changed her mind. Instead, she smoothed it out on the desk, flicked on the lamp and sat down.

There was a hole in the top corner of the paper where one of Pierre's teeth must have pierced it. Luckily, the rest of the page was intact.

Just as Emma had thought, it was a printed e-ticket showing a flight from New York's LaGuardia Airport to Nashville. It must have come from Kate's handbag. Emma was about to crumple the paper up when the date of the flight caught her eye.

She grabbed her purse and scrambled through it, finally unearthing her cell phone. She thumbed through the applications until she found the calendar. She checked the date on Kate's e-ticket again then glanced back at the calendar.

There was no mistaking it. Kate had arrived in Paris several days before she claimed to have arrived.

Meaning she had been in Paris before Guy's murder.

Emma had barely digested the potential meaning of that when a knock sounded on the front door.

Chapter 28

"OH!" Emma jumped and dropped the piece of paper as if it were a hot coal. She was suddenly acutely aware of the fact that she was all alone at Sweet Nothings. And not only that, no one knew she was there. It was Sunday morning, and she should have been snuggled up in her bed resting after yesterday's triumphs.

Emma had left the blind down on the door. She lifted one of the slats and peered out. Kate was standing on the doorstep, tapping her foot impatiently. She had a strange look on her face, and for a moment Emma almost didn't recognize her. She looked cold and somehow . . . calculating. Without thinking, Emma flung open the door.

Kate's face changed so fast, Emma wasn't sure she had really seen that other expression.

"Emma!" Kate gushed, pushing past Emma and into the shop. "I couldn't believe it when I saw the light on. And here I thought I would have to leave without saying good-bye."

Emma stammered a greeting and backed away until she was leaning against one of the cabinets.

Kate looked at her quizzically and put up a finger to slide her errant glasses back up her nose. It was then that Emma noticed the ring she was wearing. It was a huge aqua terra jasper in an elaborate setting that matched the earring she and Brian had found earlier.

Kate must have noticed her glance. "Like it?" She waved her hand around in front of Emma's face.

"It's the same design as that earring—"

"I wondered when you were going to figure that out. Yes, they were a matching set. Beautiful, don't you think?"

Emma nodded. Her mind was reeling. She had to keep Kate talking. She stole a glance at her watch. It was too early for anyone to be passing by. The first church service of the day wasn't for another couple of hours.

"It's my design, you know." Kate held her hand up in front of her and admired her ring. "If you still have the earring, I wouldn't mind having it back."

"Of course. It should still be in Arabella's desk."

"I tried to get that wretch Nikki St. Clair to wear some of my jewelry in one of her photo shoots. It would have given me quite a leg up, but she was having none of it." Kate sneered. "Makes me glad she's dead."

Emma gasped, and Kate shot her a look. "Well, I am glad. She could have helped me out, and it wouldn't have cost her a thing. But no . . ." Kate dashed a hand across her eyes. "Good old Kate, that's what they all thought. Content to be Guy's assistant forever, never wanting anything more out of life than being in his shadow."

"I don't think people really—"

"Oh, please, spare me." Kate held up a hand. "I know what everyone thought. I was invisible. Unless they needed something, then it was Kate-go-do-this, Kate-go-do-that."

Kate swiped at her eyes again. "You don't know what it was like." She gave a loud sniff.

"Were you in love with Guy?" Emma asked gently.

Kate nodded, her curtain of hair falling across her face and partly obscuring it. "I was nothing more than a piece of office furniture to him."

This time Emma didn't try to contradict her. Maybe if she just let Kate talk—get it all out of her system—then they could call the police. Because she was now certain it had to have been Kate who murdered Guy. She'd been in Paris days before she admitted to being there, and must have met up with Guy at Sweet Nothings that night. That's when she dropped her earring. Emma shuddered as the scene flashed before her eyes again.

"Why kill Nikki, too?" Emma said without thinking. "Because of the way she treated you?"

Kate shook her head. "No, although that was reason enough if you ask me." She frowned. "She realized that earring belonged to me. It's the set I was hoping she would wear for her *Vogue* cover shoot." Kate gave a bark of laughter. "Serves her right."

Emma shuddered. Kate had lost her mind.

Her cell phone was on Arabella's desk in the back room. If she could get to it, and dial 9-1-1 . . . She still couldn't believe Kate was dangerous. But she'd obviously murdered Guy and Nikki, and had nothing to lose.

A horn honked right outside Sweet Nothings, and they both turned toward the windows.

"That's my taxi." Kate gave a smile that sent chills through Emma. "I don't have much time. I'm sorry it had to end this way, Emma. You've always been very nice to me. Unlike the others." She put a hand on Emma's shoulder. "If you hadn't insisted on snooping, you might not have put two and two together and, well . . ." She shrugged.

Panic gripped Emma by the throat. She had to keep Kate talking. About something . . . anything. If she yelled . . .

Emma glanced toward the window and suddenly remembered the warning sign that had been taped to the glass. At the time, she had been so certain Angel had done it.

"Did you tape that sign to our front window?"

Kate was already shaking her head. "Yes. And I got drenched doing it. I had the taxi drop me a block away, and I waited until no one was looking."

"And you brought your suitcase with you."

Kate nodded again. "I had to make it look as if I were just coming from the airport. I saw you looking at my dress and how wet I'd gotten, but fortunately you didn't put it all together. At least not then."

Emma glanced around her wildly. A pair of scissors was on the counter, the trademark pink Sweet Nothings ribbon trailing from the handles. If she could just reach them without alerting Kate. She doubted she'd have the nerve to use them, but Kate wouldn't know that, and it would buy her some time.

Emma tried to inch her hand along the counter casually, hoping Kate wouldn't notice. Her fingers had almost closed around the scissors when Kate reached out and grabbed her hand.

"I'd put those down if I were you."

Kate's grip on Emma's hand was strong and painful. She meant business. Panic rose in Emma's throat like bile. *Keep talking.* The words went around and around in her head like a mantra.

"Those photographs—" Emma began.

Kate smirked. "I thought that was a brilliant touch, if I must say so myself. After you discovered what Angel was really up to, I had to do something to distract you. It worked, too."

Angel. "The brakes on Sylvia's car," Emma said accusingly.

A slow smile of satisfaction spread across Kate's face. "My handiwork."

"But, how—"

"I grew up with four car-obsessed brothers. Some of it rubbed off on me."

"So you didn't really fall on the steps that day . . ."

Kate laughed and shook her head. "I wasn't about to get in a car whose brakes were soon going to fail." Kate glanced at her watch. "I don't have much more time."

"But why?" Emma cried. "Why kill Guy?"

Kate's face darkened. "You know that job at La Moda Italiana that Guy offered you?"

Emma nodded.

"That was my job!" Kate shouted so loud that Emma jumped. "Guy told me he was going to send *me* for that interview. He knew how much I wanted to work for them. But then he decided to use the job to lure you"—she stabbed an accusing finger into Emma's shoulder—"back to New York City. That's when I decided I would follow him here and confront him. But he wouldn't listen. All he cared about was getting you back again."

"But I don't want the job," Emma said, surprised to realize she meant it. "If you go back to New York, you can go to that interview yourself—"

"My plan exactly. But first," Kate said as she rummaged in her tote bag, "I'm going to make sure the police continue to think you're the murderer." She pulled a small but deadly looking gun from her bag.

Emma gasped. "What are you doing?"

"You're going to commit suicide," Kate said, getting the gun into position. "It's so sad. You were distraught over what you'd done and decided to take your own life."

Kate leveled the gun at Emma's temple.

Chapter 29

EMMA stared at the pistol in Kate's hand. She thought her heart would stop. Her mouth had become as dry as the Sahara, and her legs were as wobbly as two Slinkys. Surely Kate didn't mean to . . . to . . . shoot her?

She thought she heard the rattle of cans next door. Perhaps Mr. Tharpe was putting out the garbage? And maybe if she screamed? Emma pictured Mr. Tharpe and her heart sank—he was nearer to eighty than seventy and walked slower than a tortoise. He would be no match for anyone, let alone someone with a gun.

But she had to try. Emma opened her mouth.

Kate shoved the pistol against Emma's temple. "I wouldn't do that if I were you."

Emma immediately clamped her mouth shut. She felt tears spring into her eyes and blinked them away angrily. She wouldn't make a fool of herself in front of Kate.

She had to do something. She couldn't let poor Aunt Arabella walk in and find her like she'd found Guy. A sob rose in Emma's throat, and she swallowed it quickly. She had to keep her wits about her.

The noise next door had stopped. Even if it had been old Mr. Tharpe and his waste cans, she wasn't going to get any help from that quarter. She thought about O'Connell's Hardware across the street. She risked a glance out the front window. Unfortunately, the façade of O'Connell's was as dark as it had been earlier. O'Connells was open a half day on Sundays, but Brian wouldn't be rolling up the shutters for a few more hours. He was probably still home in bed.

Emma glanced around. Kate had moved the scissors out of reach. She needed something to knock the gun out of Kate's hand. Arabella's walking sticks were in a stand by the front door, but there was no way Kate would ever let her reach them.

They heard a horn honk outside, and Kate steadied the gun in her hand.

"I've got a plane to catch, so I'm afraid I can't hang around here much longer." She held the gun up so it was level with Emma's head. "I really am sorry about this." Kate gave a crooked smile. "I always liked you, Emma. But you insisted on snooping."

Kate held the gun pointed at Emma's head.

Emma's mind was whirling faster than a tornado. She had to do something. She couldn't let Kate get away with this. The look on Kate's face was frightening, and Emma was momentarily paralyzed.

There was a noise—Emma thought it sounded like the rattle of the front door handle. She held her breath. Had Kate heard it, too? She didn't seem to have. Emma picked up another noise—the squeak of the front door. She'd been at Sweet Nothings long enough now to recognize all the little sounds the shop made.

Someone was coming in! Maybe the taxi driver had seen something through the window and had come to investigate.

Emma would have crossed her fingers, but Kate had a steel grip on her hand.

"Hello? Emma? Arabella?" The front door squeaked open wider.

Kate let go of Emma's hand and whirled around to face the intruder. Emma noticed that the gun in her hand wobbled slightly.

Brian pushed the door open the rest of the way and stepped into the shop.

"What the . . ." he said when he caught sight of Kate and Emma.

"Don't move," Kate commanded, leveling the gun at Brian.

Brian put his hands up in the universal gesture of surrender. He stopped where he was, but Emma noticed his eyes moving this way and that, taking in the scene.

Brian's mere presence made Emma breathe easier. She felt some of the tension easing from her shoulders. Brian would know how to handle Kate. Emma still couldn't believe that Kate meant to kill anyone. But then she remembered Guy sprawled on the carpet and Nikki dead in her hotel suite, and panic returned in a wave the size of a tsunami.

Perhaps while Kate's attention was focused on Brian, she could find something to use as a weapon. A headless bust stood on the counter and despite the fact that it was sporting a bullet bra, Emma didn't have any illusions about its effectiveness as a weapon. But she had to do something, and she might distract Kate long enough for one of them to grab the gun.

Emma hesitated for a second, but then Kate leveled the gun into a position that showed she meant business. The thought of anyone hurting Brian heated Emma's blood to the boiling point. She grabbed the bust from the counter and swung it in an arc toward Kate's head.

The decorative metal finial on the top of the bust caught

Kate just above her left ear. It was hardly a deathblow, but it was painful enough to make Kate drop the gun and grab her head. Emma noticed a thin trickle of bright red blood dripping down the side of Kate's face and felt a spark of satisfaction.

The gun skipped across the floor, like a stone thrown across the surface of a pond, and came to rest with a thud against the underside of one of the cabinets. Kate made a move toward it, her hands still clutching her head, but Brian dove in front of her and went after it like a football player retrieving a fumble.

Emma held the bust at the ready, prepared to take another swing if necessary.

Brian scrambled to his feet, the gun held firmly in his hand. He stood for a minute, catching his breath.

"What on earth is going on?" He looked from Kate to Emma and back again.

Before Emma could open her mouth, Kate blurted out. "Emma killed Guy and Nikki, and now she's going to kill us."

Emma was so shocked she could do no more than sputter.

"Nice try."

"It's true," Kate protested. "Guy gave her the brush-off, and she was furious with him. Then she killed Nikki in a fit of jealousy."

"I still don't believe it."

Kate stamped her foot in frustration.

Brian nodded at Emma. "I think it's time we called the police."

IT was barely six a.m. when the blare of sirens once again disturbed the warm morning air of Paris, Tennessee. Brian kept the gun trained on Kate, but the fight had gone out of her and she was slumped in one of the toile chairs, a sulky expression on her face. Emma found herself seized by a fit of violent shivering despite the fact that she had yet to turn on the air conditioner and the thermometer was already flirting with eighty degrees. She pulled a throw off the love seat and wrapped it around her shoulders.

"You okay?" Brian looked up in concern.

"I'm fine. It's just a reaction to . . . everything." A sob caught in Emma's throat, and she swallowed it quickly. She wouldn't cry—not here, not now. Later, perhaps, while in the shower where the rush of the water would drown out the sounds, she'd give in to the emotions that were making her shake like a leaf in a storm.

The front door burst open and two patrolmen, already sweating in the early morning heat, burst into the shop. Emma recognized one of them—Flanagan his name was—from the day she found Guy. She shivered and pulled the throw around her more tightly.

They weren't there for more than five minutes before the door burst open again and Chuck Reilly swaggered into the room.

"Well, well, well." He looked from Emma to Kate and back again. "What do we have here?"

THREE hours later, Chuck Reilly and several policemen had all gone, having taken Kate into custody, and Emma and Brian were left alone in Sweet Nothings. Emma had finally stopped shivering, and she realized that it was actually quite warm. The hair around Brian's forehead was damp, and she could feel her blouse sticking to her back and sides. She had never gotten around to turning on the air conditioner.

Brian's cell phone rang, and he pulled it from his pocket, said a few terse words and snapped it shut again.

"I guess you'd better be going."

Brian shook his head. "I don't want to leave you here alone like this." He put out a hand and smoothed a lock of hair back from her forehead. "You've had a terrible shock. Bobby said he'd open the store for me."

"I can call Aunt Arabella."

Brian smiled. "Arabella is a dear and quite the woman of the world, but I'd still like to think that I can do a better job of taking care of you."

Was Brian playing the big brother again or . . . was this something else? Emma tried to read the answer in his eyes. Emotion swept over her, and she stifled a tiny sob.

Brian put his arms around her, and she let her head drop against his chest. His arms tightened, and she felt him bury his face in her hair. She inhaled the fresh scent of his clean shirt and the slight aroma of soap mingled with deodorant. It was intoxicating. Brian kissed the top of her head, and Emma felt herself smile.

Everything was going to be okay.

MONDAY was their first official day of business, and Emma was relieved to see that their first customers arrived shortly after they opened the doors at ten a.m. Emma was pretty sure they'd been drawn by the rumors of the police having been there the day before, but she didn't care.

Arabella had been shocked to hear about Kate, but, as usual, she had taken things in her stride. It had hit Sylvia a little harder—she and Kate had become quite close. Sylvia wrung her hands, and said she was sorry she hadn't paid more attention to the prediction her precious tarot cards had made about someone deceiving her. Fortunately, when she saw the customers spilling into the shop, she rallied. They were run off their feet all morning and afternoon as they racked up sale after sale.

Finally, the clock ticked to a minute past four thirty, and

Sweet Nothings was empty, the sound of the last customer leaving still echoing in the silent shop.

"Well," Arabella began when the front door opened again.

Their collective indrawn breaths were nearly audible as Deirdre Porter walked into the shop. A strong equine odor clung to her hair and clothes, and she was dressed in jodhpurs and a white shirt with the sleeves rolled up to the elbows.

Arabella plastered her best shopkeeper's smile on her face, although Emma could see the lines of fatigue that had settled around her mouth. "Can I help you?"

"Not at the moment," Deirdre said. She didn't look around but made her way directly to the counter. She had a backpack-style purse slung over her shoulder. She plopped it on the counter, loosened the drawstring neck and pulled out a photograph. She tossed it down.

"I thought it would be best if I satisfied you all's curiosity once and for all. Mama always said the best way to stop a rumor was to face it head on."

Sylvia held the photograph in her blunt fingers and settled her reading glasses on her nose. "It's a horse?"

Deirdre nodded. "A quarter horse to be precise. A sixteen-hand gelding named Lancelot."

Emma glanced at the photograph and nodded politely. Her feet ached and all she could think about was curling up on her window seat with a long, cool drink. She couldn't imagine why Deirdre had stopped by to show them a picture of a horse. Unless . . .

"That," Deirdre said, and stabbed the photo, sending it spinning across the counter, "is what I did with the money from the sale of my sapphire bracelet. Are you satisfied now?"

"Oh." Emma said in a very small voice, quickly echoed by both Arabella and Sylvia.

"I know what you all were thinking." Deirdre tucked the photograph back in her purse. "But there's nothing between me and Skip Clark except for a mutual love of horses. He was boarding Lancelot for old Mr. Everest, and when he passed, his family wanted to sell him. I'd fallen for the old dear myself, and Peyton was okay with me selling my wedding bracelet to buy him."

Emma must have looked skeptical because Deirdre continued.

"Peyton said if he'd realized I was so crazy about horses, he would have bought me one instead of a piece of jewelry." She looked around at Emma, Arabella and Sylvia. "I know you all think we're rolling in dough, but we're living on the salary Peyton makes working for the family business, and I didn't want him to go asking his mama for the cash." Deirdre rolled her eyes. "We'd never hear the end of it."

AT five minutes after five, Emma gratefully locked the front door and pulled down the shade.

"Lord, am I tired." Arabella plopped down on the love seat where Pierre had already taken up residence and was snoring softly, his white ear flipping back and forth in the stream of his breath.

"You can say that again." Sylvia came out from behind the counter, eased off her right shoe and rubbed the ball of her foot. "So now you going to tell us what happened this morning?"

Emma knew she couldn't put it off any longer. She'd told them very briefly about the police and Kate but without any of the details. She took a deep breath.

"Imagine the nerve!" Sylvia exclaimed when Emma told them about Kate's tampering with her brakes, and how she had posted that threatening note on the window of Sweet Nothings.

"I just can't believe it. She seemed like such a nice young lady."

"I was getting quite fond of her," Sylvia admitted with what Emma thought was a sniff.

"Thank goodness that drama is over. The shop is up and running and is going to take all of our time and energy," Arabella said.

"I've had enough drama for a lifetime." Emma admitted. The thought of going upstairs to her cozy apartment and putting her feet up while savoring a glass of ice-cold white wine made her almost quiver with anticipation.

Sylvia was gathering up her things, and Emma and Arabella were turning out the lights when someone began hammering on the front door.

"Keep your shirt on," Sylvia yelled as Emma hastened toward the door.

Another knock rang out, a different sound this time.

"What on earth?" Arabella mumbled as Emma reached for the doorknob.

Les all but fell into the room. He was dabbing a white monogrammed handkerchief against his brow. "Arabella," he cried when he saw her. "I've been so distraught. I just heard the police were here again yesterday morning. I was so worried that something had happened to you."

"Arabella!" A gruff voice barked out right behind Les. "The boys notified me about the arrest. Are you okay?" Francis strode quickly across the room to stand by Arabella.

Les gave him a dirty look and hastened to stand by Arabella's other side.

Emma looked from one man to the other and then smiled at Arabella.

And here she'd been worried that small-town life was going to be dull!

The front door eased open again, and Brian stuck his head around the corner. "Just thought I'd check and make sure you ladies are okay." He was covered in plaster dust, obviously on his way back to O'Connell's Hardware from his latest renovation project.

Emma smiled. Not only was small-town life going to be more interesting than she'd expected, she had the feeling she was going to thoroughly enjoy it!

Finding a property's hidden potential has rewards and challenges—not to mention certain unanticipated dangers. Like murder.

FROM NATIONAL BESTSELLING AUTHOR
JENNIE BENTLEY

FLIPPED OUT
A Do-It-Yourself Mystery

Avery and her hunky handyman boyfriend are renovating a house belonging to a local news anchor who's thrilled to be filmed as part of a home-renovation TV show. But cable-TV fame proves fleeting when the man is murdered and Avery faces the task of nailing the killer.

Home-renovation and design tips included!

penguin.com
facebook.com/TheCrimeSceneBooks
jenniebentley.com

M1093T0412

Penguin Group (USA) Online

What will you be reading tomorrow?

Patricia Cornwell, Nora Roberts, Catherine Coulter,
Ken Follett, John Sandford, Clive Cussler,
Tom Clancy, Laurell K. Hamilton, Charlaine Harris,
J. R. Ward, W.E.B. Griffin, William Gibson,
Robin Cook, Brian Jacques, Stephen King,
Dean Koontz, Eric Jerome Dickey, Terry McMillan,
Sue Monk Kidd, Amy Tan, Jayne Ann Krentz,
Daniel Silva, Kate Jacobs...

You'll find them all at
penguin.com

Read excerpts and newsletters,
find tour schedules and reading group guides,
and enter contests.

Subscribe to Penguin Group (USA) newsletters
and get an exclusive inside look
at exciting new titles and the authors you love
long before everyone else does.

PENGUIN GROUP (USA)
penguin.com